4

THE TRENCH

Recent Titles by Max Marlow

ARCTIC PERIL*
THE BURNING ROCKS*
DRY *
GROWTH*
HELL'S CHILDREN*
HER NAME WILL BE FAITH
MELTDOWN
THE RED DEATH
SHADOW AT EVENING*
SPARES*
WHERE THE RIVER RISES

* *available from Severn House*

THE TRENCH

Max Marlow

This first world edition published in Great Britain 1998 by
SEVERN HOUSE PUBLISHERS LTD of
9–15 High Street, Sutton, Surrey SM1 1DF.
This first world edition published in the U.S.A. 1999 by
SEVERN HOUSE PUBLISHERS INC of
595 Madison Avenue, New York, N.Y. 10022.

British Library Cataloguing in Publication Data

Marlow, Max
    The trench
    1. Suspense fiction
    I. Title
    823.9'14 [F]

    ISBN 0-7278-2237-3

Typeset by Palimpsest Book Production Ltd
Polmont, Stirlingshire, Scotland.
Printed and bound in Great Britain by
MPG Books Ltd, Bodmin, Cornwall.

CONTENTS

Chapter 1   The Hole   1
Chapter 2   The Haven   24
Chapter 3   Picking up the Pieces   46
Chapter 4   The Trench   72
Chapter 5   Decisions   91
Chapter 6   Ashtead   113
Chapter 7   Sutton   136
Chapter 8   Towards the River   162
Chapter 9   Mitcham   187
Chapter 10 The River   211
Chapter 11 Evacuation   232
Chapter 12 Beyond the River   255

It cracked and growled, and roared and howled,
Like noises in a swound!

Samuel Taylor Coleridge.

The Hole

D avid Barnes switched off the car radio when the pro-
gramme changed from music to chatter as he swung off
the A3 junction towards Oxshott. Instead he whistled happily,
partly at relief at being at last out of the heavy traffic on the
trunk road, but equally because he was nearly home, with
two days of leisure ahead of him. It was a splendid evening,
with hardly a cloud in the sky, and if it was a trifle warm,
one expected that in the middle of June. The forecast for the
weekend was equally good.

David did not suppose there was any feeling quite compar-
able with driving down from London on a Friday afternoon.
And for David it was more pleasurable than for most, because
his life was so entirely his own. He was thirty-three, in the best
of health, and had a comfortable job as a manager in the Victoria
branch of the City and South Bank, an occupation which many
would have found prosaic, but which he thoroughly enjoyed;
having no problems himself, he genuinely enjoyed trying to
help others who really did have problems – no matter what
these were, at the end they always came down to financial
matters, from loans to simple arrangements. Thus he could
delve into other people's lives, attempt to sort them out,
and then walk away from them to continue his own utterly
enjoyable existence.

He slowed to cross the railway line and then pass through Oxshott itself, before opening up the big Toyota through Prince's Covert for a brief spell before he reached the lane leading down to his house just east of Stoke D'Abernon.

David Barnes was a tall man, well built without being heavy. He had dark, wavy hair and a handsome, slightly aquiline face with blue eyes. He enjoyed sport, having recently abandoned cricket in favour of golf, as more befitting a bank manager, and he also played a lot of tennis. More importantly, he enjoyed himself, and nothing so much as his lifestyle. This centred on the house. He had inherited it from his mother; his father had died some years before. Now, sadly, Mother herself was dead. But her memory lived on, in the house and their garden, the swimming pool and the tennis court. With four bedrooms, it was far too large for a bachelor but, as he had been born and grown up there, David had seen no reason to sell it in favour of the dubious comforts of a London flat. He got on well with his neighbours, liking most of them and playing tennis with some, both on his own court and at the local tennis club where he was an enthusiastic member of the inter-club team; one could never be sure of one's neighbours in London.

He quite enjoyed the drive in and out of town every day, except in heavy rain and traffic jams, and would never use the train even to avoid such irritations. As for companionship, he had never lacked for that. Currently it was Alison, who would be joining him later this evening. She actually lived in London, with her parents in Brompton, and delighted in escaping into the "country" in the company of a handsome man who would allow her to mess about in his kitchen. Though an enthusiastic diner, he had never been interested in food production and welcomed any attractive girlfriend who was prepared to satisfy the inner man . . . and the other, for that matter. Just so long as they didn't start trying to run his life, get serious and talk about "settling down". He had yet to meet the woman for whom he would willingly sacrifice his freedom.

He swung round the last corner, saw the gap in the trees and the high black and white mock Tudor gable of his house in front of him. And in front of the house, a large crowd of people including both policemen and firemen, complete with their light-flashing vehicles. A policeman stepped into the middle of the road behind the crowd, waving him to stop. "No further, sir." He came to stand at David's driving window as the Toyota came to a halt. David frowned at him. "Has there been an accident?"

"You could say that."

"Anyone hurt?"

"No, I don't believe so."

"I see. Well, I'll have to get by. I live over there at The Gables."

"One of these houses down here?" The constable turned to look at the houses, which on this country lane were fairly well spaced. "Which one?"

"The one with the wrought iron gates," David snapped, pointing straight ahead. Not that he could see them through the crowd, but he was starting to feel a little irritated.

"Good grief!" The policeman's eyebrows shot up. "Well, I'm afraid you're going to have to leave the car here."

"Are you telling me I can't drive into my own front garden?" David demanded, growing even more irritated.

"Your garden. Yes, well . . . you don't have a front garden any more."

David pushed open the car door and leapt out, hurrying into the crowd.

"David!" It was Marion Pope. "What a terrible thing!"

3

"Tell me about it." David hurried past her, shouldering people left and right.

"Rum show what, David?" Bill Foster, his neighbour from the other side. "Never seen anything like it."

Hurrying past him as well, David was restrained by another uniformed policeman. "No, further, sir."

David stopped. In front of him, the road running past his front gate had suddenly disappeared. So had the wrought iron gates, and several of the flowerbeds his mother had nurtured so carefully, and which, with the aid of a weekly gardener, he had attempted to maintain. He was not an overly keen hands-on gardener himself. In place of the well-ordered front garden, with its paved drive up to the waiting garage, there was nothing but a huge hole. "What the hell—?" He looked left and right.

"Do I understand you live here?" The police inspector was checking a list attached to his clipboard.

"That's right. What on earth has happened? Has there been an explosion?"

"Let me see, you'll be Mr David Barnes?"

"Of course. Tell me—"

"You live alone in there?"

"Yes, I do," David shouted. "Will you please tell me what happened?"

"Well, sir, we're hoping you may be able to shed some light on that. There wasn't an explosion, or at least, your neighbours didn't hear anything – save for the rumble when the earth gave way."

"But—"

"It appears to be a sinkhole," Foster said knowledgeably. "Happens all the time in Florida. I've seen them."

"This happens to be England, sir," the inspector pointed out.

4

"Well, they've happened here too," Foster maintained. "Read about them, what?"

"And what causes a sinkhole, sir?"

"Well . . . really can't say, old boy. Movement of some sort under the surface."

"An earthquake," pronounced a woman who had just driven up in a Land Rover. Her property was immediately behind David's. He had met her in the local from time to time, and recalled that her name was Moore. She was distinctly horsy, and her hair was concealed beneath a headscarf. "That's what it is, an earthquake."

"We don't have earthquakes in England," Foster protested.

"Oh, yes we do," Mrs Moore declared. "There used to be very severe earthquakes. There was a tremendous earthquake just after the Battle of Hastings."

"Lady, that was nine hundred years ago," Foster pointed out.

"Listen," David said. "I need to get into my house. There may have been structural damage. I can climb across that trench. Or I can go round the back of the property."

"I can't let you do that, sir," the inspector said. "We don't know when something else might give."

"Gas," someone said. "I can smell gas."

"The mains are fractured."

There was a press forward to look down, and indeed the hole resembled a bomb crater. All of the mains down there had been snapped off, as well as the sewage link, David estimated, from the smell rising even above the gas. The whole area smothered in a steady stream of water from a fractured mains pipe. "Please get back, ladies and gentlemen," the inspector said. "We don't want anyone falling in, right?"

The hole was about ten feet deep, and six wide, while the

trench itself stretched some fifty yards. "We have radioed for some experts to come down . . . ah, here they are now," the inspector said, with considerable relief.

Men emerged from various vehicles, wearing hard hats and looking terribly efficient. Behind them was a television van from the local station, from which other men immediately began unlimbering cameras and yards of cable. "Right," said the man from the council, taking charge. "Get all of these people back a hundred yards, please, Inspector. Dave, check that gas leak and seal the main. Charlie, get on to the water company and tell them to shut this supply down, until we can have that pipe sealed. Jim, check those electrical cables. And take it easy. Wally—"

David sidled back through the onlookers. He had no desire to be forced to appear on television, and he felt a little dazed, that this should have happened to him, that his so well-organised life should have been so disrupted by such a totally unforeseeable event. "Rum do," Foster said again, walking beside him. "You reckon there's any damage to the house?"

"I have no idea," David said morosely. "And I'm not being allowed to find out. What a bloody mess!"

"Still, you're insured, what?"

"Well . . . I suppose I'm covered for holes in the ground."

"Unless your people claim it's an Act of God, eh? Ha ha ha."

David stifled the desire to be rude, sat in his car, gazing at his mobile phone. He wondered if this would make the South-East News. Probably it would, in which case Alison would be going spare. Alison was a delightful girl as regards face and figure, and she enjoyed a good time, but she could also be somewhat querulous. He did not really feel like speaking with her at this moment, but he was still considering the phone when another head presented itself at his window. "Mr Barnes?"

David looked up, and was pleasantly surprised. The young woman had good features, surrounded by straight yellow hair that fell below her shoulders. That she wore horn-rimmed glasses was in no way a detraction. Her blue suit was neat, the hem just above the knee, her shirt white and crisp.

"That's me."

"You're the owner of that house where the hole is?"

"I'm afraid I am."

"I'm Deborah Owen, reporter for the *Epsom Courier*."

"Ah," David said. Well, obviously they would eventually turn up. On the other hand, looking at this young woman he no longer had quite such a revulsion to being interviewed.

"Do you mind if Martin takes your photograph?"

He looked past her and discovered that she was accompanied by a large young man carrying a camera. "Why?"

"To feature in our report," Deborah Owen explained.

"Why me?"

"It's your house began the whole thing," she pointed out, and flushed.

"I think you should rephrase that," David suggested. "However, I suppose he can take my photograph." He got out of the car.

The camera clicked twice, as David smiled politely. "One more," the large young man requested.

Photocall over, David turned back to the car. "Now," the reporter said, "I would like to ask you some questions."

"You'll need to sit down," he said, and opened the passenger door for her. He hoped it wasn't a risky move, he didn't want to get stuck with her, but on the other hand she looked quite harmless . . . and she was attractive. Super legs.

He glanced at the car clock as he climbed in beside her.

He really should start thinking about Alison. She was due in a couple of hours. From her large shoulder bag Deborah Owen produced a small tape recorder and thumbed it. "Testing," she said, and looked up. "Okay?"

"Shoot."

"Did you see the hole appear?"

"No. It was there when I got home."

"Do you know how it happened? Or why?"

"Haven't a clue."

"Is the house damaged?"

"I haven't been allowed in to find out."

"Surely the other residents know."

"There are no other residents."

Deborah looked through the windscreen at the house. "You live in that great big place alone? No wife?"

"No wife," he grinned, adding, "Or boyfriend. Or, so far as I am aware, any children."

Deborah frowned slightly and looked as if she wanted to make a comment, but changed her mind. "May I ask what your job is, Mr Barnes?"

"I'm a bank manager."

"Bank?"

"City and South."

"I see. When do you expect to get into the house?"

"No idea. When it is eventually pronounced safe, I suppose. I gather the experts are afraid of a gas explosion from the broken mains."

"And you have absolutely no idea why or how that hole happened."

"As I said, not a clue."

"Do you own the house or is it rented?"

He thought she had a bit of a nerve to ask, but of course it was her job. "It belongs to me, lock, stock and barrel."

He looked at the car clock again. "Six o'clock. Look, I've no idea how long I'm going to have to wait to get in, so why don't we backtrack into Oxshott, and have a drink. I certainly feel like one. And I know a good pub over there. Your cameraman Martin can come too, if he likes. He has wheels, hasn't he?"

"Sure. But how will you get home? Or will you be sticking to Coke?"

"Not likely. I'll take a taxi and pick the car up in the morning. I do that quite regularly."

"I'm sure." She had already shut down her tape recorder. Now she replaced it in her bag. "Afraid I still have work to do, if you'll excuse me. If you would be kind enough to leave me your phone number I may call you later, after you've got into the house, to find out if there is any structural damage."

Disappointed at being turned down, he said "Please do. But if you hung around you'd be in at the death, or the beginning, anyway, when I'm allowed in."

"I'm sure you'll have plenty of things to do," she said, and got out to join the waiting Martin.

"Have fun," David said, and watched them disappear back into the crowd. He thought Deborah Owen looked just as attractive walking away from him as she had walking towards him.

Now, why had she made such an instant impression? Because he was feeling browned-off, tired, and thirsty? That should have made him take an instant *dislike* to her. He started the car, did a three-point turn with difficulty because by now quite a lot of other cars were parked behind his.

He was also, although he was trying not to admit it even to himself, very apprehensive. Over the years his parents had accumulated a great many treasures in that house, both personal momentoes and some quite valuable objets d'art they had picked up when Dad had been an area manager for Shell Petroleum. But the house looked solid enough, he told himself, as he drove into Oxshott. It had to be all right.

"Bit of a flap on in your neck of the woods," remarked Harold the barman.

"You can say that again," David said, taking a deep drink of his scotch and water.

"You're not involved?"

"It's my property."

"Goddam," Harold said. "That's bad luck. Subsidence, is it?"

"Something like that."

"Much damage?"

"Haven't found out yet."

"Have another," Harold suggested, seeing that David needed it. "On the house. I'll get you a taxi when you're ready."

"I had that in mind," David said.

They both looked up at the television set above the bar, as did all the other customers. There was nothing on the national news, but the local had the story. "The appearance of a sinkhole in rural Surrey has raised several questions," said the reporter.

There were shots of the hole and the house; David estimated they had been taken while he was being interviewed by Deborah Owen.

"These phenomena," said the presenter, "are common enough in certain parts of the world, but they are not usual in England. To explain why, we have with us Professor Murray of the University of London. Good evening, Dr Murray. Good of you to come in at such short notice."

"My pleasure." Dr Murray was bald but made up for that by wearing a huge handlebar moustache.

"Can you explain exactly what a sinkhole is?"

"A sinkhole," Dr Murray said, "also known as a 'doline', is a depression formed as underlying limestone bedrock is dissolved by groundwater. It is considered a fundamental structure of karst topography." He paused, with the air of a magician who has just pulled a rabbit out of a hat.

The presenter naturally took the bait. "What exactly is karst topography, Professor?"

"That is a description of the sort of landscape in which these holes occur. The name comes from a limestone area along the Dalmatian coast of Yugoslavia, where it is very prevalent; nowadays it is used to describe any such area. You will find karst topography all over the world, in places like the Causses of France, the Kwangsi area of China, the Yucatan peninsula, the Middle West of the United States, and also Kentucky and Florida."

"But not in Britain," the presenter suggested.

"It is not usual, to be sure," Murray agreed.

"So what exactly causes these sinkholes?"

"As I said, it is caused by the action of underground water on limestone. Limestone dissolves fairly easily in water. It is this action that creates all the great caverns of the world. Water gets into fissures in the earth and sinks down, working away all the time. Some depressions are too big to be called sinkholes; these are known as 'poljen', and are often of great value for cultivation."

"Cheer me up," David muttered into his second whisky.

"In some places, sinkholes are known as 'cenotes'," Murray went on, warming to his theme. "This is a particular feature of sinkholes in the Yucatan peninsula, where the roof of some underground caverns may collapse, exposing water underneath. The ancient Mayans regarded these events as being sent by the gods, and would make sacrifices to the relevant deity, throwing gold and silver objects into the fissure, and sometimes, in extreme conditions, sacrificing small children."

"Hell," David said. "Bang goes my insurance. Look, I'd better be getting back. They must have finished with the house by now."

Harold nodded. "I've your taxi waiting. Listen, if you can't get in, come back here, David, and we'll find you a bed for the night."

"I'll keep that in mind."

David went outside, contemplated his car. He had left his mobile inside, and he had no doubt that if Alison had been watching the news it would be red hot by now. He retrieved the phone – he felt rather naked without it – but as he felt even less like trying to explain it all to her at this moment he left it switched off. He was starving, and not at all sober. "Some foul-up," remarked the taxi driver.

"Dolines," David said disgustedly. "Cenotes. Did you see that bit?"

"Can't say I did. What do you reckon?"

"That we'll probably have to sacrifice a child or something." What rubbish! he thought.

The crowd had dissolved; it was time for dinner. Even the experts had gone away. Only two policemen remained on duty, and a ROAD CLOSED sign had been erected at each end of the road, either side of the hole, whilst immediately surrounding it stood red and white painted barriers and temporary lamps. "Hang about, will you, while I see if I'm able to get in yet," David told the taxi driver, and went towards the hole. "What's happening?" he asked the policemen.

"There's this hole—" he peered at David. "You were here before. David Barnes, is it?"

"Yes. And I want to get into my house."

"Ah, well, yes. I think you can do that. There doesn't seem to have been any more movement. I'm afraid there's currently a power outage. They've had to cut it off till they can make proper repairs in the morning. Have you got candles?"

"If I can find them."

"You'll need a torch," said the other policeman. "For when it gets dark."

"Yes. I've a big one in the garage." He turned back to the taxi. "Seems I'm going to be okay," he said, and paid the driver. "Can I book you for tomorrow morning, to fetch my car?"

"Sure thing. What time'll suit you?"

"Let's make it ten o'clock." He had an idea he was going to sleep in. "What about phones?" he asked the policeman.

"I'm afraid the lines are down, because that telegraph pole went in. They're hoping to get everything back to normal tomorrow. They had to be sure that hole wasn't going to widen, or anything, you see." David nodded.

"Now you be careful," said the other policeman.

David stood on the edge of the hole, and surveyed the situation. There was still an offensive smell coming out of the ground; they hadn't been able to do very much about the broken sewage pipe. But the smell of gas had gone, and he observed that most of the water had gone too; as the main had been blocked and with the supply cut the escaping water had sunk into the earth. Had the Mayans sacrificed children before or after they had seen water at the bottom of their holes? Murray hadn't been clear about that.

Carefully he skirted the edge of the hole, anxiously watched by the two policemen. When he reached the wall round his

13

garden, which was about five feet high, he paused again. The end of the wall, together with the gate, had fallen into the hole. And climbing over what was left was going to make a mess of his suit, which he had been trying to avoid. But that was a better bet than either trying to swing himself round the exposed end – the bricks looked somewhat loose – or clambering in and then out of the muddy pit. He placed both hands on the top of the wall, vaulted up and over, landing in a flower bed on his hands and knees. He got up, dusted himself off, and had to skirt the rest of the pit, which had entirely swallowed his paved driveway. He supposed he was lucky no trees had come down.

Cautiously, he advanced up the side of the drive, looking down again and again at the tangled broken mains, wondering if there *was* water under there waiting to come bubbling up, and sighed with relief when he saw that the fissure had stopped some twelve feet short of his front steps. When he stood on this particular piece of ground he could not help but feel uneasy, but it seemed perfectly firm. He activated the electronic eye on the garage door with his car key and fetched the torch, came out again, reclosing the door before edging round the bay window of the drawing-room towards the front door. Cautiously, he went up the shallow steps and pushed the Yale key into the lock.

Considering the chaos outside, everything in the house seemed remarkably normal. The drawing-room, with its old-fashioned chintzes, gilt-framed landscapes and large portrait painted of his parents and himself when he was only five, the hairy hearthrug in front of his mother's tapestry firescreen all bathed in the pink glow of evening sunshine, offered the same comfortable, welcoming effect as it always had, ever since he could remember. Leaving his briefcase in the study he wandered through the oak-panelled hallway into the kitchen. Something was definitely different in here. He paused, frowning, then realised it was the silence . . . no hum of fridges or other modern gadgetry. He would need to be careful not to leave the freezer door open longer than necessary as he hunted for supper for himself and Alison. The power should be connected again by tomorrow.

In the dining-room David poured himself a beer; he had had enough whisky, especially if he and Alison were to share a bottle of wine with supper. He pushed his cuff back to see the time – nearly eight-thirty, Alison should be arriving fairly soon so he had better get her on her mobile to warn her of the problems getting into the house. "What on earth is happening?" she demanded. "And where have you *been*? I've been trying to get you for the past hour."

"Things have been rather fraught. Do I gather you have seen the news?"

"Yes. Are you all right?"

"I'm all right."

"What about the house?"

"The house is fine, Where are you?"

"On the A3. I was held up in the office. I should be there in just over half an hour."

"Well you'd better be sure to arrive before dark," he laughed. "As I said, the house is fine but—", he tried to explain the hazards of trying to climb over the wall.

"What!" she exclaimed. "Forget it! I'm wearing high heels and nylons and my new Gucci suit! They'll be wrecked."

"Haven't you got anything in the car you can change into?"

"What, a swimsuit and wrap? You joke. Nothing doing! I'm turning for home. You can come and join me if you like."

"Can't. I've been drinking and my car is at the pub. Why

don't you come down in the morning in more suitable clothes. I have a tennis match at eleven, remember."

"What's that? You're getting very faint and I think your battery warning beeper is going."

"Yes," he shouted. "See you tomorrow." Damn, he swore silently as he switched off. Without electricity he couldn't recharge his battery. His thoughts returned to food and the still hard-frozen chicken Kievs on the drainboard. He picked them up and dropped them back into the freezer . . . he didn't really feel like Kievs in solitary state tonight. In fact, he wasn't particularly hungry – he had had an enormous lunch at Ristorante Lucarno, a few doors down from the bank, with the area manager and a visiting inspector. The tinned food cupboard offered Heinz tomato soup and there was a large chunk of Cheddar in the fridge. Great. But there was one problem . . . how to heat the soup without gas for the hob or electricity for the microwave? Right. Cold soup! Quite nice, actually on a warm June evening, with chopped cucumber and chives. A bit like *gaspacho*. He grinned to himself. Just as well Alison wasn't coming down, she'd never stop moaning. He emptied his pockets, threw his suit in a corner – it would have to be cleaned, anyway – put on a pair of chinos and a loose shirt, and returned downstairs.

There was a large, sliding glass door beside the kitchen breakfast area, a brilliant idea of his mother's a few years ago. With the door open, fake *gaspacho* and cheese and crackers on the table, along with half a bottle of red wine left over from a couple of nights ago, he sat watching the sunset stretching the shadows across the lawn.

He soon realised he was not alone; the neighbourhood tabby had arrived to share his cheese. She was very fond of cheese. "Hello, Miranda!" he greeted her as she wound herself round his legs. "What do you think of that whopping great hole in the road, then?" He bent to scratch her ear, wondering what to make of the situation himself. It really was an enormous pit: it would take tons of rubble to fill it in before the council could think of remaking the road surface. And meanwhile he would need to devise some rather more satisfactory method of gaining entry to his property. He couldn't expect the postman and the milklady to vault over the wall every morning. He would have to get the gardener to open up a gap further along the road, well away from the hole, with a temporary path leading to the house. In a way, one might be tempted to laugh at the whole thing, if it wasn't so darned inconvenient. The cat nuzzled his hand, purring very loudly, so he cut her a corner of cheese and dropped it onto the floor.

"You love this house almost as much as I do, don't you, Miranda?" Miranda! Damn silly name for a cat, he thought for the umpteenth time. She was often on the front doorstep when he arrived home in the evening, always keen to get inside and make herself at home, and David loved to see her on the hearthrug in winter. His parents had always kept a houseful of cats and dogs, and he had been encouraged to keep rabbits and guinea pigs as a boy. The pair of elderly King Charles spaniels had died soon after his father went. Mother had been heartbroken, thankful to have old Munge, the smoky grey who had been adopted as a kitten and ruled the house for years. He had lasted only six months after Mother died, and it hadn't seemed fair to get another pet and leave it shut up alone all day while he was at work. So he was always happy to see Miranda stroll in. He had no idea to whom she actually belonged.

The last streaks of sunshine disappeared. "I'd better go and find the candles before it's too dark to see," he told the visitor, heading for the old-fashioned pantry. They weren't there, but he finally ran them to earth in a box at the back of

17

a cupboard in the utility room. Then he collected silver candlesticks and candelabra from the dining-room, plus a book from the study, placing them all on the breakfast table. "Without radio, television or Internet, it looks like this is going to be an evening of continuous reading, puss." Matches proved a problem. The gas hob was self-igniting, when there was gas, so there was no need of matches in the kitchen. Where would Mother have kept them? An inspiration sent him to the drawer of placemats in the chiffonier in the dining-room and he returned triumphant to strike some light into the gathering gloom. The result wasn't brilliant, but passable, and he settled into his chair, bottle of wine at his elbow, a faint draught from the doorway flickering the candle flames.

The cat leapt on to his lap. David opened his book and smiled at the strange light reflecting through the wine in his glass. The flames continued to dance, but why, he wondered, should the faint breeze ruffle the surface of the wine . . . A cup rattled on the old kitchen dresser . . . Miranda stopped purring and dug her claws into his thigh. "Hey! Stop that—" The cup fell off the shelf and shattered on the floor.

"Oh my God!" He clutched the cat as he jumped to his feet. The whole house was trembling and he realised with horror that the floor was tilting, and the things on the formica table were sliding away. "The house is going!" he yelled into the air, and dashed out through the open door into the back garden, followed by the tremendous din of timbers snapping like rocket fire. The lawn trembled and seemed to sway under his feet. He ran diagonally northwest to the side hedge, glancing over his shoulder in time to see the tall, brick chimney stack with its four terracotta pots on the far side of the house, slowly lean over and hurtle thirty-five feet to the ground with an almighty crash. Aware of a strange, sucking noise, he turned his head in the direction of the swimming pool. It was emptying fast and as he watched it seemed to split in two and the rows of beautiful blue tiles simply slid away into a void.

A vast trench was opening up through the garden, swallowing up the pool as it went, and was heading for the tennis court, the far netting of which marked the boundary which abutted the property of his rear neighbours. Suddenly aware of the chasing horror, Miranda yowled and tore at the flesh of David's arms as she freed herself and dived under the hedge. David followed. It was an elderly privet with gaps underneath large enough for him to wriggle through.

"What the hell's happening?" shouted Bill Foster, encased in a plastic apron and wielding a spatula over his barbecue.

"Run," David yelled back. "Get out down the road. Anywhere but here. The sinkhole is spreading!"

"But I can't leave the steaks, they're just about done!"

"Damn the steaks," shrieked Deirdre, his wife. "Here, put them on this." She shoved a paper plate in his hand before gathering up her glamorous sarong, kicking off her high heels and running barefoot down the side of the house towards the road, yelling at their supper guests to follow. David was close behind. Foster brought up the rear clutching in both hands a paper plate precariously loaded with fillet steaks. "Great Scott!" he exclaimed as he emerged into the lane, then glancing up and realising that The Gables had disappeared, his mouth opened and shut like a fish. "Great Scott!" he repeated with a roar.

David stood rooted to the tarmac. Paralysed. He couldn't breathe. He just gaped at the empty space across the road in total disbelief. His home, everything he possessed had vanished! It was as though, in a matter of seconds, his entire previous existence had been wiped out. But surely something must remain over there, beyond the wreckage? Family things.

Photographs. The grandfather clock which had been handed down through generations of Barneses. Suddenly his limbs took life. He had to know – find things, anything, and he dived back towards his property, or what was left of it. The sinkhole had widened, stretching sideways now, across two-thirds of the front and into the side garden of his neighbours, the Pikes to the south-east. Worst of all, it had lengthened right across the roadway and into the field opposite. He wondered how far it had reached by now through his back garden and into the property beyond. He paused in the Fosters' front garden, trying to work out in his mind how on earth he could approach the place to hunt for salvageable items when there was a loud cracking noise followed by a subterranean firework display.

"What the hell is that?" Foster said at his elbow. "Looks like a massive electrical short circuit to me, what?" Through the hedge they could see sparks flying up out of the pit.

"There is no electricity," David said absently. "There must have been a gas pocket formed under the house when the mains broke, and my candles have gone into it."

"Holy hell," Foster commented.

Truly, a vision of hell, David thought, as flammable material exploded into a ball of flame. But in the gathering gloom it lit up the scene quite effectively, showing that the ground had actually sunk away through the drawing-room hearthrug, and the northwest wall of the house had fallen outwards across the side garden towards the Fosters' boundary hedge. The chimneys this side had separated from the wall and flattened the hedge a little way away. The rubble formed a bridge and David scrambled across it, great patches of soot discolouring his off-white chinos. He felt a pressing urgency to get as near as possible to save all he could. "David!" Foster called after him. "David, come back. Don't be a fool! You'll be killed! That fire is spreading!"

David scarcely heard him above the noise of the fire and the shouting of all the other people gathering in the road. And then he was standing on the wall which was now lying flat and almost intact. Gingerly, he stepped forward, down the length of the bedroom wall to where the floor-joist had been ripped away before plunging into the pit. He progressed further into what had been the drawing-room . . . and gasped. There, lying at his feet and apparently undamaged was the family portrait! And just beyond it was Mother's tapestry firescreen. Admittedly the frame was smashed, but the stitchwork appeared to be intact. All at once he snapped out of his trance as he realised he was almost teetering on the edge of the huge sinkhole which had now become a vast trench. Everything that remained of the house and its contents was at least twenty feet down . . . and burning. Even up here on the surface the heat was becoming intense. And all that remained was this wall on which he stood. Another gush of heat and flame shot up in his direction. Frantically he grabbed at the tapestry, then at the portrait. He had to save something. The wire which had suspended the picture was firmly attached to its heavy hook, stuck fast in the masonry. David tugged. It wouldn't budge. He could feel the skin on his face beginning to scorch. Dropping the tapestry his fingers fought to unwind the wire. "Never mind about that, man! Come on! Quick!" A policeman had chased after him and was grabbing at his arm.

"No! I must have it!" David elbowed him away, angrily.

"I can't let you stay—"

Suddenly the wire was free. "Take this for me, please," David said, pushing the dilapidated firescreen into the man's arms. And with enormous effort he heaved the weighty gilt-framed portrait upright and dragged it along the flattened wall.

Seeing that David was not to be thwarted, the policeman shoved the tapestry at Bill Foster and returned to help with the picture, and together the two men were able to lift it over the rubble, across the Fosters' flowerbed and out into the road. The canvas alone measured some three foot six inches by five foot six, added to which the frame itself was six inches wide, meaning it stood nearly as tall as David himself. Foster, his wife having relieved him of the steaks, but still in his plastic apron, stared at the picture in amazement. "Great Scott!" he commented.

The fire brigade arrived in answer to somebody's summons, but there was little they could do: the entire remainder of the timbered house was well alight, flames shooting up into the darkening sky. Sightseers were assembling, much to the annoyance of the police, adding to the throng of people in the narrow roadway. "What are you going to do with that?" asked Mrs Moore, his horsy neighbour who had lost part of her garden into the hole.

David, holding the picture upright, the wrecked firescreen at his feet, scratched his head with his free hand and gave her a lopsided grin. "I don't know. I really haven't got the faintest idea."

"I'd invite you to bring it into my place, but the police have told me I have to vacate. Damned annoying. They won't even let me go in to retrieve anything." She was a large, rawboned woman with big yellow teeth and a hearty laugh who seemed to live in trousers or jodhpurs and long, hairy jumpers. But she was a friendly soul. David couldn't help liking her.

"If I could get it to Oxshott maybe Harold at the Laughing Cavalier could find somewhere to put it, and me, for the night."

"How will you get there? It couldn't possibly fit in a car." She studied the vast frame for a moment then slapped David's shoulder. "I've got it! I'll hitch the horsebox onto the back of my Range Rover. It will fit in there beautifully," and she was off, circumnavigating the trench by striding through the field, determined to put her plan into action before he could argue. Not that he wanted to argue: no alternative immediately sprang to mind.

Mrs Moore disappeared into the darkness and the gathering crowd. David listened to sirens blaring and the shouts of the onlookers. He still felt utterly dazed at what had happened to him, could only gaze at the burning house which had been his home for all of his life. "This doesn't appear to be your night," remarked Deborah Owen.

The Haven

D avid blinked at the blonde young woman; he was so dazed he could not remember who she was for a moment. As she recognised. "Remember me?" she asked. "Debbie Owen? We talked, this afternoon."

"You're from a newspaper." He looked past her, seeking the large photographer.

"He'll be along," she said. "Don't tell me that was your house?"

"Yes," he said.

"Didn't you have any warning?"

"No."

She looked at the painting. "Is that all you saved?"

"And this." He held up the broken firescreen. "My only remaining belongings." He did not know whether to laugh or cry.

"Shoot!" she commented.

"David!" Bill Foster panted up to them. "I say, old man, could you possibly give us a hand? The police say we have to evacuate our house. It's too close to the edge of your hole. Everything's shaking—" He was even more upset than David.

"Of course I'll help," David said. "If I can find some

24

place for this thing—" he looked at Debbie. "I don't suppose—"

"Leave it in the care of one of these policemen," she
recommended.

"Oh," he said, disappointed.

She grinned at him. "I'm coming to help too. This is a
story. It really is *your* hole, isn't it? I mean, that is your
house down there."

The police sergeant accepted a watching brief over the
painting, but was doubtful when he realised where they were
going. "You want to be careful," he said, unnecessarily.

"Helping a friend," Debbie explained.

By now the crowd was increasing, as word of what had
happened, or might still be happening, spread, and people
poured out of Oxshott on the one side and Stoke d'Abernon on
the other, appearing from each direction, blowing their horns,
shouting at each other and overlapping the ROAD CLOSED
signs that had been erected. They were being physically
restrained from approaching the fissure by the policemen
as they gazed at acquaintances across the gap and shouted
even more loudly.

Now there was a fresh blaring of horns as more emergency
vehicles came roaring up, lights flooding through the gathering darkness, followed, as before, by the television vans. "I
don't think Martin is going to get through all that," Debbie
muttered, and remarked again, "Shoot!"

On top of everything else, it was now starting to drizzle.
"Hurry," Foster begged.

At least they were on the right side of the fissure. David
caught a glimpse of Mrs Pope, on the far side, waving her
arms at people who were attempting to help her get some gear
out of her house, also teetering on the edge of the opening.
He wondered how Mrs Moore, whose property was behind

his and reached by a narrow cart track between himself and the Fosters, was getting on; he really did not expect to see her returning with her cart and Land Rover for some time – she'd have to go the other way.

He and Debbie ran behind Foster, skirting what was left of David's property. Debbie slipped and he had to catch her arm, only then realising that beneath her coat she was wearing a dress and high heels. As usual, she seemed able to read his thoughts. "I was having a candlelight supper with a friend when I heard the news," she explained.

"Where's the friend?"

"God knows. Somewhere about, I should think."

"Bill! Oh, Bill—" Deirdre Foster stood on her front porch, two policemen beside her. They had carried one or two articles out of the house. "They say we must go, now. That crack might come this way any minute."

"It's not supposed to do that," David said, somewhat inanely, remembering Professor Murray's theories on television – was it only a couple of hours ago?

"You get away, darling," Foster said. "We'll just—" he paused uncertainly, gazing at Debbie.

"Oh, don't bother about me," Debbie said. "I'm working." Another hesitation, then Foster went into the house.

"If you go in there, Miss Owen," said one of the policemen, who obviously knew her, "it's at your own risk."

"Point taken," Debbie said, and went behind Foster.

David grinned at the policeman and followed. He still didn't know whether he was standing on his head or his heels, still couldn't believe what had happened, still couldn't accept that it was anything more than a bad dream. A nightmare! Foster was in the kitchen, emptying drawers of silver into a carrier bag as if he were a burglar. "Can't you just lock the place up?" David asked.

"And suppose it goes up, like your house?"

"You mean down," Debbie suggested.

"If you think this is a joke—" David began, nettled.

"It's an incident," she told him. "No use losing your shirt, especially when it's all you have."

"My golf clubs—"

"Golf clubs! What about your wife's jewellery?" Debbie exclaimed. "Do you know where it is?"

Foster looked annoyed at her sense of priorities. "There'll be some in the casket on her dressing-table. The rest is in the safe and she has the key."

"Come on," said David, and ran up the stairs, Debbie's heels clattering behind him. They reached the landing and he turned left for the master bedroom. As he did so, there was a creaking sound. "Christ!" he muttered, checking.

Debbie ran into him. "Oof. It's not going yet. In there?" She brushed past him, while he hung on to the door jamb. There had been virtually no warning when his house had gone. Miranda! Whatever had happened to Miranda? But cats had nine lives.

Debbie had taken a pillow from the bed and removed the slip. Now she was seated at the dressing table, opening drawers and the jewel casket and emptying their contents into the slip. She too looked like a burglar. "I'm sure this stuff is insured." David was standing at her shoulder.

"Not if this is an Act of God," she said.

"Oh, my God!!" If it was an Act of God, he could be destitute. Even if . . . he realised for the first time that when she had said he was down to his shirt she had been speaking the absolute truth. He was not even wearing a jacket. His wallet, cash and credit cards were all on his own dressing table . . . in that burned out mess a few yards away. There was another creak, followed by a tearing sound. The floor tilted, and Debbie gave a little shriek as she slid across it and into the far wall.

"We're getting out!" He slid across the floor behind her to grab her arm, at the same time realising that this was what might be called an ordinary subsidence; the house was collapsing towards the fissure, rather than straight down into a new opening as his had done. Which did not mean they were not in grave danger.

He held her wrist and tried to pull her up the sloping floor to the door, but then the house tilted again, and they both went sliding back down in a tangle of arms and legs. "The window!" Debbie shouted, realising they weren't going to make it.

She brought up both legs, and her high heels crashed into the glass. This shattered, and she threw up the frame, inserted herself into the opening, skirt up to her thighs, giving a little squeak as some of the broken glass slashed her tights and the flesh beneath. Then she was gone, giving another shriek as the drop remained further than she had expected.

David crawled through the window in turn. "Are you all right?"

"Jump!" she bawled, looking up at the overbalancing house.

He obeyed, and went down in what seemed a flurry of chimney pots. He landed on soft earth and fell to his hands and knees. Debbie was waiting, grabbed his arm to get him up, and was then struck by some falling object. This time she made no sound, just went down into the flowerbed. David grabbed her by the armpits, heaved her up, and threw her away from him. Then he was hit himself and sent staggering, but he kept his feet and leapt behind her, picked her up again and rolled her away from the crashing masonry. They fell off some kind of border and landed on a path, panting, while rain-shrouded dust rose around them accompanied by an immense rumbling sound. He found his face against hers. "Are you all right?" he shouted.

"You hit me!"

"I did not. The house hit you. And me."

"There is no necessity to shout." She sat up, pushing mud-stained yellow hair from her face; amazingly, she still wore her glasses. "Christ Almighty!"

The Fosters' house lay on its side, the walls cracked open, the roof having slid off into David's pit to join the remnants of his own. "Can you stand?"

"Of course I can stand." She demonstrated, and then promptly fell down again. "Where are my shoes?"

"I have no idea. Listen—"

"Is anyone there?" A fireman picked his way through the rubble.

"Yes. Us!" Debbie shouted.

The fireman approached behind the beam of his torch. "Where have you come from?"

"We were in that house," Debbie explained.

"You were in *there*? You are jolly lucky to be alive."

"We were helping the owner, Mr Foster, to pack up," David said. "Is he all right?"

"Someone got out the front," the fireman said. "You people come round and get yourselves examined."

"We are perfectly all right," Debbie said.

The fireman shone his torch up and down her. "What's that blood, then?"

Debbie looked down at her torn dress, her disintegrated tights, and the blood on her leg. "Oh hell! That must have been the broken glass."

"Get yourself examined," the fireman said. "Can you walk?"

David held out his hand and pulled her up. "Ow!" she grumbled, as her bare feet encountered a stone.

"I'll carry you," David said, gallantly.

She didn't object, but she was heavier than she looked, and the way, round the far side of the Fosters' shattered house, was uneven. Holding her against him, with her head resting on his shoulder, was pleasant enough, but he was panting by the time they emerged into the glare of the arc lights and the full concentration of the media and the emergency services. "You can put me down now," Debbie suggested.

"They were inside," the fireman was explaining to an incredulous superior.

"Medics!"

"Now listen," Debbie protested as they were led to a standby ambulance.

"Okay, love. Let's have a look at your leg," said one of the paramedics.

She and David submitted to the ministrations of the enthusiastic young man and his colleague. Their cuts and bruises were somewhat more extensive than they had supposed, although none were very serious. They were also covered in mud and dust, solvent in the rain; this was cleaned away where necessary and various pieces of plaster applied.

Then one of the medics noticed the bruise on Debbie's head, and insisted on peering into her eyes. "You could have concussion," he explained.

"You'll have concussion if you don't let me out of here," Debbie said. "I've a story to file."

As the medics retreated with their bandages and plasters, a voice shouted "Debbie!"

"Martin!" She jumped down from the ambulance and embraced the cameraman.

"Was he the chap you were having a candle-light dinner with?" David asked.

"Of course not. Martin! Where's your camera?"

"Here."

"Have you taken any shots?"

"One or two. I was worried about you."

"Well, get all you can now. Wait. Would you mind lifting me up again?" she asked David.

"Not at all." He swept her from the ground, and some of the onlookers cheered.

"Get this one," Debbie said.

"A bit more of the leg," Martin suggested, focussing.

"Look, just take it. He keeps wishing he was working for *Penthouse*," she explained. "All right, Mr Barnes. You can put me down again now."

The penny suddenly clicked in David's mind. "Is that photo going to be in the papers?"

"*The Courier*, certainly. Front page. But if we handle it right, it should make at least one of the nationals, as well."

David tried to remember which daily Alison's family took. But it couldn't possibly get into tomorrow's edition. "Move back there, move back," called the police inspector, and peered at David. "Oh, it's you. This is quite a mess," his tone almost suggesting that David might have started the whole thing.

"David!" Bill Foster panted up. "Thank God you got out. And you, Miss . . . ah?"

"Owen," Debbie said. "I got out too."

"Oh, quite. Did you . . . ah?"

"I did," Debbie said. "But I lost them all, getting out." She gestured at the still dust-shrouded wreckage of the Foster house. "They'll be in there, somewhere." Foster stared at the house in dismay. "Well," Debbie said. "I must be getting on.

I have one hell of a story to put in." She looked at David. "You resemble a drowned rat."

"So do you," he pointed out. "Wait till you see that photo. Ah . . . my God, what's that?" Something very wet and very furry clawed up David's body into his arms.

"Talk about drowned rats!"

David hugged the cat. "Oh, Miranda! I was so worried."

"Martin!" Debbie shouted. "Camera!" The flash exploded. "And another! I can see it now," Debbie said. "Banner headlines. Local hero rescues girl reporter *and* cat. Did you say its name was Miranda?"

"Is," he pointed out. "She's still alive."

"And she's yours?"

"Well . . . from time to time. I'm not sure where she actually lives."

"Looks to me like you're stuck with her. Well, like I said, I have work to do. So—" she held out her hand, then frowned at him. "You do have some place to go?"

"Ah . . . do I?"

"There's an hotel in Oxshott."

"Trouble is, I don't have any money or cards. They're all in there." Harold had said he'd take him in, but he knew where he'd rather be.

Debbie looked at the smouldering abyss. "My night for taking in stray cats," she said. "But there could be a story in it."

"That's awfully kind of you," David said, feeling obliged to protest. "But I couldn't, really."

"Listen," she said. "Even if you had all the credit cards in the world, I doubt any self-respecting hotel would let you in in your condition. You need a hot bath before you catch pneumonia, and feeding. And the cat is probably starving."

"I've already eaten but . . ." the thought of a hot bath and a drink and a safe place to put Miranda, plus the prospect of Debbie's company, was certainly preferable to that of Harold. "But . . . the painting!"

At that moment he saw headlights moving around the field opposite the hole. They approached and stopped. "Yoohoo!" It was the redoubtable Mrs Moore.

"Hallo," David responded. "Is your house okay?"

"I hope so. I only went as far as the back door to fetch the dogs. I've got them aboard. Now what about your picture?"

David frowned. "But what about your horses? Won't you need the horsebox?"

"No. They're over at my brother's place, three miles away. Now, let's get this thing loaded. Where did you say you were going?"

"He is coming to my place. There is room to park the horsebox outside." Debbie spoke with some authority.

"Where exactly is your place, dear?" Mrs Moore enquired.

"Ashtead," Debbie said.

"Well, that's only a couple of miles," Mrs Moore remarked.

"Yes, but there is no way you'll get that painting up the stairs to my flat."

David's mouth opened and shut, but he said nothing as the two bossy women took over his shattered life. Martin wandered around, his camera flashing repeatedly. He rejoined them as the loading was completed. "Why don't you hitch the horsebox to your car, Debbie?" he asked. "It would save Mrs Moore driving right over to your place and back."

"Because one has to have a towing hook, stupid!"

"But you've got one. I've seen it." He looked offended.

"I have?"

"Don't you know anything about your car?"

She gazed at him, innocently. "I know it usually goes if I

33

put petrol in. And I had to buy a new battery last month. How does that sound to you?" She looked at Mrs Moore.

"Well . . . you mean you want to borrow my horse box?"

"If you wouldn't mind."

"For how long?"

"Just tomorrow. You'll have it back as soon as David finds a home for his painting."

"Well . . . I suppose I can put the dogs in the car."

The police allowed Debbie to bring up her car. Martin was right, it had a hook and the horsebox was soon hitched on and the electrics connected to work the rear lights. "Ever towed before?" asked Mrs Moore.

"No. But I guess there's a first time for everything. Come on, David. Come on, Martin." David climbed into the back seat with Miranda, who commenced a continuous yowling.

They dropped Martin by his car which was parked some distance up the crowded street, and Debbie drove on to Ashtead, to her flat. Driving with the horsebox in tow was comparatively easy. Parking the beastly thing was not. David and Miranda got out to shout instructions, which didn't seem to help, and eventually Debbie abandoned the exercise, leaving the box parked at an awkward angle to the kerb. "I hope the lock on that box is strong," she said anxiously, then grinned. "I can't see anyone wanting to pinch that painting, anyway. They'd need a van to get it away."

Upstairs, she pushed a large bath towel into David's arms and showed him to the bathroom, while Miranda prowled from room to room, examining every nook and cranny, yowling constantly. She obviously felt dazed and lost. Things improved when she was fed; as Debbie did not own a cat of her own, this was a tin of beef stew, which Miranda clearly thought was a good idea.

David still felt out of this world. Now that the initial

sense of urgency had passed and all that need for action, he felt limp and exhausted. Waves of sickening horror at what had happened washed over him as he gaped at the unrecognisable apparition in the mirror over the wash-basin. Where was the image of the immaculate banker or the debonair sportsman? What possible relationship did they bear to this dirty, dishevelled, hollowed-eyed monstrosity now staring back at him. Bathing one-handed was difficult, but he didn't want to wet the clean dressing on the other and the hot water stung the gouges from Miranda's panicky claws: apart from which the hot water was relaxing, temporarily.

"Use the towelling robe on the back of the door, David," Debbie shouted. "I'll bung your things in the washing machine." She hoped the editor would appreciate the trouble she took to get an exclusive story!

David emerged in the large robe as instructed. Miranda had stopped yowling and selected the only armchair as a suitable place for a thorough grooming. A young man and woman were on the settee drinking wine, while Debbie busied herself at her computer. She still wore her mud-stained clothes and looked bedraggled. She looked up. "Oh, hi! Does that feel better? Meet Tom and Penelope Clarke from the flat below. They've heard about the sinkhole on the news and popped in to talk about it."

David was not in a very sociable frame of mind. "Oh. Hallo." He tightened the girdle of the robe before shaking hands.

"Sit down, David," Debbie instructed. "I'm just finishing this so I can fire it off to the office for the early morning edition."

"I wish I could have vetted your report before it goes," he said.

"Don't worry. I haven't said one unkind word about you."

"Debbie says your house was the first to fall into the hole," Tom said. He was chunky with a lot of unruly brown hair and a lived-in face: well matched to the mousey, freckled girl beside him who was watching David's every move with interest.

"Ye-es," David nodded, looking around for a spare seat and finally picking up the cat and resettling her on his lap.

Penelope was eyeing the dressing-gown. "You two knew each other before, did you?"

"No," Debbie replied for him. "I just dashed over to the scene to get a story. I asked David a few questions and then brought him back here to clean him up and maybe get a proper interview." Then registering Penelope's interest in the robe added, "His clothes were filthy. They're in the washing machine."

"Oh." Penelope looked disappointed.

"I can only offer you a glass of wine, David. I don't normally keep a stock of the hard stuff."

"Wine would be great, thanks." What he really wanted was to be left alone to think. To sort out what the hell he was going to do in the morning, like getting some new clothes. And contacting the insurance people. And fetching his car from Oxshott . . . And then finding some place to live and . . . his thought processes were interupted by the doorbell.

Debbie lifted the door phone. "Hi! Yes, it's okay. Come on up." She replaced the receiver. "The neighbours over the road want to come up for a chat. You don't mind, do you David?"

"No, of course not," David lied, stifling a weary sigh.

Three girls and a bearded young man poured into the flat. "Hope you don't mind us coming up so late, but we saw your sitting room light was on."

"Not a problem. Help yourselves to wine. You know where it is."

David was introduced and promptly cross-examined by all six visitors, and he was aware of Debbie sitting at her desk in the background making notes. He sincerely wished he hadn't come, thinking of the comparative peace of the pub. He attempted to be sociable, but his subconscious mind refused to co-operate. Would the insurance people pay up? Would there be sufficient money to buy something as nice, complete with tennis court and swimming pool? But was it worth replacing The Gables with such a large house, just for one person? On the other hand, why not? Presumably he would get married at some time and have a family. Not that marriage was an immediate priority: he would have to find a suitable mate first. Someone other than Alison. She could be great fun when she was in a good mood but, by Christ, she had a foul temper when she chose. Her tennis was her best asset – and her legs – though the latter were not as good as Debbie's. He remembered his view of them as she was getting into his car, for that first interview. He looked at his watch . . . and blinked. Had it stopped? Was it really only three and a half hours ago? Hell. If only all these people would go, or he could retrieve his clothes and escape.

"Okay, chums. Time to pack it in," Debbie called above the chatter. "Everybody out, please. I've got work to do." Actually she could see that David was exhausted and wanted to get a bit more out of him before he fell asleep.

The final goodbyes took twelve minutes. David timed them, thinking how strange it was that folks could bid farewell and then take so long actually to exit. As her guests' chatter died away on the stairs, Debbie locked the door. "I'm going to shower. Don't nod off. I'd like to ask you a few more questions."

She disappeared into the bathroom, and David poured himself another glass of wine. Maybe the best thing to do was pass out.

To keep awake until Debbie's return, David wandered around the lounge, which had a dining alcove in the corner. The furniture was inexpensive, but quite tasteful, the dining table in light wood and the settee and armchairs in matching chintzes. The gas fire was a good imitation and the flat appeared to be adequately served by radiators, although on a June evening none were on.

Thus far the flat was utterly anonymous; he wondered how long she had had it. But the pictures and ornaments gave slightly more of an insight into her character. The prints were all of human beings, of varying sexes and occupations; people were her business, although there was a tasteful flower arrangement in the centre of the dining table. The ornaments were mainly animals, a collection of small bears and one or two elephants; she definitely did not go for inanimate objects. Which suggested a possible solution to another of his problems, if he played his cards right. He had no home for Miranda, until and unless he could find her rightful owners. And he couldn't possibly traipse her around London while he looked for some place to stay.

Debbie returned, wearing a dressing gown and slippers; she had washed her hair, which was now wrapped in a towel. "That feels better. Now, you say you've eaten?"

"A bite."

"I think you could do with a sandwich. And coffee?"

"If it's decaf. I really need to sleep."

"I'm sure you do." She disappeared into the kitchenette and busied herself, returning a few minutes later with a tray which she placed on the coffee table before seating herself beside him. "Please tuck in. Are you totally shattered or can I ask you a few more questions?"

"Well, just a couple. I don't suppose I'll get much kip tonight, but I surely need to try!" He bit into a ham sandwich, chewed slowly, trying to relax. "So. Fire away."

Debbie looked down at the big yellow notepad on her knee. "You may find some of these questions slightly repetitive, but if you wouldn't mind answering them, I can correlate all the details later. First of all, why did you continue to live in that big place, all by yourself, after your parents died?"

"It was the only home I have ever known. I can't imagine ever living anywhere else." He sighed. "I'm going to have to now, aren't I?"

"Have you any plans to marry?"

"I hope to one day."

"Engaged?"

"No."

"Girlfriend?"

He hesitated. "Ye-es. Someone I go out with. Play tennis with."

Debbie raised an eyebrow. "But not a marriage prospect?"

David frowned at her. "Look, you're not going to put all this in print, are you?"

She grinned. "What? That you are currently running a girlfriend but have no honourable intentions towards her? No. I promise I won't."

"I suppose I should be grateful," he commented, not smiling.

"When you left, how far had the sinkhole developed to the rear of your property?"

"It had swallowed up the swimming-pool and was heading across the tennis court towards Mrs Moore's place."

"Swimming-pool? Tennis court? You did have a big place. Are you a keen swimmer?"

"Not particularly, but it is nice to cool off with a swim after tennis." He sighed. "I am keen on tennis. I'd just bought myself a superb new racquet."

Debbie's businesslike features relaxed. She sounded quite human as she asked, "What will you do now?"

"Now? You mean tonight, tomorrow or next month?"

"Well . . . all three. I mean, as for tonight, I hope you'll accept the offer of this settee. It really is very comfy and quite long."

He guessed it would be pretty difficult looking for a bed elsewhere, especially in a bathrobe. "Thanks very much. I imagine tomorrow will be taken up buying clothes and sorting out insurance. I'll need to go into all the various legal implications. And I may have to get someone to stand in for me at the bank until I get things sorted out."

"Forgive me pressing on with these questions, but there may not be another opportunity."

He gave her a thin smile. At least she had the grace to sound apologetic. And with legs like those emerging from the dressing gown in front of him, even if dotted with pieces of sticking plaster, you could forgive a girl almost anything. "It's okay."

"So will you buy another house in the same area, or might you prefer to move into London?"

His head dropped into his hands and his fingers dug into his scalp. The idea of living in a streetful of houses in London, or in any town or city, made him feel physically ill. But the alternative prospect of house hunting in the country, decorating and furnishing from scratch, was equally daunting. He look up and stared at her, shaking his head. "I really haven't the remotest clue," he said.

Debbie stood up. "This isn't fair. I am sorry. Look, I'll get out the spare duvet. It's time you tried to get some sleep. But do you mind if we just catch the late news?"

Nobody had ever spoken to him like that since his mother died. Maybe it was the combination of whisky he had had earlier, the wine with his supper, and then the two glasses he had drunk here, but suddenly the enormity of his devastating loss hit him, and he wanted to weep. "Go right ahead," he said.

She switched on the national news, and they sat through various international and financial entanglements. Then the presenter said, "There have been strange goings on down in Surrey, where a large sinkhole has swallowed up several houses."

"Only two," Debbie objected.

"Fortunately," the presenter went on, "there has been no loss of life, but the damage is extensive, and because of the uncertainty as to whether the hole may spread, the police are evacuating all other houses within an area of a quarter of a mile. With me in the studio is Dr Winston Murray, of the University of London, an expert on topographical matters."

"Not him again," David muttered.

"Dr Murray," said the presenter. "Are these sinkholes common?"

"Indeed," Murray said, and went into his spiel, leaving the presenter looking rather impatient.

"But are they common in England?"

"No. But there have been sinkholes in England before."

"As large as this one?"

"Well," Murray said, "as I understand it, this is two sinkholes which seem to have joined up."

"That's not true," David said. "It was one sinkhole which suddenly extended."

"Not a lot of difference, surely?" Debbie asked.

"Would you expect another sinkhole to appear in this vicinity?" the presenter asked.

"I should think that is highly unlikely," Murray said. "It is not unusual for two sinkholes to join up. But it would be highly unusual for more to appear in an area which does not topographically contain the right features."

"He almost sounds disappointed," Debbie said, and switched off the set. "Now let's get you to bed."

"Thanks," David muttered. "That would be great."

The four-seater settee was just adequate but really quite comfortable. Debbie lent him a pillow and tucked the duvet round him. Again it was a long time since anyone had done that for him.

"Now," she said, "I hate to be an utter nuisance, but I just have to get off that copy. Won't be long." She seated herself at the desk in the corner and he heard her fingers rattling over the keys. She was very efficient.

Having her in the same room, working, gave him a sense of intimacy he hadn't felt before, even when using her bathroom. He at last did begin to relax, nodded off, and awoke again when he heard the high-pitched tone of her fax as she despatched the copy. Then he heard her chair move, and hastily closed his eyes. He knew she was standing above him, looking down at him . . . and the doorbell rang. And again. "Bugger it," Debbie muttered under her breath.

David listened to the latch being turned. "Debbie?" The voice was loud and aggressive. "Where the shit have you been? I've hunted everywhere for you."

"I was at the scene," Debbie explained.

"So was I. I didn't see you. You just shot off—"

"Look, Richard, I'm a working girl," Debbie said. "And this happens to be a story, right?"

Half-asleep, David sat up, as he realised that this had to be the candlelit supper partner. Perhaps he shouldn't have moved. "What the shit—?"

"Listen," Debbie said.

Richard, who was an extremely large young man, moved Debbie to one aside by the simple method of grasping her shoulders, lifting her from the floor, and setting her down again. Then he advanced into the room, kicking the door shut behind him. "Who the shit are you?" he demanded.

David threw aside the duvet and stood up. "David Barnes. And you?"

"What the hell is he doing here?" Richard shouted. "Sleeping here! Wearing my bathrobe?"

"It happens to be my bathrobe," Debbie reminded him, "which you have been allowed to borrow, on occasion. David happens to be the owner of the house which collapsed."

"Yeah?" Richard's expression suggested that he was disappointed David hadn't stayed with his house. "Then what's he doing here, with nothing on?"

"His clothes were wet and muddy, and are presently in my washing-machine," Debbie explained with great patience. "And he has nowhere else to go."

"So you brought him home for a quick shag," Richard declared.

"You bastard," Debbie said. "Look, get out. Out, out, out."

"I'm not going anywhere unless he does," Richard said, and pointed. "You! Get your fucking clothes on and get out of here."

"Just don't move, David," Debbie commanded.

David looked from one to the other. Exhausted as he was, or perhaps because of it, he was starting to feel distinctly irritated. He was not used to being treated like either a piece of furniture or a stray cat. Miranda had prudently removed herself under the dining table. "I said, out!" Richard repeated, advancing.

"You're being both rude and absurd," David pointed out. "I only met Miss Owen today for the first time. If you are suggesting—"

"Right," Richard said. "You can go in the altogether." He reached for David's bathrobe, which slipped from David's shoulders and fell to the floor. That was too much. Now as embarrassed as he was angry, David hit him.

The big man seemed utterly taken by surprise as David's fist thudded into his midriff. He took a step backwards, hands clasped to the affected part, then gave a roar and came forward again. So David hit him again, this time on the chin. He was not as big a man as Richard, but he was in the best of health and fitness. Richard hit the floor with a crash that seemed to shake the entire building. "My God!" Debbie said. "What a super punch!"

David was nursing his right hand; he felt that he had broken the knuckles, not to mention the wrist; the knuckles were certainly split and bleeding. Richard sat up and rubbed his jaw.

Debbie opened the door. "I think you'd better leave." Slowly, Richard climbed to his feet. He didn't seem able to speak.

"I didn't hurt you, did I?" David asked, anxiously. Richard gave him a look, then staggered through the door.

"Debbie?" Tom Clarke called up from the next landing. "You all right?"

"I'm all right," Debbie called back. "Sorry about the noise. Richard fell over." She closed the door, gazed at David, and started to laugh. Then she picked up the bathrobe and handed it to him. "I think you should put this on."

"I do apologise."

"I'm quite partial to naked men," she said. "But there is a time and a place for everything."

"I meant, about that friend of yours. Have I ended a beautiful romance?"

"There was never anything romantic about Richard. He is entirely physical. Look, sit down and let me do something about your hand."

David obeyed. His entire arm was throbbing and he had a suspicion the hand was swelling. Debbie returned with antiseptic cream with which she smothered the cut knuckles, surveying as she did so the plaster on his left hand, applied by the medics. "I imagine you could do with another glass of wine. No, wait! I've just remembered, I have some brandy. It's been there a long time, but I reckon it's still drinkable."

It was. There was enough for two glasses, and they sat together and sipped. "Now you really need to get some sleep," she said. "Shoot, it's past midnight." She wished him goodnight and turned out the light at the door.

Of course he didn't sleep, even with the effects of the brandy rambling about his brain. Not even the most comfortable bed in the world could have overcome the hours of nightmarish insomnia, as images of the collapsing house, Richard's angry face, and Debbie's pretty one, flickered through his mind. He retrieved the duvet from the floor and punched the pillow a dozen times or more. Finally, only utter exhaustion forced him into oblivion just before dawn.

Picking Up The Pieces

D avid awoke to the smell of a cup of coffee being placed on the table beside the settee, and the weight of Miranda sitting on his chest. "She loves you," Debbie remarked.

He moved the cat, sat up, gazed at Debbie, fully dressed in a smart grey suit over a white blouse, hair dressed with a tortoiseshell comb. She was even wearing make-up. "Well, hi," she said.

Now he could smell bacon, as well. "Breakfast is ready," she said. "And your clothes are all dry and pressed. And I've fed the cat."

"You didn't need to do all that," he protested.

She gave him a glass of orange juice. "I did, you know, or you would have been arrested for vagrancy. And the cat was starving. How're the hands?"

The mention of them made him realise that his right hand was still extremely painful. "It's okay," he said.

"Well, I do hate to rush you," she said. "But I have to get to work. Could you shower and dress and have a quick meal? I don't, well—"

"You're not keen on leaving me alone in your flat."

"We did only just meet, yesterday. I know you're a bank manager, but . . . are you really a bank manager?"

"I manage the loan department."

"Ah. Maybe I'll ask you for a loan, one of these days. Until then—"

"I'll rush," he promised, and hurried towards the bathroom, then checked, stroking his chin. "I don't have a razor or a toothbrush."

"You can use my razor," she said, following him. "Toothbrush . . . I have a new spare in the drawer. You'll have to use my paste. But for shaving foam . . . how does soap take you?"

"You really are a treasure," he said. "A million girls would be having the heebee-jeebies."

"You're my story," she said, and placed his neatly pressed and folded shirt, pants, drawers and socks on the chair before closing the door on him. All he possessed. She had even cleaned the mud off his shoes and given them a rub.

When he emerged, she was seated at the dining table, drinking coffee and reading the newspaper. "Well," she said, "you look a whole lot better. I'm afraid I can't supply you with either a jacket or a tie. Shall I try Tom, downstairs?"

"I'll manage. Is that yours?" Pointing at the newspaper on the table.

She shook her head. "No. I write for the *Epsom Courier*. This is the *Telegraph*. But you're in it." She held it out and he read the rather small news item: HOUSES COLLAPSE IN SURREY.

"Don't worry," she said, "We're giving you a much bigger spread, complete with those photos."

"You think that's a good thing."

"The girlfriend? Do you want to give her a call?"

David ate toast and bacon while he considered the situation. "I don't think I want to do that, right this minute. I would like to ring my insurance broker, and have him meet me on site, though. And I should ring the bank—"

"Today is Saturday," she pointed out.

"Good grief. I'd forgotten that. Hell . . . I still have to get hold of my broker. I mean, I have nothing. Not even a cheque book." He grinned. "And no PIN card, either."

"Can't you open your branch?"

"By doing a lot of telephoning."

"Cards," she said. "You have to report the loss of your cards. Did you have a lot?"

"Doesn't everyone? But they're not an immediate problem. I mean, they haven't been pinched. No one is rushing about running up great charges in my name. They're all incinerated."

"They'll still want to know. All the companies, I mean. So they can issue new ones." She reddened. "Sorry! I'm trying to teach my grandmother to suck eggs!" She held her lower lip between her teeth for a moment. "Okay," she said. "You have one hell of a lot of phone calls to make. There's a book over there. I just have to go."

"You mean you're leaving me here, after all?"

She shrugged. "If you can't trust a bank manager, who can you trust? Listen, just slam the door behind you when you go." She gathered up her briefcase, went to the door. "And put the dishes in the sink."

"I'll wash up."

"There's no need to go OTT. There's a dishwasher."

"Well, I'll load it. What about the cat?"

Debbie regarded Miranda, who was leaning against David's leg and purring.

"I suggest you get in touch with the owner."

"I don't know who the owner is."

"Say again?"

"She lives someplace in the neighbourhood, but I don't know where. She just comes in, regularly, and I feed her."

"If you don't know her owner, how come you know her name?"

"It's on her collar."

"But no phone number?" Debbie looked as if she wanted to drive her fingers into her hair, but she decided against upsetting her *coiffure*. "Then she'll have to go to a cattery until you can find out where she belongs."

"I don't think that's practical, right now. I don't have any wheels or any credit. It'll only be for a day or two."

"You're asking me to keep her? I'm out all day and most nights. I don't have any cat food. I don't have a cat litter. She's already put one down in the corner, and I've cleaned it up."

"I love you."

"Grrr."

"Listen. I'll buy cat food and a litter."

"What with?"

"Ah . . . good thinking. I don't suppose—"

"I haven't any money on me," Debbie said. "All right, leave the damned cat. I'll draw some cash and buy cat food and a litter and try to get back here for lunch. I assume you will be gone by then?"

He couldn't determine whether she was hoping so or not. "I am going to try to get things moving, yes. I'd be eternally grateful . . . I mean, I am eternally grateful. And so is Miranda. It'll only be for today."

"Send me a cheque for the phone," she suggested. "When you get a cheque book."

The door closed, and David drank coffee, while trying out his right hand, stretching and then closing the fingers. They weren't going to be a lot of use for the next day or two. What on earth had made him hit that fellow? He tried to remember. Self-defence, of course. But it had been more than that. It had been the thought of that uncouth lout in bed with Debbie . . . he didn't know they had, but if that fellow had worn the bathrobe . . . ! What did women see in men like that?

It was none of his business. Save that, he should be feeling more depressed than any man on earth. He had lost every single possession, his entire family background, as if he'd been hit on the head and developed amnesia, save that he could remember every moment of it . . . and, strangely, he felt more elated than at any previous moment in his life. Because all of that family background had been a weight pulling him down? Or because he had, inadvertently, met the most gloriously attractive woman? Who had a crop of friends, and boyfriends, outside of his ken. While he . . .

Alison! My God, Alison! She would certainly know what had happened by now. She was the first person he should call. But the thought of speaking with Alison right now was unacceptable. If only because, in some unfathomable fashion, the whole thing would turn out to be his fault. As for explaining where he was calling from . . . ?

First things first. Miranda had gone to sleep on the settee. He riffled through the phonebook, punched the numbers. A woman answered. "Mrs Bryson? David Barnes. May I speak with Wayne, please?"

"He's just leaving to play golf."

"Well, can you grab him? It's urgent."

"Ah—" she was clearly looking out of the window. "He's just driving out of the yard."

"Well, can you give me his mobile number? I simply have to get hold of him."

"Are you a client, Mr Barnes?"

"Yes, I am."

"Well, don't you have his mobile number? If you're a client?" Clearly she didn't intend to give the number to anyone who shouldn't have it.

"Yes, I did have his number," David said, trying to be patient. "But I don't any more. It has burned up, with my house and all my possessions."

There was a moment's silence; no doubt she was now thinking, there goes Wayne's golf date. But she gave him the number.

"Dave, old son," Wayne Bryson's voice was, as always, loud and cheerful. "I was just coming down to your neck of the woods."

"Well, then, you can pick me up," David said.

"You playing today?"

"No," David said. "I need your help."

"Ah . . . it's Saturday, old boy."

"This won't keep. Where are you now?"

"Just coming up to Epsom."

"I'm in Ashtead. I'll give you the address."

Wayne digested this. "Would you mind telling me what's going on? Holy Jesus Christ! You're not involved in this cave-in?"

"I am the very centre of this cave-in," David said.

"Jesus!" Wayne said again. "Okay, I'll get down there right away. Meet me at the site."

"You have to pick me up. I'm separated from my car. That's in Oxshott. And my only possessions are the clothes I'm wearing, and there's not a lot of them."

More digestion. "I'll be with you in half an hour," Wayne said at last.

* * *

Wayne Bryson went with his voice, big and brash and cheerful. And reassuring. "Cute place," he remarked when David let him in.

"It belongs to a friend." David had spent the intervening half-hour telephoning his various card companies and was feeling a lot better; he had been promised a new set on Monday morning, addressed to the bank. But that still left forty-eight hours of virtual non-existence to be paid for.

"Cute friend. Hey, what a precious cat." Wayne sat beside Miranda. "I adore cats." Miranda purred as she was stroked.

"Well, you may have to get to know this one a lot better if we don't get things sorted out PDQ," David told him.

Wayne seemed to register David's state for the first time. "You look like something the cat dragged in," he remarked, and gave a shout of laughter. "This cat? What happened to your hand?"

"I hit someone."

"Friend, or enemy?"

"I don't think he's a friend, at this moment. Look, are you going to help, or not?"

"I've cancelled my golf game," Wayne pointed out in an aggrieved tone.

"Well, that's something. Thanks. What do we do first?"

"You sit down and tell me exactly what happened, and what you've lost." David did so, and Wayne made notes. "Quite a list. What do you value the house at? I know I have the figures at the office, but I don't carry them about in my head."

"Four hundred and fifty thousand for the property and a hundred thou for the contents."

"And personal effects?"

"Something like thirty thousand. You keep upgrading it."

Wayne nodded. "I think I'd like to get down there and see the damage for myself."

"I'd like to do that too. But I need some kind of instant cash or credit. I have nothing, and no place to go."

Wayne looked around him. "What's wrong with here?"

"The lady is committed, and not to me."

"What an exciting life you bank managers live," Wayne remarked. "We'll have to sort something out. You say your car is in Oxshott?"

"Yes. But I've just remembered, the keys were in my jacket pocket."

"And your jacket—?"

"Is burnt . . . at the bottom of the pit."

"Let's rush," Wayne said. "What about puss?"

"She's allowed to stay here, temporarily." He gave her some more of the tinned meat Debbie had been doling out. "Now," he told her, "you behave until that nice lady comes back."

Miranda, eating vigorously, ignored him.

They got downstairs at the same time as a traffic warden arrived from along the street. "You wouldn't know who this monstrosity belongs to?" the warden asked, tapping the side of the horsebox.

"Ah . . . well, yes, I do, as a matter of fact."

"Well, it can't stay here. It's parked half on the pavement as it is."

"I'll try to get hold of the owner and have it towed away," David offered.

"If it's here in half an hour, I am going to have it towed away," the warden said.

"God, what a hassle! Just one goddamed thing after another," David said as he sat beside Wayne in his car.

"Does it belong to the lady friend?"

"No, it doesn't. But it has my painting inside."

"You'll have to explain that," Wayne suggested, and listened with interest. He had also been thinking. "Use my phone," he said. "Call your garage, and have them make a spare key for your car. That'll be a start."

David obeyed. By the time he had managed to convey the situation and get a satisfactory response, they had arrived at the scene of the cave-in. He got out of the car with a feeling of wonderment: had it all really happened? The ROAD CLOSED sign was a quarter of a mile away from the actual hole, but once again the road was crowded, mostly with removal vans and their crews, hard at work. "Isn't it ridiculous," complained one woman. "They say we all have to move out. What on earth for? There's nothing happening now."

David led Wayne forward, up to the barrier, where they were checked by policemen. "I'm David Barnes," David explained. "My house went in."

A consultation, then they were allowed through, this time finding themselves in the midst of a crowd of council work men, as well as some very important-looking men, standing on the edge of the hole and peering into it; two men in yellow helmets and boots were actually down in it. "Whew!" Wayne remarked. "That is really something. Must be a hundred yards long."

"At least. And a few wide," David said. "Not to mention a good thirty feet deep."

"And that was your house," Wayne said. "Mind if we look around down there?" he asked the policeman who had escorted them from the barrier.

"I wouldn't," the policeman said. "Could be dangerous."

"We may be able to find something," Wayne explained.

"Well . . . mind how you go."

They picked their way over rubbled earth, upturned slabs of concrete that had once been a garden path, tangled flowerbeds, and stood immediately above the burned remains of David's house. "There's absolutely nothing there," Wayne said in wonderment.

"Well, after the collapse, it caught fire," David explained.

"I see that. Well—" he clambered down the ladder at the side of the hole, getting mud on his coat and pants. David followed, suffering similarly.

"Who are you?" asked a man in a hard hat, tramping through the mud in wellington boots.

"This was my house," David explained.

"Ah! My name is Montrose. The council has asked me to look into this."

It was Wayne's turn to say, "Ah! Do they accept responsibility for sinkholes?"

"This isn't a sinkhole," Montrose said.

"Isn't it?" David asked. "Professor Murray—"

"With respect, Mr Barnes, Professor Murray is a pompous windbag. Oh, he knows about sinkholes. He's made a lifelong study of them. But he hasn't actually been on site to look for himself. This is a subsidence."

"You mean there was a cause," David said.

"Of course."

"And you have found out what it was," Wayne suggested.

"No, we haven't at the moment. But we will."

"What exactly are you looking for?"

"Well, the most likely possibilities are, firstly, that there is an underground stream of which no one is aware, which has been eroding the earth . . . we have a diviner working on it now. The second possibility is that there was some structure under here, dating back several centuries, possibly Roman or even earlier, which may have crumbled away and caused the subsidence. We have an archaeological expert looking into that. But you may be able to help us, Mr Barnes. What sort of warning did you have?"

"I didn't."

"Oh, come now. There must have been a shaking, or some kind of noise—"

"I wasn't here when the original sinkhole . . . I beg your pardon, when the original opening occurred. When it extended, a few hours later, there was virtually no warning. A few cups rattled then fell off the shelf and the ground just opened up. I was lucky to get out before the house caved in."

"Hm. Strange, You'd think there would have been . . . Yes?" He looked round as a man hurried up.

"Mr Wadkin, the diviner, has covered the whole area, Mr Montrose. There is no water under here. Apart from the mains, of course."

"Bang goes one theory," Wayne remarked.

"Yes, well there is always the other," Montrose said, somewhat sourly. "You'll excuse me." He picked his way back along the trench.

"Talk about pompous windbags," Wayne remarked, and surveyed the disintegrated house, hands on hips. "Feel like having a dig?"

"Not really. That sight totally depresses me. What are you hoping to find?"

"Well . . . silver?"

"It won't be worth anything. It's probably melted."

"Hm. Yes, I suppose you're right. I'll have to get on to the insurers. But I can't do anything much before Monday."

"Meanwhile?" David asked.

"Yes. Right. We will go together to a bank cashpoint and I will withdraw a couple of hundred to tide you over. Then we will find you an hotel for the weekend. I will put it on one of my cards. Then I will . . . where do you shop? I mean for clothes and things. Not Armani's, I hope."

"Well, no. I use a place called Trotter's in Epsom."

"I assume they take cards. I will telephone them, give them my number, and tell them that you will be coming in to buy some gear, and that it is to go on the card. I assume they know you?"

"Yes."

"Then there'll be no problem with identification. Right. I'll give you a limit of three hundred—"

"You have got to be joking – that won't buy one suit! Then there'll be shirts, pants, shoes and socks; toiletries too, and—"

Wayne held up his hand. "Okay, okay! Message received. Double it if you must!"

David slapped him appreciatively on the shoulder. "I'll owe you one!"

"You'd better believe it! And meanwhile we'll both pray that the insurers will stump up!"

"Er . . . will they fork out for my hotel accommodation?"

"We can try them, but they certainly won't wear the Savoy. Have you anywhere in mind?"

"There is a chain hotel not far from my bank."

"Sounds reasonable. Go for it. Now, shall we go into Oxshott, get some money first, then see if you can get into your car yet?"

A mechanic was waiting in his van in the Laughing Cavalier

car-park. "Afraid I have to ask for proof of identification and your signature," he said.

"No problem with the latter, but I can't do anything about identification," David replied.

"Don't worry," Bryson cut in. "Here is *my* proof of identity. I'm his insurance broker, God help me. I'll vouch for him." The mechanic removed his greasy baseball cap and scratched his head, but eventually allowed himself to be persuaded, probably so he could get home early.

"I'll buzz your hotel and make sure they have a room for you." The broker punched his mobile for enquiries, got the number and punched again. "Done," he told David as he snapped it closed and put the tiny machine back in his pocket. "Anything else before I go?"

"Can't think of anything else, except to say thanks a bunch for everything, and sorry about your golf. I really would have been up the creek without your help."

Wayne Bryson grinned. "At least I'll know where to come for a loan to buy my first yacht."

After watching him drive off, David decided that his first priority should be to phone Alison: she would probably be spitting bricks by now. The public phone in the passageway outside the bar was not the ideal spot, but the nearest available. He'd have to replace his mobile first thing on Monday. He got change from the bar and dialled. Alison's mother answered and David could almost feel the icicles in her voice as she called the girl to the phone. "Well?" Alison demanded aggressively.

"Look, I'm terribly sorry, but I'm afraid there has been a major catastrophe—"

"Like the start of a nuclear war, perhaps?"

He was irritated by her tone. "Similar. There has been a massive subsidence where I live . . . lived—"

"I know that! You told me yesterday evening. And it was on the news. But I can't see how that excuses you for not ringing me—"

"It was my house that fell into the hole—"

"Oh yes! Ha ha! Pull the other one."

"My home," he continued, trying to suppress his anger, "and every damn thing I possess. Even my clothes and credit cards, passport and driving licence are gone. The lot."

There was silence at the other end of the phone. Then she said, "Seriously?"

"Too damned right it's serious. Just a minute," he added as the pips denoted the money was running out. He shoved some more coins into the slot. "Look, I literally have only the things I stand up in and I must get into Epsom for new kit."

"Oh! Oh darling!" At last she sounded as though the information was sinking in. "You poor thing! How terrible! Do you want me to join you? I could help you choose some clothes, perhaps. And we could have some lunch together."

It seemed a good idea. He wasn't particularly good at buying clothes – at least that was what Alison repeatedly told him. If she came along it might stem the flow of criticism. "Great," he tried to enthuse. "I'll see you in the main entrance to Trotter's at noon." In fact, he decided, it would be nice to have her along if only for company. Normally, he was not bothered by his solitary existence but right now, with waves of sickening horror washing over him every few minutes, it might be good to have a sympathetic companion. He kept having these mental images of precious belongings – the cricket bat signed by Denis Compton when he visited David's school years ago, his father's flying helmet and medals from the war. Sports trophies, photographs, the list was endless. Thank God he had that family portrait and Mother's firescreen. Portrait! It was still parked outside Debbie's flat! Being towed away! He must ring her and make arrangements to have it rescued. She was out. He left a message for her to phone him at the hotel that evening.

Alison could not have been sweeter. "My poor, poor darling," she moaned, and kissed him affectionately on Trotter's doorstep. "You must tell me all about it!" She was tall with thick, tawny hair curling over suntanned shoulders, heavy bracelets jangling on her bare arms, the short, skin-tight sundress revealing a Miss World figure.

But David was not in an appreciative frame of mind. "Over lunch. Let's do some shopping first."

She looked slightly disappointed; all the drama of his tragedy was so exciting. Then she noticed the plastered knuckles and the swollen hand. "What on earth happened to your hand?"

"I . . . ah . . . hit something. Not intentionally."

She raised her eyebrows. Something else to be told over lunch. She fell for a splendid suit. "You'd look marvellous in this," she cooed.

"I should bloody well think so at that price! There would only be enough money left over for a pair of socks. Cheap socks at that!" He moved on to a more modest department.

Alison's beautiful pink lips pouted, but she agreed that the light-weight grey he picked out did fit him. He let her choose some shirts, refused to be seen dead in the tie of her choice, and pulled some ordinary socks off a stand. The assistant, who was on commission, thought he had won the lottery as his customer's purchases piled up on the counter. David made his number with the department manager who knew of the arrangement with Wayne Bryson, and soon the couple were laden with big plastic carriers and heading for the exit.

Alison said she would treat him to lunch at Penney's, a restaurant on the first floor of an old Tudor building not far from the car-park. "Now," she said eagerly as they sat down, "Tell me all about it."

"Hard to know where to begin." In fact he didn't want to begin. He didn't want to talk about it. All he needed was a glass of wine and something really appetising by way of food which would slide down over the leaden ball in his gut, and give him strength to face the ordeal of the next few days. Weeks.

Sunglasses on the table in front of her, Alison's enormous hazel eyes were fixed on his, waiting. She could have kicked herself for turning her car round and going back home last night. If only she had gone on she could have been part of the drama. "Your hand."

"There was this fellow being hysterical. So—"

"You hit him? Oh, David! What a thing to do!" She sounded admiring. "Was this before, or after, your house collapsed?"

"Well," David started reluctantly, "The cups on the kitchen dresser were the first to go."

Bit by bit, with nagging questions, she managed to drag some of the details out of him, happily overlooking the hand as she heard the story. "Burnt!" she exclaimed eventually. "You mean you won't be able to salvage anything?"

"No. All I got out was a picture and a firescreen. My brand new tennis racquet has gone, and my golf clubs."

"You can easily buy a new racquet." She didn't add "and golf clubs" because she hoped he wouldn't. She hated the time he wasted on the golf course. "So where did you spend the night?"

"Er, a newspaper reporter put me up," he elected not to mention the gender and quickly went on, "Wayne Bryson, my insurance broker, kindly fetched me this morning for a site meeting and to fix me up with a temporary loan."

The waiter appeared pushing the dessert trolley. "Ooh! What are you going to have?" Alison's little pink tongue strayed out over her lips.

David eyed the exotically decorated glasses of strawberry mousse, the chocolate gateaux and lemon meringues, and said, "A plate of cheese, thanks."

With Alison in tow, David went into Boots after lunch to buy toiletries – a razor, hairbrush and deodorant and a zipped bag in which to put them. He could have managed better without his girlfriend's assistance – she had to sniff a dozen aftershaves before she was satisfied. He paused outside the window of a computer shop eyeing the mobile phones, but decided to wait until he was alone after the weekend before purchasing one. "Can we go and look at the hole, now?" Alison asked as they entered the car-park.

"There is nothing to see except a pile of rubble." He didn't want to go back there, yet. "Anyway, the police don't allow sightseers anywhere near it."

"But surely they would let you—"

"I would like to get to my hotel and hang up all this new gear before it gets crumpled," he went on, but then, seeing her disappointment he added, "I was hoping you might come along, too. Women are good at that sort of thing."

Mollified, she beamed at him. "Just tell me where the hotel is in case I lose sight of you on the way." She climbed into her white drophead Golf and waited for him to lead the way in his Toyota.

Traffic was light and Alison managed to keep David in her sights by jumping a traffic light and cutting up a furious Jag driver. It took a while to get through the reception staff – starting with a trainee, a pimpled youth, and his immediate senior who argued that there was no record of his reservation, followed by the reception manager who wanted every detail repeated, and finally the hotel assistant manager who had taken Wayne Bryson's call and card number.

The bedroom was adequate; ideal for the travelling businessman with a desk for his briefcase and space for his overnight bag, but sadly soulless for a homeless refugee. A large-patterned red and orange tartan folkweave material hung over the windows and covered the two small double beds, the carpet was of a blending fleck, and the statutory matching pair of tall, bedside lamps had pseudo-antique metal bases and hessian shades which reduced the lighting in the room to a fashionable gloom. The window looked out over a backyard. David wondered how long he would have to be there. How long he could stick the décor.

The drive had taken over an hour, and by the time his meagre possessions were put away and he had used his new hairbrush it was six o'clock.

"What are you doing about dinner?" Alison asked.

"I'll eat downstairs, I suppose." The prospect of sitting alone did not appeal. "Would you like to stay?"

"Of course I'll stay, you poor lamb." She wound her arms round his neck. "I couldn't possibly leave you here all by yourself." Gazing up into those compelling blue eyes, watching a black eyebrow arch at her invitingly, she wondered how she could possibly ever get cross with him. He was so gorgeous, even if he did keep their relationship on a rather too casual footing. Which reminded her of the problem at home. She bit her lip. "I would have asked you to come and stay with us . . . but you know how it is with Daddy and Mummy."

Yes, David did know how it was. Mr and Mrs Bates were

extremely anxious to see their lively daughter married and settled down, and the fact that she had been going out, on and off for some months, with a promising prospect who had not only failed to pop any vital questions but hadn't even made any hopeful noises, had not endeared him to them. In fact they were becoming quite impatient, convinced that David was "stringing her along". David, on the other hand, was well aware that he was only the latest in a long line of Alison's escorts, and he wasn't at all sure which attracted her, and her parents, most, himself as a person, or his apparently healthy income. As far as his own feelings were concerned, he was quite fond of her when she was in a reasonable mood, admired her body and enjoyed playing tennis with her. But he found her frequent tantrums a terrible turn-off and if it wasn't for the sex interest they had little else in common. Maybe if he ever got to know her well . . . After all, she was very beautiful, and right now he was in dire need of consolation. He slid his arms round her waist and was kissing her soundly when there was a knock on the door.

David and Alison drew back, frowning at each other. "Must be a maid with more towels, I guess." He went to the door, flung it open . . . and Debbie bounced in.

"Hi! I got your message, so I was able to track you down." Parking herself on the end of the bed, facing the door where David still stood with his hand on the handle, she failed to notice Alison standing by the window. "Now look. What do you intend to do about this?" She waved a piece of paper at him.

"What is it?"

"A reclaim ticket for you to collect the horsebox from the car pound."

He allowed the door to slam shut as he peered at the paper. "Oh, shit!"

"What are you going to do with it when you get it?"

"God alone knows! I suppose I'll have to get in touch with Mrs Moore."

"Well you'd better make up your mind pretty pronto. They charge by the day for keeping it there."

"Would you care to introduce us?" Alison's tone was frigid.

Debbie swung round rapidly, her large spectacles nearly falling off her nose. "Oh! Hallo! Didn't see you there. I'm Debbie. Who are you?" She got up and held out her hand.

It was ignored. "I'm Alison. Do I gather you are a friend of David's?"

David sensed big trouble. "Debbie is a reporter with the . . . er . . ." he began, then wished he hadn't. Too late.

"The one you slept with last night?"

"Yes . . . er . . . no. Well only in a manner of speaking."

Debbie's head swung from one to the other, mouth open.

"You mean that after your evening's disasters you weren't able to make the grade?" Alison grabbed her handbag and flung it at David's head, screaming, "You bastard! No wonder you phoned and put me off coming!"

He ducked, and the contents of the pink leather bag spilled over the floor. "Shut up, you idiot! It wasn't like that!"

Debbie was blushing, but she had an urgent desire to giggle. "No it wasn't like that. Truly. Are you David's girlfriend?"

"I thought so, once upon a time. Now," she stormed across the room and glared at David, "You can help me to pick up my gear. I'm leaving."

"Oh no!" Debbie cried. "Look, I'm sorry. You've got it all wrong. I've got to go, anyway." She stood looking down at the pair who were on their hands and knees ferreting under the bed for straying lipsticks and perfume. "I'll leave the ticket on the dressing table, here."

"Just a minute!" David jumped to his feet. "What about Miranda?"

"And who the hell is Miranda?!" Alison yelled.

"A pussy cat!" Debbie yelled back. "And with ten times as much brain as you have, you stupid cow!" She flung the door open. "I wish you joy of her, you poor sod," was her parting shot before slamming the door.

"The bitch!" Alison snarled.

"She is not a bitch. She is a very decent girl who kindly allowed me to doss down on her settee overnight. You owe her an apology."

"Apology! How the hell was I to know that you weren't – well, I mean—"

"Just calm down, will you?" David sat on the end of the bed, running his fingers through his hair. "Perhaps I had better explain, though it shouldn't be necessary." He went into great detail, especially in regard to the settee, exaggerating its discomforts, stressing Debbie's relationship with Richard.

"You hit her boyfriend?" Alison demanded.

"Well, he was trying to throw me out into the street, in the altogether."

"And is Miranda really a cat?"

"Yes. In fact you've met her at The Gables a number of times. She always comes in and makes herself at home, particularly at mealtimes."

"You don't mean that scruffy stray?" Alison was proud owner of a pair of pedigree Siamese yowlers, and regarded tabbies as beneath contempt.

David was too exhausted to argue. After all, it wasn't as though Miranda could hear her. "Yes. Now are you satisfied?"

"Yes. I suppose so." She picked up her handbag and David

instinctively ducked. But she carried it away into the bathroom to fix her face before dinner.

The dining-room décor was infinitely better than in the bedroom. So was the wine list, but as David intended to drink sufficient to give himself a really good night's sleep, he ordered a bottle each of house red and white. No point in getting soused on expensive vintage Châteaux. The menu was excellent and stimulated his appetite and as Alison was an avid gourmet on occasion they ordered both coquilles St Jacques and a chilled vichyssoise before a main course of tournedos steaks. They discussed their joint shopping trip while waiting for the first course, then talked of tennis, neither of which topics were very demanding or controversial. David realised his mind was drifting back over the events of the past twenty-four hours . . . so he poured another glass of white wine.

The steaks were tender and delicious and he was developing a welcome sense of euphoria when Alison asked, "Where are you going to put your horsebox?" David hadn't the faintest idea and said so.

"What I don't understand is what on earth you want it for. You haven't got a horse, have you?"

"No, of course not. It belongs to a friend."

"Not another female?"

"As a matter of fact, yes."

"So what are you doing with it?"

"It's got the family portrait in it."

"Eh?"

"I've already explained to you upstairs. That's why it was parked outside Debbie's place last night."

Alison looked even more beautiful when she was baffled. "But for heaven's sake why do you want to keep it in a horsebox?"

"I don't *want* to keep it in there. I simply borrowed the horsebox from Barbara Moore to keep it in until I've somewhere else to put it."

"Who is Barbara Moore?" Alison demanded suspiciously. "And why couldn't you pack up the picture in a parcel and put it in the back of your car?"

Mellowed by the food and wine, David threw back his head and laughed. "Barbara Moore is a dear friend and neighbour, utterly charming, old enough to be my grandmother and with a face that would stop a clock." He had the grace to feel slightly guilty at the description, before adding, "And the picture is roughly six foot by five and weighs half a ton. Satisfied?"

Alison looked surprised. "Oh. So where *are* you going to put it?"

David sighed. "Good question. I suppose I could get it up into my bedroom here, with the help of a strong man. Or maybe Wayne Bryson might let me store it in his garage, though I hardly dare ask. He has done so much for me already."

"Where is his garage?"

"That's a point. I don't even know if he has one."

"Where are you planning to keep the horsebox?"

"I'm not. I have to get it back to Barbara Moore."

Alison giggled. "You have got yourself into a mess, haven't you?"

"I have not!" David retorted indignantly. "I was just sitting there minding my own business when Fate stepped in and dropped my house down a hole!" Alison giggled again. "You are too tight to drive home, my girl. You had better stay the night."

Alison grinned happily. "Ooh! Do you think I should?"

"Yes. Finish your wine and we'll go upstairs."

Alison was definitely tipsy as they walked out to the lift. David held her arm and said, "Sshh!" as she continued to giggle, much to the amusement of other diners. In the bedroom, she kicked off her high heels, staggered as she tried to reach the zip on the back of her dress and eventually called for his help.

Watching her wriggle out of the little pink number, David thought it was a very pleasant way to end an horrendous day. "If you are very good I'll allow you to take first turn with my new toothbrush," he said. They stood together on the tiled bathroom floor in their briefs, sharing the imitation marble wash-basin.

"I'll have this bed and you can have that one," David ordered.

"What!"

"All right. Only joking!" And together they wriggled down between the clean sheets of the window bed. Her skin felt good, as it should have, judging by the time she spent pampering it, and he nuzzled into her neck, enjoying her perfume. They had slept together many times before, but he still found her interesting, even exciting when she was in one of her erotic moods. As she was now. After they had kissed extensively she rolled him onto his back, kissed both his ears, his neck and nibbled at the black hair on his chest, gradually working her way done his hard-muscled body.

After the recent tragic events in his life, David had wondered if he could possibly come up to scratch: now he realised he need not have worried. He stretched luxuriously, sighing deeply in appreciative enjoyment of Alison's ministrations . . . and the telephone beeped in his ear. "Don't answer it!" Alison commanded.

He had no desire to, but it continued persistently. "Shit,"

he said, rolling onto his side and nearly tipping her onto the floor. Furious, he grabbed the receiver, and snapped "Yes!"

"Sorry to disturb you, David, but I thought you would want to know—" it was Debbie Owen's voice.

"Know what?"

"Your sinkhole has more than doubled in size. It's now a bloody great fissure and has swallowed three more houses."

David sat up. "Good God. It must be enormous. Do you know which other houses have gone?"

"Yes. The Popes' place, the other side of you, and Mrs Moore's, beyond your tennis court, plus one other."

"Shit! Are they all right? The people, I mean."

"They should be. Weren't they all evacuated?"

"I think so. Hell, I must get down there."

"To do what?"

"Well . . . I feel kind of responsible."

"Don't be a noodle. You have nothing to do with what's happening."

"I'm going down. You?"

"I'm actually on my way."

"I'll see you there." He put down the phone, looked at Alison.

"Who was that?"

"Ah . . . a friend, to tell me that fissure is opening even more." He began dragging on his clothes.

"So what are you doing?"

"I'm going down to see what's going on."

Alison sat up, pushing her hair out of her eyes. "Now? It's damn near midnight. And you're not sober."

"I haven't had a drink for two hours." He grinned. "And I don't think the police will be out breathalysing in south Surrey right this minute."

She got out of bed in turn.

"So what are *you* doing?"

Alison pulled on her knickers. "Coming with you. I don't think you're fit to be out on your own."

The Trench

"I think this is the most crazy idea," Alison grumbled as, using David's car, they drove out of the hotel car-park and headed for Chelsea Bridge. "Gallivanting around the countryside in the middle of the night—"

"Tomorrow is Sunday," David pointed out. "You can sleep in. *We* can sleep in." He was keeping his fingers crossed that there wouldn't be another scene when they encountered Debbie.

"But what are you planning to do? Or see?"

"I'm not planning on doing anything, personally. But it's my neighbourhood being torn up. Remember, I've known every stick and stone of the area since childhood."

He switched on the car radio as they crossed the river, got a midnight news bulletin. ". . . definitely spread in an easterly direction," said the newscaster, "and is now reported to be a quarter of a mile long. Experts are at a loss to explain the phenomenon, which appears to be unprecedented. Certainly it can no longer be classed as a sinkhole, and it has already caused over a million pounds worth of damage."

"Phenomenal," Alison commented, shaking her head in disbelief.

David was concentrating; there was more traffic than he had expected at this hour. He decided against trying the A3, and swung south through Wandsworth and Wimbledon towards Merton, and thence to Sutton and Epsom. That way he would approach the fissure from the Ashtead side, which was obviously the side from which Debbie would also appear, as she lived in Ashtead. But when they got to Merton, there was a traffic jam. "At one o'clock in the morning?" Alison remarked.

"Must be an accident," David suggested.

After half an hour he realised that it couldn't be an accident; in that time they had advanced less than a hundred yards. "We have to get out of this," he muttered.

"Amen," Alison agreed.

Slowly they crept towards a side street, and David swung down it. He had no idea where they were going, but after twisting to and fro through various residential areas he found himself at a junction of the A217. Unfortunately, this too was blocked with traffic, and it took him another half-hour to edge his way in. "Where are all these people *going*?" Alison demanded.

"I imagine to the same place we're going," David said. "The hole."

"Shit!" she commented. "All these people are as stupid as we are! Well, we're not going to get there. David, let's go back to the hotel."

"Just let's give it a while longer, now we've come this far," he said.

She made an inaudible sound of disagreement, sank well down in her seat, and appeared to go to sleep. David let her settle, and then used the phone. "Are you there?" he asked.

"I'm in Sutton."

"Doing what?"

"I've been at the office in Epsom, and now I'm at my parents', just reassuring them."

"In Sutton?"

"Well, that's not so very far away," Debbie pointed out. "It's all go in Epsom. There's talk that the Meeting may have to be cancelled, or at least postponed, until they discover just what is going on."

David had forgotten that the following week was the Derby. "The racecourse is nearly four miles from the fissure," he pointed out.

"Right, at this moment in time, to utilise a very well worn cliché. But," she added, "At this time yesterday, it was rather *more* than four miles. Correct?"

"That's ridiculous. Anyway, listen, I'm stuck in a monumental traffic jam in Merton. Are all these people going to the site?"

"I think they would like to. But there's a huge police cordon, so our man on the spot tells me. Listen, stick with it, and come into Epsom." She gave him the address. "Come here, and I'll wait for you. I'm Press and, more important, local press, so I should be able to get us through. But be as quick as you can – I'm supposed to be there now, working."

"I'll do my best," he said, and switched off.

"Who was that?" Alison asked, drowsily.

"Just a contact," David said. She went back to sleep.

Slowly they crept forward, and now he was having a job keeping himself awake. Around him was a mass of lights, and occasional shouts and curses; he doubted they'd get through the night without a road rage incident. Maybe it had been a stupid idea after all.

The phone buzzed. "Where are you now?" Debbie asked.

"God knows. Some place on the outskirts of Sutton."

"Well, listen. All the roads are blocked. So I've arranged alternative transport. How close are you to Cheam Common?"

"About half a mile, I reckon."

"Well, when you get there, turn off and go into the car-park. Someone will meet you there."

"But not you?"

"You'll pick me up later."

"You sure you know what we're doing?"

"Listen," she said. "I'm doing you a very big favour, and costing my people money."

"I'll see you," he agreed.

Alison stirred, but she appeared to be fast asleep.

Another half an hour, and at nearly two a.m. he finally managed to pull off the road and into the car-park. The common should have been deserted at this hour, but to his amazement he saw a small helicopter waiting in the nearest open patch, its rotors turning idly. A man in flying gear hurried towards him. "David Barnes?"

David got out of the car. "You waiting for me?"

"Yeah, and let's get the hell out of here. We're going to be in all kinds of trouble with the noise abatement society as it is."

"I have a passenger."

The man peered into David's car. "She alive?"

"And how. Hey." David shook Alison's arm. "You staying here, or you want to go for a ride?"

"Eh? Eh?" She sat up, blinked at the co-pilot. "Are we being mugged?"

"We are being rescued," David said, and dragged her out of the car.

"Oh, gosh," she said, blinking blearily at the helicopter.

Someone was shouting from across the street. David caught the words, "bloody noise!", then he was pushing Alison into the rear seat of the helicopter, and squeezing in beside her.

"Name's Roger," shouted the pilot. "This is Hal. Strap in now."

David and Alison obeyed. "What's happening?" Alison asked. Nobody heard her.

"Who do you work for?" David mouthed at Hal; he had no intention of competing with the din.

The rotors whirred, and the machine lifted off. "At the moment, this machine is on charter to the *Epsom Courier*," Hal yelled at him. "We're to get you and their reporter to the site. Say, you guys media people?"

"Yes," David nodded, jabbing Alison in the ribs with his elbow.

"Some show," Hal yelled.

David looked down at the lights; most of the households below him were awake, and he didn't suppose the noise of the helicopter's engine had affected more than a few. The roads were solid masses of snaking headlights. "We're not the only ones up here, either," Roger shouted, pointing at a flashing light only slightly above them and a short distance to the right. "Buzzing around here in the dark is for the birds. You'd better get a good story." We already have a good story, David thought.

Hal nudged Roger's shoulder and pointed at a seemingly clear patch of the ground. The machine dropped out of the sky towards the dark area. Below them someone was flashing a torch. "That's our girl," Roger shouted.

The helicopter settled, and Debbie hurried forward. "Her?"

Alison exclaimed at the top of her voice. "I didn't know she was involved."

"She set it up," David tried to explain in the hope she could hear.

Hal had opened the door, and Debbie, her headscarf dislodged by the draft from the rotors, clambered in; she was wearing what looked like battle gear, pants and a flak jacket, and heavy boots. "What's *she* doing here?"

"Well—" David began, then gave up. It was impossible to talk above the noise, which increased as the helicopter lifted off. It was very crowded in the back. Debbie leaned forward. "How close can we get?" she bawled into Roger's ear.

"We've checked with the police," Roger told her. "We have to put down in Prince's Coverts. The bottom end. Just a matter of minutes."

"Can't we overfly the site?"

"Not a chance. There are police machines up there."

Debbie grunted disconsolately, then grinned at David. "We'll approach on foot."

Now the traffic beneath them was an even bigger jam, and from the flashing lights it seemed there were both ambulances and police cars in the mix-up. "Must be all London," Hal shouted over his shoulder.

They were coming down again. To their left Ashtead was a huge glow of light. "Miranda sends her love," Debbie yelled at David. "Have you made arrangements yet?"

"Haven't had the time." She gave Alison a significant glance, indicating that he seemed to have had the time for some things.

"I feel sick," Alison groaned.

"Nearly down," Roger assured her and a moment later they were on the ground, and surrounded by a crowd of people, amongst whom were several policemen.

"What the hell do you think you're doing?" roared an inspector through the open doorway.

"We have permission," Debbie shouted confidently. "Press." He peered at her card.

"You want us to hang about?" Roger asked.

"At your prices? We'll find our own way home," Debbie told him. "But thanks a million. Send in your account."

He nodded, and they ducked away from the rotors as the engine roared. "He needs his head examined," the police inspector growled. "And so do you, Miss Owen."

"Look, it's a story, right? A big one. And I was first to use it. How do we get to the site?"

"You walk," he said.

"Walk?" Alison's voice went up an octave as she looked down at her high heels.

"Walk," Debbie said, stamping her boots. "How far?"

"Half a mile, maybe," the inspector said.

"Oh, good lord," Alison said. "I can't walk half a mile in these shoes."

"Maybe you could take them off," David suggested.

"And go barefoot? You must be out of your tiny mind."

"Well, then, you have a choice," Debbie said. "You can stay here, or David can carry you." She grinned. "He's good at carrying people."

"I have no idea what you are talking about," Alison said, coldly; she had not seen the *Courier* and Martin's photos had not yet made the nationals.

"Come on," David said. "I'll help you."

"Just a minute," the inspector said. "Oh, get these people back, sergeant," he said, as they were now surrounded by quite a throng. He *had* seen the *Courier*. "Your name wouldn't be David Barnes, by any chance?"

"As a matter of fact, yes."

"Well, you're not going anywhere, Mr Barnes. You're under arrest."

"What?" Alison and Debbie shouted together. The crowd cheered.

"Arrest?" David demanded. "What am I supposed to have done? Dug the hole?"

"Grievous bodily harm," the inspector said. "Charges brought by a Mr Richard Tobey."

"Good grief," David muttered.

"It was self-defence," Debbie said. "I was there."

"Well, really," Alison commented.

"Do you admit striking Mr Tobey, Mr Barnes?"

"Well . . . I suppose I did."

"He has a fractured jaw."

"What? I didn't hit him that hard."

"You don't know your own strength," Debbie said, admiringly.

"You'll have to go along with one of my constables," the inspector said. "There won't be a magistrate's sitting until Monday morning, but your solicitor will probably be able to arrange police bail before then."

David couldn't believe this was happening, on top of everything else. "Listen," Debbie said. "How are you going to get him out of here?"

"Eh?"

She waved her arm; the noise of hooting horns seemed even louder than before. "That traffic is backed up for twenty miles. It'll be tomorrow morning before he reaches the cell. Look, you know me, Probert. I'll vouch for him."

Inspector Probert peered at her; they were old acquaintances. "You said he'd get police bail," Debbie said, winningly.

"I'm sticking my neck out," he grumbled.

"Listen, I guarantee to deliver Mr Barnes to you on Monday morning in time to attend magistrate's court," Debbie said. "If I don't, you need never give me a story again."

"I'll give you my office address and telephone number," David said. "City and South Bank, Victoria Branch."

"You work in a bank?"

"He's a manager," Debbie said proudly.

"Oh, well . . . I want him at the station nine'clock Monday morning, Debbie."

"He'll be there. Let's rush." She led the way across the open ground, now in the midst of more than a hundred interested onlookers.

"Well, really," Alison commented again, staggering after them. "All I can say is . . . ow! Ouch!" She collapsed on the grass and was nearly trodden on by the man behind her.

"Now what's the trouble?" Debbie demanded.

"I twisted my ankle," Alison sobbed. "I told you I couldn't walk on this grass in high heels."

"Well, now you'll *have* to take them off," Debbie said, brutally.

David knelt beside Alison, at least partly to stop other people stamping on her in the darkness. "Can you walk?"

"Oh, I suppose so." Alison took off her shoes. "My tights are going to be cut to ribbons. I could hit you."

"Save it."

He helped her to her feet, and they resumed their advance, crossing the last of the open land and coming to a road, jammed with traffic. The crowd on foot flowed round, in between and even over this, to the accompaniment of much shouting and swearing. David wound up half carrying Alison after all, as her progress was punctuated by little screams of distaste or pain, depending on what her stockinged feet contacted. "Not far now," Debbie said. "Just . . . what the hell is going on?"

*   *   *

They were now across the road, accompanied by a steadily growing crowd of would-be sightseers; David got the impression that some people had just abandoned their cars in the middle of the road. In front of them were even more people, and beyond was a large body of policemen, protecting a gang of council workers, who were erecting a wooden and wire fence beyond the temporary barricades. The crowd was loud in protestations at being checked, and those nearest to Debbie protested even more as she insisted on pushing her way through them to reach the police cordon. "Sorry, miss. No one is allowed beyond this point. It's too dangerous, see?"

At Debbie's shoulder, David peered across the next field at the huge arc lamps – obviously generator-powered as they were mounted on trucks – illuminating the scene. He could make out several partially collapsed houses, various clouds of steam, and a great number of people wearing hard hats and looking official. Some of them had to be media, he realised, noting other trucks with ladders mounted, carrying men and women perched with their cameras, while overhead several police helicopters buzzed to and fro. The fissure itself was out of sight.

"Listen, Johnson, don't come over all official with me," Debbie said. "I have to get in there, for the *Courier*. And besides, Martin is in there somewhere, has been for hours. I have to find him."

"Oh, it's you, Debbie," the sergeant said. "Well, I suppose . . . who're these?"

"My assistants," Debbie told him.

"Come through, quickly." The sergeant spoke to his constables, and they let the three of them through. The crowd surged forward, complaining loudly. "Media!" Sergeant Johnson bawled. "Media! Nobody else."

Debbie was already hurrying forward, but Alison again collapsed to her hands and knees. "I can't," she wailed. "I simply can't."

David thrust one arm under her knees and the other round her shoulders and scooped her up. "I never knew you were this heavy," he gasped.

"Bastard!"

He staggered after Debbie, who was now being checked again, by some more policemen, and required to show her card. But now they were within sight of the fissure, and David put Alison down, while he gasped both for breath and in consternation.

It actually could no longer be called a fissure. Rather it was a culvert or, he thought of Spain, a *barranca*. Only this wasn't a dried-up river bed. The opening was some four hundred yards long, stretching out of sight into the darkness beyond the arc lamps mounted on the trucks. It was also about fifty yards wide, and at least fifty feet deep. As though the men were digging a new Underground line, David thought.

In the bottom of the huge crevasse, various mains pipes jutted out of the earth; it was from these that the steam was rising, as well as from the remains of the several houses that had collapsed and lay in rubbled ruin, half in and half out of the fissure, a pitiful collection of shattered chimney pots, cracked and broken walls with paint peeling off, and a heart-rending accumulation of human debris, from broken bathroom fittings to torn and spring-exposed furniture, littered with treasured photographs and paintings. My God, David thought: the horse-box! He was going to court anyway on Monday morning . . .

Down there were also a large number of hard-hatted workmen, labouring in the light of the arc lamps, while in their midst other men poked and prodded and held anxious little conferences.

"Mr Lawrence!" Debbie had spotted someone she knew, and hurried across, taking her notebook from her jacket pocket. "Debbie Owen. Can you give me an update?"

Mr Lawrence looked dazed. "It's unearthly. It just happened. The original hole . . . you saw that?"

"My associate lived above it," Debbie said.

Lawrence gazed at David, who gave him what he hoped was an optimistic grin. "That suddenly opened up. Like as if someone was drawing a zipper. Three hundred yards in a matter of seconds. It stretches all the way back to those houses outside Oxshott."

"Has anyone been hurt?"

"I don't know, we are still searching down here. These houses were mostly evacuated before the fissure opened up, but the emergency services have had a lot to do."

"What exactly are those men doing now?" Debbie asked.

"Sealing off every mains outlet we can locate," Lawrence explained. "But I've recommended that all mains be switched off at source until we sort this lot out."

"Grim," Debbie said, writing vigorously. "But if you're shutting down the mains . . . does that include electricity and telephone?"

"Telephone," Lawrence snorted. "There isn't any of that, anyway. A dozen telegraph poles have come down. But yes, we're recommending the electricity and gas be entirely shut down in this area. There's too much risk of a fire, or an explosion."

"But . . . does that include Ashtead?"

"Of course it includes Ashtead."

"It's a fact it's gone dark over there," David said.

They looked at where the glow of the town had been. "Shoot!" Debbie commented.

"Miranda won't like it much."

"Blow Miranda. I don't like it much. When do you expect to get things under control, Mr Lawrence?"

"Barring accidents, and if this thing doesn't open up any more, we should have things under control by mid-morning."

"Thank God for that."

"I want to go home," Alison moaned. "My dress is ruined, my tights are cut to ribbons, and my feet hurt."

"Soon," David assured her. "Just how are we going to get home?" he asked Debbie.

She ignored him, pointing. "Isn't that someone we know?" The bald head and walrus moustache were unmistakable. They hurried across. "Dr Murray," Debbie shouted. "A word for the press."

"I've already spoken with the press," Murray said irritably.

"Different press. Can you explain this phenomenon?"

"No. No one can."

"Then it isn't a sinkhole?"

"Well, of course it's not a sinkhole."

"Then what is it? You must have some theory? What about an old Roman fortification which has collapsed?"

"A quarter of a mile long?" Murray demanded.

"Well, then, underground water, eroding—"

"There is a stream," Murray said. "But it's not big enough to cause this kind of damage."

"So you have no idea at all what might have caused this?"

"No," Murray said. "It's unearthly."

"Perhaps that's it," Alison cut in sarcastically. "Maybe it's from outer space. A space ship that crashed and burrowed into the earth."

"God Almighty!" Murray remarked. "Who is this woman?"

"It's as good a theory as any. It could happen," Alison sneered.

"If you believe in space ships," David agreed.

"If it was a space ship," Debbie said, "where is the entry point? There'd have to be a huge hole in the ground."

"We have a huge hole in the ground," David pointed out.

She stuck out her tongue at him. "Then where is the ship now? And all its little green men?"

"Lunatics," Murray growled, and wandered off.

"Debbie!" Martin hurried towards them, camera swinging on his shoulder.

"Where have you been?"

"Trying to get here."

Martin looked at David. "You're the chap with the painting."

"Was. Don't remind me," David said.

"What have you got?" Debbie asked.

"Not a lot, really."

"You mean you weren't here when it opened up? I told you to keep an eye on it."

"A fellow has to eat," Martin said, huffily. "Now I want to know how I can get this material to the office."

"I've an idea about that," Debbie said. "Let's go somewhere quiet."

"Like where?"

"Oh . . ." she pointed. "Over there," which was in the shelter of one of the trucks. She and Martin hurried across.

David made to lift Alison again but she pushed him away. "I can manage."

"Be like that. Look, I hope you're not going to say this is my fault."

"It certainly is your fault that I am standing here in my bare feet, aching," she snapped.

"You wanted to come with me. Come on."

They followed Martin to where Debbie was speaking into her mobile. "I know," she said. "I know. But this is pretty hot stuff. Time is of the essence. . . . Won't the original permission do? . . . Okay, you work on it. . . . You're a dear. We'll be waiting."

She switched off. "I'm trying to get that chopper back," she said. "Once it's daylight, which will be in an hour. We need police permission for it to come within the perimeter, of course, but my boss is going to work on it. So . . . I wonder if there's any chance of a cup of coffee?"

"There's a WRVS mobile canteen over there," Martin said. "They might be able to let us have something."

The canteen was much closer to the edge of the fissure, but situated just beyond where the crack had reached. They picked their way cautiously towards it, stared at by the various people who had accumulated within the perimeter, dodging hand-held camcorders and eager reporters, listening to the shouted reports and commands issuing from inside the fissure. "You know what," Debbie said. "There's a lot of heat coming out from down there. You don't think we could be witnessing the start of a volcano, or something?"

"In England?" Martin asked.

"There's a first time for everything."

"A volcano would have made far more noise over a long period of time," David pointed out. "Rumblings and that sort of thing."

"Well—"

They reached the canteen. "Coffee?" Debbie asked hopefully.

The Trench

The woman in a green uniform serving, smiled sweetly. "Of course. Milk and sugar?"

"You wouldn't have any sticking plaster?" Alison asked. "I think I've cut my foot."

"I don't think I've got any here, dear. But there's an ambulance just over . . . what's that?"

There was an enormous sound, a massive groan and a noise like giant hands tearing an oak tree apart. The ground on which they were standing swayed and then dissolved. "Aaagh!" screamed the woman, as her caravan began to sink.

Alison was leaning against the vehicle and falling over. David grabbed her round the waist and threw her towards what he hoped was solid ground. Martin had done the same to Debbie, who hit the earth with a thump, then rolled over and sat up. "It's moving!"

They were surrounded by screams and shrieks as the huge groaning continued, and Debbie gave a shriek as the ground once again gave way and she went tumbling down into the extending fissure, accompanying the caravan, inside which the WRVS lady was screaming even louder. "Help me! Help me!" Alison was shouting.

But she was on reasonably firm ground; David was more concerned about Debbie. He stood on the edge of the opening, watching more pipes and conduits being exposed as the earth fell away, gazing at the shattered remnants of the caravan, from which someone in a very dirty, bottle-green uniform was crawling. Debbie was further down yet, sprawling on wet mud. "Are you all right?" he called, hardly able to make himself heard above the cacophony of yells and screams which surrounded him, for the crack was still opening, away from them, and a truck was now caught in the sudden collapse.

Debbie sat up; she had lost her scarf and glasses and was

pushing muddy hair out of her eyes. "I'm coming down," he shouted, and began clambering and sliding down the new embankment.

"No," she shouted. "Get back. It's moving—" She tugged at her foot to drag it out of a sudden opening beneath her, threw herself again to one side. Only a few yards away the truck, complete with its arc lamps, slid down the embankment and then turned right over into the mud, wheels spinning.

A police inspector appeared above them. "There are people in there!" he bawled. "Get ladders and ropes! Medics! Get that ambulance over here."

Still the ground was opening, beyond the truck. Debbie was now clambering towards it, showered with earth and stones as part of the embankment spilled over her. David realised she could be buried alive at any moment, and went for her, arriving beside her in a whoosh of debris. "Idiot!" she bawled, clawing at the door of the truck, which was sinking, roof first, into the abyss.

David stood beside her and they wrestled the door open. Two policemen and two medics now slid down to join them, and between them they dragged out the two men inside. Both were cut and bruised and only half conscious. "Get them up here!" shouted the inspector from above them.

"It's going again!" someone yelled.

From their level, David and Debbie stared along the pit. Even in the darkness they could see the earth just splitting in front of them, and now there was a gush of water as either a main burst or the crack encountered a subterranean stream. Debbie was knocked off her feet and almost disappeared. David scrabbled after her, caught her jacket, and pulled her out of the morass, gasping and spluttering. The policemen and the medics had also been scattered by the sudden surge of water, and the men they had dragged out of the truck were submerged. "Find them!" Debbie shouted, and they waded and splashed forward, grasping under the water, which was now fortunately subsiding, suggesting that it had after all been a mains.

"Here!" David dragged one man up. By now there were several people above them on the embankment, and ropes were being passed down. The medics returned, and the first man was dragged up. Debbie found the second.

"Oh, gosh," she gasped. "Hell and damnation."

David helped her hold him above water while the medics tried to find pulse or heartbeat. But his face was suffused, and his eyes stared sightlessly. "Send him up," the inspector commanded.

Ropes were attached, and the apparently dead man was pulled to the top. "Now you," the inspector shouted. "You'd better get out of there."

The trench was being evacuated throughout its length, workmen and boffins scrambling up the sides to safety. The original fissure had hardly altered, but it was extending . . . "I think it's changing direction," Martin said.

"Don't be daft," Debbie snapped. Water was running out of her boots and streaming from her hair, and she was blinking myopically.

"Just an idea. You'd better get changed."

"Chance would be a fine thing."

They were surrounded by pandemonium, people shouting, trucks revving their engines, shouts from the people outside the perimeter, many of whom had had to be hastily pushed back as the fissure opened up only a few feet away. Obviously there was no chance of getting through that mob. Except perhaps by ambulance. The two truck drivers were being loaded in. "I'm sure they'd give you a ride," David suggested.

"Listen," Debbie said. "I'm wet, not wounded. Where's your girlfriend?"

"God Almighty! Alison!" He'd completely forgotten about her.

"She was on the ground, over there . . . if she fell in—!"

"She didn't," Martin told him. "She fainted, and they put her in the ambulance." Which now had its doors closed and was moving slowly towards a possible exit, bumping over the uneven ground.

"Right," Debbie said. "Did you get any photos?"

"I've run out of film," Martin confessed.

"You silly ass!" Debbie commented. "My phone! Where's my phone."

"You had it when you went in," David said.

"God! And my glasses!"

"Them too," Martin said, unhelpfully.

"What a bloody awful mess!" She gazed along the length of the trench, the end of which was now lost in darkness as the arc lamps had cut out. From all round them were shouts and screams, but the dreadful groaning had ceased.

"I think it's stopped again," David said.

"I feel sick. Must be something I swallowed."

He helped her away from the fissure, sat her on the ground in what seemed a secure place. People hurried to and fro; it seemed that there had been some other casualties, farther back, as the trench had not only extended, but also widened, and deepened. Certainly several trucks had gone in. "It's damn near a mile long," someone said.

"What do you want to do?" David asked, sitting beside Debbie.

"Get out of here," she muttered.

*   *   *

90

Decisions

D awn broke about an hour later. By then it had started to drizzle, which added to the general melancholy of the scene. The crevasse now stretched out of sight in either direction. The western end, David knew, was just beyond what remained of his property, the eastern must be nearly a mile distant.

It was some fifty yards wide, and at least fifty feet deep, a snaking obscenity across the face of what had once been attractive country. Several houses had collapsed, some into the abyss itself, others subsiding as the Fosters' had done, half their foundations torn away. Not all had been previously evacuated; it had been supposed that those at the eastern end were in no danger, and now ambulances were busy up there, their sirens wailing. More household goods lay scattered in all directions, some thrown aside by the crashing walls, some being rescued by distraught owners. Other houses were still being evacuated; most of the occupants were happy to go, even at a distance of some quarter of a mile from the great rift itself. Nearer at hand the crowd had hardly thinned, awestruck by the immensity of the catastrophe, setting up a gigantic murmur across the morning. Mostly they were young – teens and twenties – sensation seekers, the older

91

people more conscious of impending dangers and anxious to distance themselves and their families from the area. An isolated child wailed; occasionally someone screamed.

Out of the morass itself there rose a thin vapour, creating a sinister impression. Men in yellow hats and anxious policemen stood around, few actually approaching the edge as no one knew when it might move again or in which direction. Overhead, police and media helicopters whirred, looking down on the scene. On the ground, a few more intrepid cameramen were still filming.

It occurred to David that everyone was in a state of shock.

Debbie appeared to have dozed off, leaning against him. He looked down on a crown of yellow hair, but lower it was smothered in mud. As was the rest of her. He was no better. Now she suddenly stirred as Martin approached. "I raised a phone," he said. "That chopper is coming back, but they won't allow it in here. There's a field about a mile away over there . . ." he pointed east. "We'll have to walk over."

"Then we might as well walk home," Debbie said, somewhat acidly. "Ashtead is only a couple of miles beyond that." She held up her hand, and David pulled her to her feet. "You coming?" she asked.

"I don't have much else to do." He felt a strange intimacy with her he had never shared, or wanted to, with anyone before.

They trudged across the shattered area, picking their way in and out of trampled gardens, round the rubble of collapsed walls, houses fatally cracked and through a mêlée of parked cars. And everywhere they met people who just stood, staring vacantly at the ruins of their homes. Policemen stood guard in appropriate places and patrolled the flimsy ribbon markers and barricades – but there was no looting; the sightseers and potential felons were restrained by fear more than anything else. Despite her brave talk about walking back to Ashtead, Debbie was grateful to see Hal and Roger waiting beside their chopper as they approached. She and David were both soaked to the skin, filthy, her boots and his shoes filled with squelching mud. Martin was merely weary.

Hal strode across the grass to meet them. "We nearly gave up waiting. Thought you were never coming." He eyed the mud. "Hell! Are you getting aboard in that state? It'll take a week to clean out the chopper!"

"We could always crawl into plastic body-bags, if you've got any in there," she joked, her grin exposing teeth shining white against the dirt on her face.

But Hal jumped at the idea. "Good thinking. I'll fetch some."

She peered short-sightedly at him. "Hey! I wasn't being serious!"

"I am, dear girl." He returned moments later with thick black plastic sacks. "Here," he shouted as they stepped under the whirling blades to the door, "Get into these."

The narrow sacks allowed only inches in which to shuffle their feet, and climbing aboard meant sitting on the edge of the floor of the machine and swinging their legs in. But they made it, and despite their filthy condition found it a great relief to sit down – if only briefly. It was nearly six o'clock, and already the sunlight was glowing beyond the house roofs of Ashtead, tinging pink the trees and chimney pots.

Roger dropped the machine down to the empty playground at the end of Debbie's road. "You can keep your body-bags," he shouted, generously, "I don't think they'll be re-usable."

"You're all heart," Debbie responded, shivering. "What about you, Martin? Are you with us?"

"No," he yelled back. "If it's okay with these boys I'll get straight to the office to develop my reels and see if I've anything worthwhile on video. I may yet make my fortune!"

"And the best of luck. I'll get down to work at home, if I can locate my spare specs. Bye."

"If you can work," David remarked as the helicopter disappeared over distant buildings.

"What do you mean, if?"

"We saw the lights go out over here hours ago. I wonder if the electricity has come on again?"

"Dammit! I'd forgotten. If it hasn't we're going to have to be jolly economical with the hot water, and I'm going to have to get to the *Courier* to write my report."

"How?"

Debbie pushed a strand of muddy hair off her face. "Good point!" As they walked down the road she said, "By the way, what about that girl, Alison? Where do you think they've taken her?"

"To the nearest hospital casualty department, I imagine. I suppose I should try to find out which one, but I haven't a clue where to begin. I've no idea which direction the ambulances were heading."

"She wasn't badly hurt or anything. I guess she'll head straight home when her foot is bandaged up."

"Yes, I suppose so," he grimaced. "And she sure ain't gonna be a happy bunny. She will have expected me to follow and look after her."

Debbie looked at his dishevelled state and snorted. "In that mess? You have to be joking."

"It'll be no joking matter when she discovers I'm not there," he said with feeling, and especially as she'll guess I'm with you, he thought. But he didn't say so; there was actually nowhere he'd rather be, right this minute, even as he surveyed the pavement where the horsebox had been parked. "Damnation, I left that ticket at the hotel."

"Were you planning to do something about it right this minute?" Debbie asked.

"Well . . . Barbara Moore will be wondering what has happened to it. And I want my painting."

"First things first. Let's get cleaned up."

"It's all right for you. You've got clean clothes to put on."

"Well one thing I promise you. There'll be no washing done without electricity."

"Debbie! David!" Tom Clarke was striding down the pavement towards them. "Have you any idea what is happening? Or need I ask?" he added. "You seem to have been up to your necks in it!"

"Hi, Tom. Yes. We have, rather. Haven't you been following events on telly?" Debbie responded.

"Unfortunately, dear girl, the TV runs on electric power, of which there is a dearth, currently – if you'll excuse the pun."

"We were afraid of that," David sighed. "Did you know that this great fissure thing has extended?"

"No! How big do you reckon it is now?" He turned to walk back alongside them.

"At least a mile long when we left. It's coming eastwards."

"You mean in this direction?"

David nodded. "Well, towards Epsom Downs, mainly."

Tom drew a hand down over the bristles on his chin. "Oh hell! But surely it can't go on getting bigger indefinitely?"

David and Debbie looked at each other and shrugged.

"That's what we thought when it appeared to be just

a sinkhole," Debbie observed as they reached the apartment block.

"Good God, what a mess you two are in!" Penelope's head appeared at a window above them. "How the deuce did you get into that state?"

"We fell down a hole," Debbie called up to her, "That is . . . in a manner of speaking."

"You don't mean *the* hole?"

"Yes. *The* hole. And unless you are very lucky, you could be the next ones in it."

"How do you mean?"

Tom looked up at his wife. "They say the hole has become a sort of fissure which is growing longer and longer and is extending more or less in this direction."

Penelope gave a sarcastic laugh. "Oh yes. And I saw an elephant's nest in a rhubarb tree, yesterday."

"Honestly, Pen," Debbie was frowning, though it was hard to tell that under the mud. "We got caught out ourselves. Like a lot of other people."

"Your neighbour, here," David tilted his head towards Debbie, "is quite a heroine. She dragged a bloke out of his upturned lorry at the bottom of the fissure."

Tom swung round to look at her. "Really?"

"Well how else do you think we got ourselves into this mess? Now if you'll excuse us, we really must go and get cleaned up. Mid-June it might be, but I'm freezing, apart from anything else."

"By the way," Tom said. "That horsebox of yours. They came and towed it away."

"Grrr," Debbie commented. "Just don't start him off."

"Do you think we ought to consider packing up and getting out?" Penelope asked, worried.

David and Debbie looked at each other. "Hard to say. I

mean quite honestly, no one knows what the thing is going to do next; or where it's going."

"Might not be a bad idea to pack up some food and clothes," Debbie suggested, "just in case."

"But how will we know whether or not to leave?" Penelope asked.

"Haven't you got a battery radio? Otherwise you could always sit outside listening to the car radio," David said, seriously. "I mean to say, you can't wait until the earth moves, literally. By then it will be too late."

"Oh shit!" Suddenly Tom looked really alarmed.

As Debbie and David walked up the front steps of the building, there was a shout of greeting from across the road. "Hi, you guys. How are you doing? Jee-sus! What have you been up to?" It was one of the girls who had come into the flat on Friday night with the bearded bloke.

"Ask Tom," Debbie replied wearily. "He'll tell you all about it. We've got to go in and clean up."

"I see that," the girl laughed. "Hey, Tom!"

"Quick," David said. "Let's get indoors before anyone else turns up to ask questions."

Miranda gave them a noisy greeting as they entered the flat. She yowled at the door, trying to get out, not happy with her new confinement. "Come on, puss. I'll open you a tin of tuna." Debbie headed into the kitchen.

David followed. "I reckon I had better get most of my gear off in here."

"Thanks. Good thinking."

"I hope your shower is not electric?"

"No, plain old-fashioned gravity. I've often wished it was electric as the water trickles out so slowly."

"Well now we can be thankful for small mercies. You'd

better get in it first. You'll need more time to dry your hair."

"Ta. But what about you? What are you going to put on?"

"I don't suppose you'd have an old pair of baggy shorts and an equally large T-shirt I could borrow, would you?"

"Possibly. I'll have a hunt after I've cleaned off some of the mud."

Which took time. Debbie stood under the shower digging the dirt out of her scalp with her nails before attempting to use shampoo. The water in the tank had remained hot and she was well warmed up before she stepped out into a bath towel. "Okay! It's all yours," she called, hoping that there was still enough hot water left for David. She couldn't help liking him. Despite the horror of losing his home and all his possessions, he managed to be a really decent considerate guy, nice to have around. He was extremely good-looking, too. Pity about the Alison female. She felt a bit guilty about her. He came in wearing his still sodden underpants, which failed to conceal everything. "Sorry about this."

She looked him up and down. "If you didn't have something to apologise for, in these circumstances, I'd be offended. But most men would be too tired. Have a shower. It's what they do at Eton, so I'm told."

The water was only lukewarm by the time David stepped in. Nevertheless, he was able to scrub off the mud and bloody scratches, shampoo his hair and finish off with a vigorous towelling before rejoining Debbie in the sitting-room. "Whew. I feel almost human again." He knotted the towel round his waist. "Now, what about clothes? Find anything?"

Debbie giggled. "Depends what you call 'anything'. You are welcome to any of that gear on the back of the settee."

David eyed the colourful, crumpled heap with misgivings;

he picked up a pair of shocking-pink cotton shorts which might have fitted, if he could summon up the nerve to try them on. There were some black ones, too, but they looked like they'd be too snug and likely to cause an unfortunate strangulation, and the legs of the tracksuit bottoms would barely cover his knees. "Ah! These look possible." He held up a pair of large navy-blue shorts. "And I might be able to get into this T-shirt." He retreated to the bathroom.

Debbie used maximum self-control when he returned: it simply would not be fair, in the circumstances, to laugh. "Excellent. It's only a pity that I can't run an iron over them."

"I never iron T-shirts," David told her.

"Do you iron anything?"

"Not if I can help it. But occasionally the drip-dry method lets me down and I have to drag out the ironing-board before going to work." He caught his breath, picturing his mother's old board, the iron, the kitchen . . .

Debbie was sitting at her desk, ballpoint poised over a yellow foolscap notepad. "Do you mind if I finish this off and phone it through? Then I'll throw some breakfast together."

"Feel free. Shall I put the kettle on?"

There was no answer. Debbie's head bent over the yellow pad, wet hair hanging dripping over the towel on her shoulders, an old pair of spectacles with one arm missing, hanging from her ear and the end of her nose. David smiled and wandered back into the kitchen to fill the kettle, and then remembered . . . "No gas!"

"That figures," Debbie said. "There's a camping primus in the cupboard, with container attached. It'll have some left."

"Do you realise it's very risky to store a gas cylinder in a house?"

"Grrr," she said. "Get on with it."

There was indeed gas in the primus; David lit it and then ferreted around opening cupboards and the bread bin. Debbie finished dictating over the phone, and came in. "What on earth are you doing?"

"Trying to make toast over a gas jet," he replied, "And not very successfully. I couldn't find any marmalade."

"I keep it in the fridge." She got it out, plus the milk. "I hope this hasn't gone off," she added, sniffing the carton.

They didn't bother to toast any more bread, just bit hungrily into marmalade sandwiches washed down with cups of instant coffee. David's head dropped forward on to his hands. "Hell, I'm tired."

"Me too. I cannot keep my eyes open. Let's go and lie down. Just for a couple of hours." She yawned.

"Pity you put away my bedding from Friday night. Now we'll have to drag it all out again."

She rolled her eyeballs at him. "To hell with that. You can lie on my bed. Just so long as you behave yourself."

David grinned. "I cannot guarantee what I might or might not do in my sleep."

"Then you can sleep on top of the top sheet – that should keep you at your distance." She yawned again. "Come on."

"May I use your phone first?"

"Feel free."

She went into the bedroom, but listened to his call, wondering if Alison was about to rear her beautiful head. She wasn't sure what she wanted to happen about that. In a day and a half they had become so intimately acquainted – she was not at all sure how she wanted it to turn out. And now they were going to bed together – in a manner of speaking. Steady girl, she told herself: you are really two ships passing in the night, however rough the sea.

But he wasn't calling Alison; he was calling the pound.

"What did you say? You have to be joking." He listened. "I'll try to get to you as soon as possible." He hung up. "A hundred pounds, and twenty-five pounds a day rent. That's daylight robbery."

"I'll do a piece on it for the paper," she promised through the open doorway. "Now come to bed."

He kept his, or rather Debbie's, shorts on. She vanished into the bathroom to reappear in a large, T-shirt-type shortie nightie with a picture of Paddington Bear on the front. They fell onto the bed at the same moment and were both asleep within minutes, neither aware they had been joined by Miranda.

David woke first, totally disorientated, to find Miranda standing on his chest, kneading. Still tired, unwilling to relinquish sleep and eyes remaining closed, he thought he was in the hotel in bed with Alison. He was conscious of the body beside him, of a head of long, sweet-smelling yellow hair on his bare shoulder. It was only when he had removed the cat and turned towards her and his arm encircled her shoulders that he was aware of a difference. She was wearing something, and Alison never wore anything in bed! She grunted in response to the weight of his arm, stretching her own across his chest. He nuzzled her hair, kissing the warm forehead and felt her whole body nestle closer. It was the sheet barrier that finally established the reality of the situation. This was not the hotel and Alison! It was the Ashtead flat – and Debbie!

His first impulse was to sit bolt upright and apologise . . . but he managed to stop himself in time before waking her up. Well! Why waken her? This dear girl of whom he had become rather fond over the past . . . how long? Was it really only thirty-six hours? After the recent intense intimacy of each

other's company it felt as though he had known her for years!
He tightened the arm across her shoulder, and smiled.

Debbie stirred, and as her face tilted up slightly it felt
quite natural to reach down and kiss her full on the mouth.
To which she responded with a gasp and sat up. "What—?
Who the devil—? David!" She rubbed her knuckles into her
eyes. "David! You were kissing me!"

He grinned sheepishly. "Yes. And I'd like to do it again,
please."

"But you promised— I mean, we put the sheet between
us—"

"Which you will note remains in place."

She groped down the bed. "Yes, well . . . but nevertheless—"

David stared at her, absorbing the strange greenness of her
eyes, the faint fair down shining on her golden skin, the hint
of freckles on her nose. "Please?" he repeated.

She opened her mouth to reply but he was kissing her
again before she had a chance to utter a word. Without thinking his hand slipped down to stroke her breast.
Minutes later she drew away, panting. "Look. We must
be sensible. What is the time?" She examined the bedside clock. "Shoot! it's nearly midday. We've been asleep
for hours!" She slid out of bed and rushed to the bathroom.

Reluctantly, David swung his feet onto the floor. "Hell. I
suppose I'd better make some attempt to get that horsebox.
I don't want to lose my painting. Apart from my car, it's the
only possession I have left. My car! It's still in that park
where the helicopter picked us up!"

Debbie padded across the carpet to kiss the top of his head.
"Poor you. I do feel awfully sad about all that." Then she
dodged away as he tried to grab her again, his hands sliding

over her thighs. "Now we simply have to get organised. If we hang around here—"

"We will get even more organised," he said. "Did I tell you that I think you are about the most adorable woman I have ever met?"

"About? And what about Alison?"

"Well—"

"You are committed," she pointed out. "Let me know when you are uncommitted, and we can . . . talk about it."

"Do you realise that I have slept more often in your flat than in any other woman's habitat?"

"You obviously move around a lot. Now, listen. I am going to get dressed to go to the paper."

"On a Sunday?"

"Every day is a working day where there is news. Tell me what *you* are going to do."

"There's not a lot I can do, until I can get some clothes. I don't suppose—?"

She raised her eyes to heaven. "Oh, very well. You'll have to telephone the hotel and ask them to let me in to your room."

"I'll give you the room number and you can collect the key."

"Hm. All right."

"How soon will you get back?"

"I must go to the office first. Some time this afternoon. Read a good book." She closed the bedroom door.

David sat down and stroked Miranda. There were so many things he should be doing. Quite apart from collecting his car and reclaiming the horsebox and his painting, there was the matter of work . . . should he be telephoning the Area Manager? But the Area Manager played golf on Sundays and would not be amused. On the other hand, he must have seen the news: would he realise that the David Barnes whose house had fallen into the original sinkhole was actually the David Barnes who managed one of his departments? Better just to turn up, and explain on the spot – save that he had to be at the police court at nine o'clock! Damn and blast and . . .

But all he could think of was the trench. He wondered if it would start moving again, and if so, when?

The Prime Minister surveyed his colleagues, scattered around the Cabinet table. Both men and women looked somewhat scruffy; a Sunday afternoon in June was the very last time they had expected, or wanted, to be called out to cope with a crisis. Especially a crisis that had developed so suddenly, and about which they knew so little.

"I truly am sorry about this," the Prime Minister said. "But this is really a very odd situation."

"What exactly is happening?" enquired the Defence Secretary. His constituency was in Lincolnshire, and he had been at home when the summons had come.

"Perhaps you would put us all in the picture, John?" the Prime Minister suggested to the Home Secretary.

"Briefly," the Home Secretary said, "A large hole, which was described as a sinkhole, opened up in Surrey on Friday afternoon. Two houses collapsed and one of them caught fire."

"And that is a national emergency?" the Defence Secretary asked.

The Home Secretary gave him an impatient glance. "The usual steps were taken, mains cut off and that sort of thing, and just to be safe, the police evacuated a number of houses in the vicinity until they could discover just what had caused the subsidence. Everything seemed under control until last night, when the sinkhole suddenly became a sink crack, or whatever you would like to call it. Without warning, it began to extend, in a roughly east by north direction. It happened, as I say, suddenly and without any prior warning, and very quickly. More houses collapsed, but the trench soon extended beyond the evacuated area and when those houses fell in the situation became critical. That is when I was contacted by the local authorities, who felt unable to cope. The movement stopped at about midnight. But then it suddenly started again early this morning. I'm afraid this time three lives were lost, and there were a considerable number of injuries. People were taken entirely by surprise, you see." He looked around the table, somewhat nervously.

"Are we talking about an earthquake?" asked the lady Health Minister.

"I don't think we are," the Home Secretary said. "This, ah, opening has shown none of the normal aspects of an earthquake. There has been no movement of the earth, apart from the actual opening. There has been no register on the Richter scale. The earth has simply opened up. I may say that I have flown over the – ah – site, myself, this morning before coming here, a quite remarkable and most distressing experience. I think the only word to describe it is ugly. It is exactly as if some mammoth bulldozer had just torn up the earth."

"Subsidence," someone said. "Heavy rain."

"We haven't had any heavy rain for the past month," the Prime Minister said. "I have asked you to come in because there are some aspects of this situation that may be of national importance. I am sure you will all agree that in view of our rather limited majority we should not be perceived by the nation as disinterested in this phenomenon." He looked around the table, daring anyone to disagree with him. "Now, the first question is one of compensation. Mark?"

"This may be a tricky one," the Chancellor said. "We will

not get a full reaction from the various insurance groups until tomorrow, of course, but I have put out various unofficial feelers, and I'm afraid the general consensus seems to be that what has happened can be classed as an Act of God."

"Well, they would say that, wouldn't they?" someone asked. "That way they don't have to pay out. What sort of figure are we talking about?"

"I'm afraid it is already into several million pounds. But that is only the tip of the iceberg. If the movement continues—"

"We have called in all the available experts," the Prime Minister said, "To tell us why this has happened. But so far they have not come up with an explanation."

"There has to be one," the Defence Secretary declared.

"Obviously," the Prime Minister agreed. "But they have not come up with one yet. Now, as Mark has said, there is going to be a hefty bill lying around waiting to be picked up. But this may be more serious than merely financial. What happens if and when this trench starts expanding?"

"Is it going to do that?" asked the Health Minister.

"I'm afraid I simply cannot answer that question, Jeannette," the Prime Minister said. "Nor will we have an answer until we find out what is causing this thing to happen."

"But—" Jeannette looked left and right. "Are you saying, Prime Minister, that this thing could grow?"

"And continue growing indefinitely?" asked someone else.

"It appears to be a possibility," the Prime Minister said. "But—"

"Our problem is how to deal with it," the Home Secretary said. "I am talking on a human rather than a scientific or a financial basis. Hopefully, the boffins will come up with an answer in a day or two. However, a day or two, just for example, takes us into Tuesday, and the Derby meeting commences on Wednesday. The buskers and bookies and sideshows are already setting up shop."

"Are you suggesting that this trench may extend as far as Epsom Downs?"

"We cannot rule out that possibility. I'm afraid I do not want to envisage what might happen if, for instance, that trench suddenly extended on to the Downs at the height of Derby Day, with a hundred thousand people or more milling about."

"How far away is the trench at this moment?" someone asked.

"About four miles."

"Do you seriously expect it to extend another four miles, Prime Minister?"

"I have said, I have no certain answer to that. No one expected it to extend one mile, but it has done that. Now, it seems to me that we have three options. One is to do nothing, and hope the trench will not extend any further." He looked around the table.

"The second is to publish a warning in the newspapers and on radio and television, telling people that the trench is there, and that it is unpredictable, and if they go to Epsom they do so at their own risk."

"Do you think any punter is going to take any notice of that?" asked the Chancellor of the Exchequer.

"Probably not."

"It could well be seen as government weakness," the Health Minister said. "You spoke of three alternatives, Prime Minister."

"The third alternative is to cancel the meeting."

There was a moment's silence. "Cancel the Derby?" someone asked. "Wasn't it run even during the War?"

"I think it was."

"With the risk of it being bombed?"

"Ah, yes," the Prime Minister agreed.

"If we cancel the Derby," the Home Secretary said, "and nothing happens, we will be damned, the laughing stock of the country."

The Prime Minister looked round their faces. "So, do I take it that the consensus is that we adopt option number one, and do nothing?"

"About the Derby, yes," said the Chancellor. "But we have to be seen to be doing something. If only to prove that it is *not* an Act of God." Clearly, he was doing his mental arithmetic about the possible eventual cost of compensation.

"Well, does anyone have any ideas?" asked the Prime Minister.

"I think we should wait on the experts," said the Health Minister. "After all, it's early days. This trench only appeared less than forty-eight hours ago. Surely they'll come up with something."

The Prime Minister regarded her for several seconds, then looked around the rest of the faces. "I'll have a chat with my people," said the Defence Minister.

Everyone looked at him; his ambitions were well-known by his colleagues. "How on earth can it be a defence matter?" enquired the Health Minister.

"Well, it would appear that this is threatening to be a national disaster. That is a defence matter. At the very least, if this trench or whatever it is keeps on growing, you may need the army to keep order. And who knows, my people may be able to come up with a solution. I am perfectly willing to take responsibility for this . . . what shall we call it, officially?"

"The crack," suggested someone.

"Ahem," commented the Health Minister.

"Is there something wrong with that?" asked the Chancellor.

"Well, crack is a well-known drug," the Health Minister pointed out. "It also, in certain elements of society, has – ah – another connotation." The Chancellor scratched his head; his background had not involved him in the seamier side of life.

"The fissure?" asked someone.

"A bit difficult to pronounce," said the Home Secretary. "Try saying how is the fissure this morning three times fast."

"I think, John, that we need to remember that this is a most serious matter," the Prime Minister remarked, mildly. "I suppose something like, the opening, would sound feeble in certain quarters, Jeannette?"

"Well—" the Health Minister flushed.

"The trench," said the Defence Minister. "Simply, The Trench. People will understand that. And it has military connotations. That is important, if the military are going to take over. Right?" He looked around the table.

"Well—" the Prime Minister also looked around the table.

"I say let William and his soldiers get on with it," the Home Secretary said. He had long suspected that the Defence Secretary was after his job, and would dearly like to have him fall on his face over this one. "If they're that keen."

"All agreed?" asked the Prime Minister. No one dissented. "Then the matter is in your hands, William," the Prime Minister said. "I would like an evaluation from you on my desk tomorrow morning, and a decision regarding the Derby. Thank you for coming in, ladies and gentlemen."

Being trapped alone in a woman's flat wearing her clothes was not David's idea of the best way of spending a Sunday afternoon, especially when the nearness of her and their brief amorous encounter had left him distinctly . . . wishful? Miranda was no real company, and she became positively unpopular when she put down a load that had to be transferred from the litter tray to the loo before the stink made the flat unlivable. He telephoned the Laughing Cavalier.

"Hello, David," Harold said. From the noise coming over the phone he was having a busy day, presumably with thirsty sightseers who had been to look at the trench. "I wondered where you had got to."

"I got tied up," David said, not altogether untruthfully. "I wondered if the hole was getting any bigger? Is there any news?"

"Not a lot. Nobody has a clue what is going on. Oh, by the way, that insurance bloke was in here just now, asking if I knew where you were. Seems he'd tried your hotel, but you weren't there and they didn't know when you'd be back."

"Ah!" But David had no desire to speak to Wayne right this minute. "I'll get on to him tomorrow. Thanks a million, Harold." He really should try to find out about Alison, he thought. But he didn't know which hospital she had been taken to. He sighed, telephoned the Bates house; it was a number he knew off by heart.

"Hello, there!" Jimmy, Alison's younger brother.

"Hi, Jimmy," David said.

"David? David! We've been trying to get hold of you."

"I've been busy."

"Is that a fact. You know about Alison?"

"I know she was taken to hospital, but I don't know which one."

"Thames General. But I wouldn't waste your time going up there. She'll be home in an hour."

"How do you know that?"

"Because Dad and Mum had a call about half an hour ago, to go and fetch her. Seems she's been under observation for several hours, but now they're satisfied she's all right. Just shock, apparently. Was she really at the sinkhole, with you?"

"She was at the fissure," David said precisely. "With me, yes. You say she'll be back in an hour? Right."

"We tried your hotel," Jimmy said. "And you weren't there. Are you there, now?"

"No," David said. "I'm somewhere else."

"Well, give me your number. She'll want to call you as soon as she gets in."

Like hell! "I may not be here. I'll call her," David said.

Then it was a business of waiting for Debbie, staring at the blank television screen, wondering what was happening. To think there was so much going on only a couple of miles away, and he couldn't tell what it was. By opening the window he could look out and see the occasional helicopter passing over, but that apart there was little noise. He was even tempted to contact the Clarkes on the next floor. But not in this ridiculous garb.

At last, a key in the door. It was five o'clock. He took shelter behind the bathrobe until he saw that it was actually Debbie, looking fairly hot and bothered, but carrying a small hold-all. *"Voilà!"* She peered at him. "You look stressed."

"I am stressed."

"Well, get dressed and you'll feel better. Look what I've got." From the bag, which was stuffed mainly with his clothes, she took two cans of beer. "They were cold when I put them in. I suggest we drink them fairly quickly."

Nothing had ever tasted so good. "What's happening?"

She shrugged. "No further movement. There's a big debate on whether or not to cancel the race meeting. That's the big

111

event, knowing us English. Almost like cancelling Wimbledon. Oh, and there's a rumour that the army may be taking over the trench."

"What for, manoeuvres?"

"Ha ha! I suppose it's to mount guard over it, prevent looting of collapsed property, that kind of thing."

"And if they shoot somebody there'll be a hoohah."

"Absolutely. No one quite seems to know what to do, because no one has any idea of what is going to happen next. Are you going to get dressed?"

"Do I have to?"

"I thought you were dead keen on getting to your horse-box?"

"I can't, now. They shut at five."

"Ah. Well, I'm sure you have a lot to do."

He put down his empty beer can, took hers from her hand, took her in his arms. "No," she said. "Absolutely not. You get yourself dressed and go find Alison."

"Listen—"

"You listen. I told you, I'm not cut out to be second in line to the throne." She freed herself, adding "Anyway, I've got other things on my mind."

Reluctantly, he retired to the bathroom and dressed himself.

Ashtead

"Good heavens," Debbie remarked. "I'd almost forgotten what you looked like, properly dressed." She had brought him his new suit and even a tie.

"Now we can go out to dinner," he suggested.

"Now we can go and pick up your car," she said, "and you can go back to your hotel, and have a good night's sleep."

"We can have dinner at the hotel."

"I have things to do," she pointed out. "And tomorrow is going to be a very busy day. What time do you go to work?"

"I'm usually there just after eight."

"Well, don't forget that you're due in court at ten, and that I have to present you to the police by nine."

"And you are prepared to give evidence on my behalf."

"I might just do that. Tomorrow you also have to sort out your horsebox, do something about your credit cards and wardrobe, and find a home for the cat."

"She's very happy here," he pointed out.

"The whole place is starting to smell of cats."

"Don't you like moggies?"

"I do, when I don't have to clean up after them."

"You mean she didn't use her litter?"

"Grrr," she said."And extremely funky it was, too."

It was only when they were on the road he remembered that she wasn't wearing glasses. "Can you read the number-plate of the car in front of us?" he asked.

"Why should I want to do that?"

"Simply because it's about twenty-five yards away, wouldn't you say?"

"I suppose."

"Well, if you can't read a number-plate at twenty-five yards distance, you are driving illegally."

"Look," she said. "If you like, you can get out and walk."

They reached Cheam Common without an accident, and even more remarkably, David's car had not been towed away, although it had accumulated a ticket. "There," Debbie said. "I have done all I can for you today. See you in court, as they say."

He held her hand. "Sure you won't change your mind about dinner?"

"Listen, we both need our rest. And I think we both need to think about things. You in particular. I would say you are in a state of traumatic shock. You may feel better tomorrow."

He watched her drive away. No doubt she was right. You simply don't fall in love over a two-day period on the basis of having shared some fairly far-out experiences – certainly not when you have another woman in tow, in a manner of speaking. In the months in he had known Alison he could not recall having felt this way once. And he was going to see Debbie again tomorrow. The thought made him hum a little tune.

He drove up to the hotel. The roads were still fairly crowded with traffic, going both ways, some to look at the Trench, others returning home from having looked at it. The beaches would probably have been half empty this weekend, although the weather had been glorious. He wondered at the mentality of people who preferred to gawp at a muddy hole? But he was one of them – although he felt he had a personal interest.

"There are some messages for you, Mr Barnes," said the reception clerk.

David pocketed them until he was in his room. Three calls from Wayne. That was predictable. But he didn't want to talk to him right this minute. A call from the Area Manager, who had, it appeared, finally discovered what was going on, and that one of his people was involved. "I'd like to see you tomorrow morning, first thing, David," Oakley had said. "I'll be in early."

Well, he wanted to see Oakley, David reflected. The fifth call, as predictably as any other, was from Alison, and consisted largely of, Where are you, you beast?

He sighed, poured himself a beer and called her home. "Where have you been?"

"Ah – sleeping, mainly."

"Sleeping? All day?"

"Well, I surely didn't sleep all night," David pointed out.

"Then how come you didn't answer the phone in your room?"

"Ah – well, I wasn't here, you see."

There was a moment's silence; Alison was clearly considering this, and working things out. Then she said, "You were sleeping, but you weren't in your hotel room."

"Good thinking."

"You were with that woman!" she shouted.

"I was in that woman's flat. But—" on the other hand, he couldn't say he hadn't touched her.

"You lousy, miserable, stinking rat. While I was in hospital. You never came to see me."

"Well, I didn't know where you were."

"You could have found out. You could have telephoned to find out how I was."

"How are you?"

"Oh—" the phone was banged down.

The end of a beautiful relationship? He doubted it; she'd get over it soon enough. More was the pity.

He had dinner in his room, watching television. There was now a considerable nationwide coverage of the Trench, with extensive video footage, and a whole host of experts, or self-proclaimed experts, offering their opinions, which covered as wide a spectrum as ever, from the collapse of a water system deep under the earth, too deep to be discovered by any diviner, through the activation of summer heat on the earth's crust – the expert being unable to explain why this should happen in England, which even in a hot summer was a lot cooler than many other places in the world – to the possibility that the trench was being caused by the activity of an alien spaceship, which had crashed into the earth eons ago, and was only now coming to life. To the question as to why the spaceship had remained dormant for those eons, the expert retorted, very plausibly, that they would not know the answer for that until the found the spaceship. He recommended boring straight down into the earth at the place where the sinkhole had first appeared. "My garden," David remarked to himself, drinking some of the wine he had ordered with his dinner.

Needless to say, global warming also received a good deal of mention. There was also information confirming Debbie's rumour that the army was taking over, although no one said exactly what, and that no decision had as yet been taken regarding the Derby meeting; this was still under discussion, both by the Government and the Jockey Club.

The fact was, David reflected as he got into bed, no

one had a clue what was happening, or what to do about it.

He had arranged an early call, but he didn't need it. Sleep was a succession of mini-nightmares, in which he saw the trench opening time and again, and Debbie falling in, to be dragged out by a gigantic Miranda, purring loudly. Presumably, he thought, Miranda was in bed with Debbie right this minute. Lucky moggie.

He was glad to be up, shaved and dressed and breakfasted, in time to be at the bank at eight o'clock. Where he was welcomed like a hero. "Saw all about you on the television," confided the head porter. "Must have been quite something."

"Your picture is in the papers this morning," his secretary announced. She was a plump young woman with short black hair, and wore horn-rimmed glasses. "Who is that girl you were carrying?"

"Let me see that." He snatched the paper from her. Martin had succeeded in selling the story nationwide, all right. Not that he cared for the caption: SINKHOLE HERO RESCUES GIRL REPORTER. There was no mention of Miranda.

"Like it says, she's a reporter," he pointed out.

"You must know her very well," Angela remarked. He had never actually carried *her* anywhere, or even been tempted to do so.

"You old devil." John from Securities bustled in. "Who's been having a busy time, then?"

David looked at him. "I suppose one would call losing one's house and all one's belongings a busy time, yes."

John frowned. "You serious?"

"Every damned thing."

"Shit! I say, old man, I'm most dreadfully sorry. What are you going to do?"

"Hopefully—" the telephone buzzed.

"I have Mr Bryson," Angela said.

"Ah! Wayne!"

"Where have you been the last twenty-four hours?" Wayne demanded.

"It would take too long to explain. Do we have a problem?"

"I'm afraid we do. The insurance people are not happy with the situation."

"Who is?"

"They feel that what has happened is an Act of God."

"So I am effectively bankrupt."

"Their attitude is that the Government will be paying compensation, and that you should take your claim to them."

"We could be talking about a year. Maybe more."

"Yes. Not too good."

"Right. I'll have to organise things here. Look, I'll send you a cheque for the money you advanced."

"No hurry, old man. I just thought I should put you in the picture."

"Thanks," David said.

"Mail." Angela placed the pile of personal items on his desk.

"Credit cards!" He slit open the various envelopes. "I actually feel solvent. Angela, I need a new cheque book and a PIN number."

"You're supposed to keep that in your head."

"Well, I kept it written down, and right now what it was written on is a piece of ash. Is the boss in yet?"

"Just."

"Buzz Caroline and see if he's available."

She hurried off, and David checked his desk diary. Walden at nine. Early bird. But a good client even if his income did not always match his expectations. Nine! The phone rang. "I have a Miss Owen on the line," Angela said, primly.

"Great! Put her through. You," he said after the click, "are the answer to a maiden's prayer."

"Are you really a maiden?" she asked.

"It's not for want of trying. Do you know I dreamt of you all night? And the cat? Tell me, where did she sleep? On your chest or tucked up against you."

"I locked her out if you must know," Debbie retorted. "She wanted to make a nest in my hair. I just wanted to remind you that you are due at Epsom Police Station at nine, and the time is eight thirty. I suggest you leave now."

"I can't. I have to see my boss. I'll be there as soon as I can."

"Don't let me down on this, David, or you'll be a wanted man."

"Sounds great. I'm hurrying."

"Mr Oakley is waiting for you," Angela said, "and Miss Bates is on the line."

"Shit! Listen, tell her I'm in a meeting and I'll get back to her just as soon as I can."

He hurried to the lift, rode up to the Area Manager's Floor. "David!" Terence Oakley was well over six feet tall, and looked it even when seated behind his walnut desk. He was a somewhat cadaverous-looking man, which entirely belied his nature, which was extremely benign, most of the time. "Sit down and tell me all about it."

"I'll have to be brief," David said, sitting down. "I'm due in court in half an hour."

Oakley frowned. This was not what he wanted to hear from one of his managers. "In court?"

"It seems, that during all the crisis on Friday night, I hit this fellow. Well, he was being obnoxious. And the blighter has

119

brought a charge of grievous bodily harm. He has a hairline fracture of the jaw. I didn't know I could hit that hard."

"Neither did I," Oakley said, now looking somewhat pleased. "Well, try to stay out of gaol. Now, what exactly happened?"

David outlined the events of the weekend, seen from his point of view, omitting such things as Debbie and where he had spent the various nights. "Remarkable," Oakley commented. "I assume all is in order with your insurance?"

"Nothing is right with my insurance. They are saying it is an Act of God."

"Good heavens. They're buggers, aren't they? So—?"

"I may need some support from the bank, sir."

"Ah. Yes. I'm sure we'll be able to go along with that, David. And no doubt the Government will stump up some compensation. Right. I just like to know what's going on. Off you go to court."

David returned downstairs, feeling as if the day had already gone on too long, although he was very grateful for the way Oakley had taken the whole thing. "I have to go out," he told Angela. "Tom Walden is coming at nine to talk about that extended loan he needs, and there are a couple of others in the diary. I'm going to ask Peter to stand in until I get back, but he will need full support as regards information."

"No problem," Angela said. "When will you be back?"

"I have no idea."

She digested this. "Well, where can I reach you?"

"Try Wormwood Scrubs," he suggested, and hurried off.

This being a working day, most of the traffic was still flowing into London, and he actually reached Epsom just before half-past nine. Debbie was chatting with the duty sergeant, another policeman she apparently knew very well; wearing one of her suits and white shirts, as always she looked good enough to eat, even if she was blinking at him myopically. "May I ask where your solicitor is, sir?" the sergeant inquired.

David looked at Debbie. "You didn't say I needed a solicitor."

"God save me from impractical bank managers," she complained.

"You'd better use the phone," the sergeant suggested. "You do have a solicitor, Mr Barnes?"

"Ah—" only the firm of old family solicitors actually, not having needed one since Mother's death. But presumably he was still on their books, as it were.

"Yes," said the prim female voice. "Darling, Darling and Carshott. May I help you?"

"Mr Darling junior, please." Better try to get the younger man if possible.

"Is he expecting the call?"

"I doubt it. Tell him it's David Barnes."

"Ah," she said, and put him through.

"David? Is it really your house that went in?"

"Amongst others. Listen, Joe—"

"And I imagine the insurance people are acting up. Yes. You'd better come and see me. Can you make it this afternoon? Three o'clock?"

"Joe," David said earnestly. "I would like to speak with you about the house, and I intend to do so. But right now I'm in a spot of bother."

"What sort of bother?"

"How does a case of GBH grab you?"

There was a moment's silence. Then Joseph Darling asked, "You?"

"Is that so incredible?"

"Well, no . . . I mean, yes. It is! It's just that, well—"

121

"I'll say it for you. Bank managers do not as a rule get involved in GBH. So I've broken the mould."

"And you are—?"

"I am about to be removed to Epsom Magistrates' Court."

"I'll be there."

"All fixed up?" Debbie asked. "Right. I'll be off."

"Just hold on one moment," David said. "Aren't you coming with me?"

"You don't need me. You have your solicitor."

"You were going to testify on my behalf."

"I'll do that when it comes to trial."

"It's not going to come to trial," David explained. "I'm guilty. I hit the chap."

The sergeant coughed. "You're not supposed to say things like that," Debbie pointed out. "And if you're going to plead guilty, what evidence can I give?"

"You can explain the extenuating circumstances."

"If you are pleading guilty, they are not going to ask me to explain the extenuating circumstances. Right now I have an appointment with my eye specialist. See you around. And good luck."

David looked at the police sergeant, who winked. "Busy girl, our Miss Owen. She tells me you lost everything when your house went up."

"It didn't go up, until after it had gone in," David explained. "But yes, I lost everything."

"All your documents, and things like that?"

"As a matter of fact, yes. Is there something on your mind?"

"Is that your car outside, sir? Can you show me your driving licence?"

"My—" David realised his mouth was open.

"Not to mention your insurance certificate," the sergeant

went on. "Now I'm sure these things are on file, somewhere. But I suggest you obtain replacements just as quickly as you can. Or you may find yourself in a spot of bother. More than you are now, eh?"

"My client pleads not guilty and reserves his defence," Joe Darling said. For a comparatively young man he was overweight and wore a gold hunter in his waistcoat pocket, its chain displayed across his ample stomach. He also exuded an air of total indifference to the rest of the world.

"Very good," the magistrate said. "I will remand him to appear at the next Crown Court." David couldn't believe his ears.

"We apply for bail, your worship."

"One thousand pounds. Next."

"They'll take a cheque," Joe said. "From a bank manager."

"Listen," David said. "What the hell were you doing? I was going to plead guilty."

"And you'd have gone to gaol. GBH is a serious offence."

"Now it's going to be hanging over my head for the next month, at least."

"While we work out an adequate defence," Joe said reassuringly. "You give your cheque to the clerk over there. And don't forget to come to see me this afternoon."

"I do have a job to go to."

"This is important. See you." He bustled off.

David slowly got into his car, turned right for London, then changed his mind and turned back for Ashtead. As he was out he might as well collect the painting and the horsebox. He stopped at a telephone booth and called Angela. "All well?"

"In a manner of speaking. There are all kinds of people trying to get hold of you. Shall I give you a list?"

"No," he said.

*   *   *

David's whole life seemed to have descended into an idiotic farce. On the one hand, every time he thought of his home, the tragic loss of his entire self-identity, his, and his family's, history, every memento, photograph, precious possession . . . he felt desperate, breathless with grief. On the other hand, he had found and fallen in love with Debbie – the sweetest, dearest and most gorgeous girl in the world. He could never remember so enjoying anyone's company: visualising her long, brown legs, silky gold hair and enormous green expressive eyes, imagining her crisp bubbly voice, his misery evaporated to be replaced with the happy feeling of sun on his face. Even when she wasn't with him! But could it be love, or was he subconsciously seeking an emotional refuge? An escape from the literal as well as mental void that had overtaken him?

Whatever. Right now he really had to be practical and make a list of all the things he must do towards putting his life back on some sort of sound footing. He needed a home, maybe a small flat to rent: a new wardrobe. Joseph Darling would have to get working on claims for compensation or insurance money to replace his losses. He should notify the Canadian cousins what had happened – except he had lost his address/computer diary in the pit. Maybe Darling Senior had some addresses of distant family on file. But first things first: his two remaining family treasures – the painting and the broken tapestry screen; they must be retrieved and housed before returning Barbara Moore's horsebox.

It cost him a hundred and fifty pounds to extract the horsebox from the pound. It occurred to him that he was spending money on the scale of a bucket with a hole in it losing water. What had begun as a mess on Friday night had now descended into a morass. Once again, farce. "Your car doesn't have a towbar," the pound attendant pointed out.

"Ah," David said.

"So how are you going to get that thing out of here?"

"Ah," David said again. "I don't suppose it could just stay here for a while?"

"It'll cost you twenty-five quid a day."

This time David said, "Shit! Well, how long *can* it stay here?"

"I can give you a couple of hours," the attendant said, his tone indicating that he was breaking every rule in the book.

"Thanks a bunch," David said.

It shouldn't be difficult, he told himself; a towing vehicle would have to be found. Surely the average self-respecting garage would help. But where to house the huge painting? His artist friend and fellow tennis enthusiast Simon Harkness? Good thinking. He had an enormous studio flat with acres of empty wall space in the dockland area. He called Angela again on the attendant's phone. "Can you look up the number of Simon Harkness, call him and ask him to call me here, please?"

She did. "Hi, Simon. How are you?" They exchanged friendly niceties. "The reason I'm calling is that I wondered if you could house a painting for me?"

Simon thought he could. "What size?"

"Six by four."

"Inches, I presume."

"Feet."

"Hell, dear boy! I will have to measure the lift."

"Amply large enough, as I remember."

"Well . . . er . . . six by four? Are you sure?"

"Yes."

"How long for?"

"Until I find somewhere to live. A couple of weeks, maybe."

He knew he was being optimistic, but Simon was sounding rather dubious about the idea: he mustn't alarm him.

"Live! I don't follow. Have you sold your house?"

"No. It fell down the hole."

"Hole! What hole? What are you talking about, dear boy?"

"Don't you ever watch television, or listen to the news?"

"Not if I can avoid it. Why? What's happened? What have I missed?"

David told him. After which Simon became extremely sympathetic, almost maudlin, and offered to accommodate David, too.

"That is very kind of you, but rather a long way to commute to the bank." And even further from Debbie in Ashtead. "However, I will bear your invitation in mind. Thank you. Meanwhile, could I deliver the painting this morning?"

"Anytime, dear boy. I shall be here."

Simon was a really nice bloke, would bend over backwards to help anyone, but despite playing a hard game of tennis, like so many artistic types he was rather 'precious': David doubted if he could spend more than twenty-four hours in his company without going spare!

A garage-hand was found to drive a pseudo-jeep with towbar. The horsebox was hitched to the jeep and David led the way north across the river to Simon's flat. The painting did fit in the lift, just, and the garage man waited outside while David and his friend manoeuvred the precious possession into the least inconvenient position. "And I'll have to get this screen repaired, sometime," David remarked as he tucked it out of sight behind a chair.

"No problem, dear boy. I'll get it to my framer tomorrow. He'll fix it in no time. He is awfully good at that sort of thing."

"Super. Thanks very much, I'd be most grateful. Just let me have his bill." He smothered a sigh, visualising his rapidly depleting savings account. "Now do you mind if I make a phone call?" He had to find out where to deliver Barbara's horsebox. No good taking it back to her house since it had apparently joined his down the pit.

David lost sight of the jeep and horsebox in his rear-view mirror twice en route to Barbara Moore's brother's place in Hampshire, waited, and they duly caught up with him. Fortunately, Barbara was out when he arrived – he really didn't want to repeat the whole story of his adventures to date and was grateful to escape after leaving a note of thanks. He paid off the jeep driver and, as he was in the vicinity and very dry, decided to drop in to the Laughing Cavalier in Oxshott for a pint of Coke and a bar lunch and an update on local news. "Place is still seething with police, army blokes and bearded experts," Harold told him, tilting his head towards two groups of men seated round tables near the dartboard.

"Good for business?" David suggested.

The publican grinned. "Never had it so good. Can't get supplies in fast enough." He went off to give David's order to the kitchen and pull more pints for one of the groups and when he returned he asked, "What about you? How are you coping? Get any of your stuff back?"

"No. But I guess I'll survive, though it was a near run thing when my house went." He explained how the cat had given the warning.

Another group of people came into the bar and Harold went to ask for their orders. They were only a few feet along the bar counter from where David was standing, and he couldn't help catching a few words of their conversation. ". . . impossible to anticipate that it would not only continue further, but actually change direction."

127

"Excuse me. Did you say the Trench has changed direction?" David interrupted.

A stout little man with a mop of ginger hair and wire-framed spectacles frowned at him. "Who are you?"

Harold didn't like his tone. "This, my friend, is the gentleman whose house was the first to fall into the sinkhole – or whatever you call it now."

"Really!" Ginger-mop immediately became quite animated. "Were you in it at the time?"

"No. Or I wouldn't be here, would I?"

"Did you see it happen?"

"Yes."

"Where were you standing?"

"I wasn't. I was running like hell."

"Why? What warning did you have?"

"What made you run?" Another man asked.

They crowded round him, eager for every detail, explaining that because they were professors of seismic geology, the army had summoned them from Oxford and other universities to assess cause and effect, and anticipate what the Trench might do next. David answered their questions as briefly as possible, then asked, "What was that someone was saying about the Trench opening up in another direction?"

"Previously it was extending directly towards Epsom. Just after lunch today it veered off slightly towards Ashstead, and—"

"Ashstead. Oh God, no!" David slammed his glass down on the counter and fished some money out of his trouser pocket. "What do I owe you, Harold?"

Harold eyed the crisp twenty pound note. "Forget it. It was on the house. I'll see you again, sometime."

"Thanks. Must dash," he called over his shoulder, heading for the car.

"What about your lunch?" Harold shouted.

"Later," David replied.

Within five minutes he found himself stuck behind an articulated lorry, unable to pass because of nonstop traffic heading in the opposite direction. And it was several minutes later before he registered that most of the oncoming traffic consisted of private cars – laden – and he realised that these must be refugees escaping from the advancing Trench. Oh God! Debbie! Was she at home? Did she know? Damn and blast this confounded lorry. He hit the car horn and got two vertical fingers from the trucker in reply.

When the huge vehicle in front finally turned off his route, David reckoned he was still five miles from Ashtead but with little traffic ahead he was able to make up some time. But only briefly. Rounding a corner into a village street he was faced with a mass of stationary cars, vans and lorries, all hooting, their drivers shouting angrily through their open windows. David got out of his car. "What's happening?" he asked the greengrocer who was collecting boxes of vegetables from the pavement stand outside his shop.

"Don't ask me! Total jam up. Been like this for the past half-hour and more. No good them shoutin' and blastin' their horns. They're not goin' anywhere."

"How far to Ashtead?"

"About a mile up there," the man replied, indicating a river of cars to the east.

"Thanks," David nodded. And began running along the pavement. He left his keys in the car – if anyone wanted to and was able to move it, they were welcome.

Twenty minutes later, as he turned into Debbie's road, it occurred to him that she might well have fled ages ago, and he would have to make his way back to that blasted village to reclaim his car – providing no one had pinched it. Then he recognised the dear girl's battered estate car and was unsure whether to be pleased or sorry – if she was still here, of course.

He knew she was at home long before she answered the doorbell, because of the noise, the thumps and bumps and occasional swear words. "What on earth are you doing here?" she demanded.

"I've come to fetch you."

"Why? You didn't know I'd be here."

"Because I love you and I needed to make sure you are okay."

Debbie flung her arms round his still panting middle, hugged and released him before he could get a firm hold on her. "Come on in and see if you can talk Miranda into behaving herself. She refuses to allow me to shut her in that cardboard box."

"Can you blame her?"

"I'm trying to save the bloody stupid animal's life! How else can I get her out of here without her running away?"

"We could carry her."

"There's a hell of a lot to be carried. And if she gets agitated she'll jump out of our arms. Likewise, if we open a car window she'll be gone."

David sighed. "True. Here Miranda. Puss, puss, puss!" Miranda ran straight into his arms.

Debbie was impressed but not prepared to say so. Instead, she rushed back into her bedroom to grab the bag she had packed. "Here," she said, throwing him the keys. "Can you get this and the cat into my car? Or do you want to take her in yours?"

"Mine's in some village a mile away."

Her soft green eyes grew wide. "You mean you walked?" He grinned at her and nodded. Her eyes rolled, expressively, and she blew him a kiss. "When you've got that gear stowed you might knock on the Clarkes' door. See if there is anything we can do to help with the children."

Miranda yowled loudly as she was carried down to the car and stowed on the back seat – alongside Debbie's computer and printer. David smiled when he saw it: the dear girl might be scared out of her wits but she remained essentially practical.

The Clarkes' front door was open.

"Hi there!" David called. "Anything we can do to help?"

"Who's that? Oh, it's you, David," Tom said. He looked harassed and his hair was standing up in spikes from agitated finger-combing. "Come in, man, if you can find anywhere to put your feet."

The place was chaotic. Black plastic binbags stood near the door, stuffed with clothes. There were two suitcases, one with a broken zip and tied with cord. The children had added precious belongings, a cricket bat, a large plastic space-station and a teddy bear amongst other things. Penelope was shouting instructions from the kitchen, where she was accumulating as much food as she could cram into the coolbox, plus a basket of tinned goods – which reminded David that he hadn't had any lunch! "No, George, you cannot take your bicycle," she said.

"But Mum—" the boy wailed.

"Where are my ballet shoes, Mum? I'll need them for tomorrow." The little girl's voice.

"There might be some room for gear in Debbie's car," David suggested, "Though I doubt if we can manage a bike."

"Of course you can't," Tom agreed, "But perhaps you might find room for one of these sacks."

David heaved a binbag up onto his shoulder. "Are you ready to leave yet?"

"Just about. Penelope! Come on. Everyone to the car."

"Let's try to stay in tandem, then we can help each other

out if necessary." David headed down the corridor to the stairs.

"Splendid. Thanks. We'll be with you in just a minute."

Debbie's face was taut as, having locked the door of her flat, she set her bags down beside David on the pavement. He raised the hatch and loaded them for her.

The girls from opposite appeared, waving their arms. "Do you really think it's coming here?" one of them shouted.

"I don't propose to chance it," Debbie said. "Are you staying?"

"Ooh . . . well—"

"I'd leave, if I were you," David said. "You have transport?"

She nodded. "But . . . what should we carry?"

"Anything you can fit in."

"Where should we go?" asked another of them.

"North of the river," her friend said. "It'll be all right north of the river."

Debbie looked at David. "I wasn't going north of the river. My parents live in Sutton. I was going to them."

"I should think that's far enough," David said.

Tom's car was a few yards away down the street ahead of them, so they got in and drove up behind his heavily laden family Volvo. "I hope his wing mirrors are at the right angle," David commented, "He can't see a damn thing through his rear window."

"They were jolly lucky they were able to get to the children's school to fetch them. The traffic on the main road is terrible, they say."

As she spoke her voice was drowned out by the sound of a loud-hailer stuck on the roof of a police car. "This is an official police warning. This area is in imminent danger of being engulfed by the advancing Trench. You are ordered to

evacuate immediately. This is an official police—" the voice
trailed off as the police car continued down the road behind
them. Tom stuck his head out of his car window. "We head
north, okay?"

"Yes, fine," David called back. "We'll follow you."

But they didn't get far. A line of vehicles waited ahead
of them to turn into the stream of traffic on the main road,
where all the drivers were too concerned about putting
distance between themselves and the advancing threat to
give way. Only very occasionally was someone prepared
to pause and let one car through. Debbie bit a fingernail.
"Honestly! Nearly all the cars from this road are loaded with
children. You'd think people would let them through!"

"Maybe they are all loaded with children themselves." David
took her hand from her mouth, kissed it.

"Yes," she agreed.

David turned to look at her and found the big green eyes
fastened on his. "A pity we had to meet in these circumstances."

"But for these circumstances we never would have met."

"Are you sure? Maybe it was always decreed we should."

"Fate? Karma?"

He slid his left arm across her shoulders and drew her against
him. "Something like that, I guess."

She leaned her head on his shoulder and bit her lip, wanting
to believe – so much. Were his feelings really any more than
a shock reaction to the events of the past forty-eight hours?
He was so gorgeous, in every way. Of course, just at the
moment he tended to give the impression of 'little boy lost',
understandably, but he could not have become a bank manager
without having personality and strength of character. So how
could he fall for a short-sighted, ordinary small-time reporter
on a third-rate newspaper?

They were stationary, but the car suddenly began to shake. Debbie shot bolt upright in her seat. "What was that?"

David stuck his head out of his window. "Can't see anything."

"We haven't moved one foot in the past five minutes!" Debbie groaned. She opened her passenger door and got out onto the pavement – which trembled.

"Oh God! David!" she screamed. She could see, beyond the roof of the railway station, the tall brick warehouse chimneys crumbling, falling and disappearing in a huge pall of dust.

"What?" David yanked on the handbrake and leapt into the road.

"Look! It's coming! It's only a couple of streets away."

"The cars are moving. Get in quick."

Suddenly they were next in line, the Clarkes having moved on into the mainstream of traffic. Then the cars closed up across their bonnet and they were immobilised again. Nothing was moving – but the car continued to shake.

Debbie got out again and David came round the car to join her. Then, above the noise of car engines, hooters and raised voices, they heard the rumbling, faint at first but growing louder by the second.

"Look! The station is collapsing!" The long roof of the building simply caved in and disappeared behind the chimneys of the houses on the opposite side of the road from Debbie's flat. Then those houses themselves seemed to fall backwards.

People around them were screaming and shouting, jumping out of their cars and starting to run. David and Debbie stared open-mouthed as the far end of the road opened up and swallowed all before it, including Debbie's apartment building. "David!" she screamed again. "Get Miranda! We must run!"

But at last the traffic was moving. Gratefully, they scrambled back into the estate car.

Sutton

"Look, there they are." Debbie reeled down her window to peer round the car in front. Half an hour ago the Clarkes' car had edged into the mainstream of traffic several vehicles ahead of her Vauxhall Estate and been lost to view; now she could see it parked on the hard shoulder. "Keep going," she told David, who was driving. "At the rate we are moving I can reach them on foot long before you draw level." She opened the door of the car as it dribbled to a standstill again, got out and ran ahead to greet her neighbours. "Hi, you guys! What's up?"

"One vomiting daughter," Tom replied.

Penelope was holding the little girl's forehead. "I think she'll be all right now. She must have lost everything that was in there. Tom, pass me another tissue, will you please."

Tom obliged, grumbling, "I don't know how we are ever going to get back on the road. Or where we should head when we do." Aware that their home was gone, he was frantically worried.

"I'm not sure that we will have an option," Debbie made a moue, "But if it is possible, I suggest we could head up to my parents' place in Sutton. There will be room for us to park both cars on their forecourt, unless you have other ideas in mind."

136

"None. Sounds as good as anything. Do you think David could hold up this traffic long enough for us to pull out in front of him?"

"Sure. But I had better just tell him the plan, then I'll come in your car if you can find room. Otherwise you won't know the way. Dad and Mum are off the main route."

"I think Jason should go with David in your car so as to make room in ours. Otherwise you'll have to have one of them on your knee. And by the way," he managed a grin, "we got Polly out before she threw up."

"I'm glad of that," Debbie grinned back – with an effort, mostly with the intention of suppressing the almost overwhelming sense of devastation after seeing her home destroyed. That had been the most harrowing experience of her life; she wanted to weep, non-stop. But the thought of how well David was coping helped her bite back the tears. After all, she had only been in the flat two years – David had grown up in what had once been his family home. At least some of her childhood possessions were still in the house in Sutton. "Come on then, Jason," she called.

The child looked anxiously at his father. "Do I have to?" He sensed the enormity of what was happening without actually having assimilated the full facts.

"Wouldn't you just love a ride in Debbie's nice car?" Tom urged, as David drew near. "You can help look after the cat."

Jason shrugged and said, "Okay." But he wasn't smiling as Debbie opened the passenger door for him.

"I'm going with Tom to act as guide," she said. "Will you let us in then try to stay right behind us."

"If I can," David grunted. He was disappointed to lose Debbie, and he wasn't enchanted with the idea of driving any distance with this solemn-faced child. He had had very little to do with young children: being an only child himself there were no small nephews and nieces, and he always felt somewhat tongue-tied in their company. But he didn't argue. "You'd better be quick, darling," he said, conscious of using the term of endearment for the first time. "The traffic is moving again." But slowly – very, very slowly – with bouts of furious hooting, shouting and arm-waving, especially from behind when David allowed Tom back into line.

They were climbing a hill, Tom praying that his engine wouldn't overheat, when Polly screamed. She had turned to kneel on the back seat and peer over the mound of luggage out of the rear window. "The houses are falling! I can see them! And there's lots of smoke." She started to cry.

Penelope released her seatbelt and reached behind her, trying to comfort the child. "It's all right, my sweetheart. There's no need to cry." But she too was frightened.

"It's coming, Mummy. It's coming, and it's going to swallow us up!"

"Nonsense! It won't reach us up here," she said sternly, almost as though forbidding the destructive force to dare! She was feeling physically sick, herself. But this was no car sickness, just pure terror.

Debbie put an arm round the little girl. "Try not to worry. It won't help. We are going to my mummy and daddy's house and we'll be quite safe there." She prayed that was true. She was not a very actively church-going type of Christian and not in the habit of communing with God, but she saw no harm in hedging her bets. If there was a God up there in His heaven, she just hoped He could hear her.

Both north and southbound lanes were packed tight with traffic heading north for the hoped-for safety of the capital, and gradually they were progressing a little quicker when Debbie instructed Tom to edge across to the right-hand side. "You'll need to turn right about a mile further on," she said. Then she asked Tom to open her window with the electric switch so that she could signal to David to follow. David acknowledged her instructions with a wave of his hand.

Their manoeuvres met with aggressive responses from their fellow travellers and Tom was glad they were moving too fast now for any road rage maniac to dare leave his car to come and start a fight. "This is the turning coming up now, by that lamp post," Debbie said, leaning over Tom's shoulder. "That's it! Great. Then second on the left."

It wasn't easy. Cars were stacked up trying to get out and head north, too, but at least most of them were on their correct side of the road. "That's it. There's the forecourt just beyond that sycamore tree."

With a sigh of relief, Tom turned the wheel and the car bounced up over the footpath onto the paved area in front of a redbrick house with a white front door. David drew Debbie's car in alongside. Jason was first out and rushed into his father's arms, tears streaming down his face. He had struggled to be brave for so long and now was time to give way.

"Debbie!" Her father opened the door and flung his arms round her. "Oh, Debbie, we have been so worried." He was a rather frail-looking man with white hair.

A tall woman with fading blonde hair appeared. "They've been showing video footage taken from a helicopter over Ashtead," she said, putting an arm round the girl. "Not a pretty sight even when you don't have your nearest and dearest living in the area. We couldn't tell exactly what part was swallowed up – do you know—?"

Debbie nodded and made a quick check over her shoulder that the Clarke children couldn't hear hear before answering. "Yes. My whole building went."

"Oh no!"

"And we've brought a family from one of the other flats with us."

"Us?" her father asked.

"Yes. David! Come and meet my parents."

They shook hands, the older couple slightly bemused.

Penelope rushed up to the door with Polly. "Do you think we could use your loo, please? It's rather urgent."

"Yes, of course. Follow me." Mrs Owen hurried up the stairs, leaving her husband to usher all the surprise guests, including Miranda the cat, into the house.

They had an alfresco meal, part lunch and part tea, on the back patio. None of them had had any proper lunch. Tom and Penelope insisted on opening their coolbox. "We virtually emptied our fridge into here," Penelope explained. "We might as well eat the stuff up before the icepacks melt." She busied herself feeding her family, while Elizabeth Owen produced plates and cutlery and the men concerned themselves with liquid refreshments.

David looked at his watch. It was four o'clock. He had left the office that morning at half-past eight, and hadn't been back.

He wondered if he still had a job, toyed with the idea of calling Angela, and decided against it. There was no way he could go in now, or cope with any banking problems. Even supposing he could get there without a car. Car! he thought. My God, my car! Abandoned just outside Ashtead. Probably it too was in the pit by now.

There was an automatic, unspoken agreement not to talk of the terrifying events they had escaped whilst the children were within earshot, so conversation was limited to trivialities like traffic and weather and how pretty the garden looked. "And how long have you two known each other?" Elizabeth had been itching to ask since they arrived, teased further by the intimate glances between Debbie and David. Until now she had thought she was her daughter's confidante and was surprised Debbie hadn't mentioned him before – they appeared to have been close for quite some time. So she was totally unprepared for the answer.

"Er, let me think—" Debbie looked to David for help.

"Just three days. Since Friday night," he said. Then he added, "That's incredible! It feels like forever!"

"I'm not sure I know how to take that!" Debbie raised her eyebrows at him. John and Elizabeth Owen both saw him wink at her.

Their energy quota refuelled, the children asked to explore the garden. As they skipped away, Penelope looked anxiously at Tom. "What are we going to do? The children will be ready for bed within the next hour."

"We haven't discussed yet where we are heading. I think you and the children should go up to your folks in Yorkshire."

"Tonight?"

"Of course not, dear," Elizabeth cut in. "You must sleep here at least for tonight. Then you can continue north when you have made your arrangements."

"But we can't impose—"

"Rubbish. I would be most hurt if I thought you saw it as an imposition. We would be delighted to have you. It will mean the children sharing a room with you, but surely that will be better than trying to find an hotel, or driving all night."

Penelope gave a sigh of relief. "You are so very kind."

"We would have expected no less from Debbie's mother. She is a model neighbour, you know," Tom said.

Debbie snorted. "That's only because you've brought your kids up to behave decently. They really are super.

Not like some I come across when doing interviews for the paper."

"You don't have to live with them," Tom feigned a growl. "Anyway, I'm pretty damn sure that every hotel, motel and boarding house north of here has been filled hours ago."

"Undoubtedly," said John, getting up. "Now, there's a spare mattress in the attic, isn't there?"

David jumped to his feet. "Let me help."

The patio party broke up, the women clearing away the food and dishes into the kitchen, the men heading upstairs to rearrange beds. "You'll have your old room, Debbie dear," Elizabeth remarked in the kitchen when Penelope went outside to fetch the children. "And David can stretch out on the couch."

Debbie gave her mother a blank stare.

"You mean you are sleeping together already?"

Her daughter giggled. "Only in a manner of speaking. You understand that David's was the first house to be swallowed up by this Trench. He had nowhere to stay, so when I had finished interviewing him on Friday night I offered him the use of my settee . . . And, well, things have advanced a little since then."

Elizabeth tilted her head to one side. "Oh yes?"

"Yes." The girl took a deep breath. "We think we are in love."

"You joke! After only three days!"

"No, Mummy, I'm serious. I've never felt anything like this before. Just the sight of him leaves me legless."

"That's not love, it's lust."

"How do you know that?"

Elizabeth straightened her blouse. "Just because I happen to be old enough to be your mother, doesn't mean I have forgotten how lust feels!"

"Oh Mum!" Debbie flung her arms round the older woman. "Isn't it a wonderful feeling!" Then she drew back. "But he is a wonderful person, too, you know. Terribly nice. I'll tell you all about him sometime, when this is all over." By the time all the sleeping arrangements had been settled and the children undressed, washed and put to bed it was nearly nine o'clock. "Just in time for the News," John said, turning on the television.

Gathering in the sitting-room round the television, the six adults watched with horror as endless video footage of the disaster was screened. "The Trench," said the presenter, "to use the official Government name for it, now extends approximately three miles from its starting point, the house of a Mr David Barnes outside Stoke D'Abernon—"

"Fame, forever more," Debbie murmured.

"Almost as if they're trying to hold you responsible," Tom said.

The same thought had occurred to David; he was in such a mental turmoil he was even wondering if he *was* in some way responsible. ". . . And has now cut right through the centre of Ashtead. This means it is actually travelling on a slightly east by north curve. It is at present some fifty yards wide, and at least that deep. These shots will show that it is constantly emitting smoke or steam, but the experts say that this is caused by fracturing mains rather than subterranean activity.

"This change in direction, which occurred during the night, means that it is now no longer threatening Epsom Downs or the racecourse, but the Secretary of Defence announced an hour ago that in view of the disruption caused in the area, and the possibility that the Trench may again change direction, they are requesting the postponement of the Derby meeting. It is stressed that this is only a postponement,

143

for whatever period is required to bring things back to normal.

"Meanwhile, at this moment in time, plans are being carried forward for the total evacuation of Epsom. It is being stressed that this is merely a precautionary measure, to ensure that the panic evacuation of Ashtead, in which quite a few people were injured, is not repeated elsewhere. The miracle is that so far there have been only three known deaths from this phenomenon.

"Damage caused so far is running past a hundred million pounds, with much of the centre of Ashtead wiped out. All train services on the main line to Epsom have been cancelled, as in Ashtead the line and the station have collapsed into the Trench.

"Now, I have with me tonight Dr Winston Murray, of London University. Dr Murray is an expert in sinkholes and related phenomena."

"He certainly gets about," Debbie said.

"Good evening, Dr Murray," the presenter said. "Now, the statement from the Ministry of Defence that the Derby meeting is to be postponed, just in case . . . that sounds as if the Government are expecting this Trench to grow some more. Is this what you anticipate?"

"Ah, well," Murray began, and went into his spiel, some-what extended, at the end of which it was obvious to everyone, including the presenter, that he did not have any idea of what was happening, what had caused it, and when it might eventually stop.

It was an extended newscast, and when it finished and the set switched off they all felt sick with apprehension and horror. "Just how far is it from Epsom to Sutton?" Elizabeth asked.

"Two miles," Debbie said.

"But it hasn't extended to Epsom yet," Tom said, as cheerfully as he could manage.

John looked round at the white and weary faces. "It seems to me we could all do with an early night," he said, adding, "Even if we don't actually sleep."

David was tempted to suggest that someone should sit up with a radio on, just in case the trench moved north again. But he didn't want to sound alarmist, and even if it eventually came in this direction, surely they were in no imminent danger. Not tonight. Then tomorrow he would have to head for the bank. He sighed inwardly. He had no desire to leave Debbie. "You are looking terribly serious," she whispered, sitting on the couch beside him.

He shuddered. "Just the proverbial goose, I guess."

"Me too."

"Yes, Mr Owen," Tom agreed, yawning. "We need all the rest we can get. Tomorrow is likely to be a very long day." He got up and pulled Penelope to her feet. "Come on, my sweet. Let's go up."

John eyed his daughter and David. Elizabeth had told him the news. "Are you two going up, too?" he asked.

The young couple got the message. "Yes, sir," David responded, flushing sightly. "Thank you." He wasn't quite sure what he was thanking John for – the loan of a bed or the loan of his daughter. Or both.

Debbie's bed was four feet wide: a glorified single. With the door closed, David asked, "Are you going to mess about with a barricade tonight?"

She had had her hair pinned up all day to allow cool air round the back of her neck. Now she pulled out the pins and he watched as the golden strands cascaded over her shoulders. "Only if you feel it's necessary," she replied.

He decided not to remind her of her ruling regarding Alison, and put his arms round her, pressing her head against his shoulder. "My darling. Right this minute all I want is to hold you in my arms all night . . . and sleep."

"But for the fact that I feel the same way, I should be mortally offended by that remark," she murmured into his shirt. Then she began to undo his buttons.

When she turned out the light they realised it was not yet fully dark outside; a hazy glow edged in round the sides of the curtains, faintly illuminating their faces as they lay side by side on the pillows. David's hand crept up over her features, outlining each eye, her nose, her left ear. "You are so very beautiful," he whispered.

She touched his chin. "And you have magnificent designer stubble."

"Oh! Do you mind?"

"No,' she said, and began kissing him.

He came up for air minutes later, just long enough to remark that his recent tiredness had suddenly vanished.

"I'm glad of that," she whispered, pressing herself against his warmth, all the way down the bed.

"I have with me General Briginshaw," the Minister of Defence said. "General Briginshaw, as we all know, is Deputy Chief of the General Staff, and is an expert on explosives." He paused, and looked around the Cabinet Table with a slightly anxious air. It was eight o'clock at night, and no one had yet had any dinner.

"Explosives?" the Prime Minister asked, as quietly as ever.

"What's he going to blow up?" inquired the Home Secretary. "The Trench?"

"Yes, sir, if it becomes necessary," General Briginshaw said.

There was a moment of stunned silence. "You can't be serious," remarked the Health Secretary.

"What on earth do you expect to achieve by that?" asked the Chancellor, obviously doing some more mental sums.

"Well, sir," the general said, "when I say, 'blow up the Trench', I mean detonating a large explosive across the end of the Trench, in the direction in which it is spreading. This is of course a last resort, and perhaps, one might say, a desperate one. But it does appear to my staff, and myself, that things like this Trench do not just happen. There must be a reason. An agent, causing the earth to open."

"Not little green men again," groaned the Health Secretary.

"I would not care to offer an opinion on that, madam," the general said. "But definitely, an agency. Which has to be stopped. Now, how do you stop a fire that has got out of control? How, for example, did they stop the Great Fire of London in 1665?"

"It was 1666," the Chancellor said, absently.

"Whatever. They blew up a whole street of houses."

"Surely we have advanced a little since 1666?" asked the Health Secretary.

"Anyway, I'm afraid I do not follow the analogy," the Home Secretary said. "If I am right . . ." his tone left no one in any doubt that he was quite certain he was, "the object of blowing up a street of houses was to create an open space so that the flames would have nothing to leap to, and set alight. The Trench is operating through the ground. It is creating its own open space." He looked around, but if he was expecting any response to his feeble attempt at humour it was not forthcoming.

"Quite so," Briginshaw said, unfazed. "But you have just put your finger on it, sir. The word is operating. It is working, at the behest of an agency. It must be."

The cabinet ministers exchanged glances, then looked at the Prime Minister, who had so far taken no part in the discussion. But he had given the Department of Defence its head, as it were. "Perhaps you would explain exactly what you have in mind," the Prime Minister suggested.

"Well, sir, as I said, this is a last resort. Should there be no more activity from the Trench, well then, we can let sleeping dogs lie, eh?"

The Cabinet stirred restlessly, at the steady stream of clichés. "However, should it begin moving again, it is our recommendation that we pick a position, directly in its path, and blow it up."

"Blow what up, exactly?" asked the Home Secretary.

"As I have said, we shall blow up the advancing end of the Trench, sir."

The Home Secretary scratched his head, and looked at the Chancellor.

"Let me get this straight," the Chancellor said. "You propose to blow up a trench that is already more than fifty yards wide and getting on for the same in depth? Have you any idea what will be involved?"

"It will be a big bang," Briginshaw agreed. "But desperate situations require desperate remedies."

"But . . . forgive my stupidity," said the Health Secretary. "What are you hoping to achieve? The Trench is there already. You are only going to extend it."

"It will put an end to the agency that is causing the Trench, madam."

"But you don't know what this agency is."

"Neither does anyone else, madam. But we know it is there."

"How do you know this?"

"Because it has to be."

The Trench

The Health Secretary was biting a second fingernail.

"Just where were you planning to do this blowing up?" the Chancellor asked.

"Well, it would have to be in as clear an area as possible," Briginshaw said, and indicated the map of south London on the table. "Now, as I have said, if the Trench now becomes dormant, and remains where it is, on this line here, from just east of Stoke D'Abernon to the A24 just outside Ashtead, then we shall take no action. If, however, it resumes its activity, it would appear at the moment to be threatening Epsom, then Sutton and Cheam, and then Mitcham. It seems to us that the best place to stop it would be here." He put his finger on Mitcham Common.

"Good God, man!" the Health Secretary said. "Do you mean you are writing off Epsom and Sutton and Cheam? And Mitcham?"

"Well, Madam, as I understand it, Epsom is already being evacuated. I would certainly recommend that we evacuate Sutton and Cheam, and Mitcham, as well. In an orderly fashion, of course. Just in case. If nothing devolves, the people can always go back to their homes."

"If you blow a vast bomb crater in Mitcham Common," the Chancellor said, still obviously concentrating on the financial aspects, "you are going to cause an enormous amount of damage to the surrounding neighbourhood."

"Well, sir," Briginshaw said, "the Trench is already causing an enormous amount of damage to the surrounding neighbourhood."

"There's the point," the Defence Secretary said, in support of his expert.

Once again all heads turned to look at the Prime Minister. Who sighed. "I'm afraid we have to do something. Of course I am still hoping the various boffins will come up with a solution, but this far they have failed to do so. I'm going to give the go ahead on this. It's a carefully thought out plan, and it may just work. So . . . John, will you organise the evacuation of all these areas? In an orderly fashion, as the general recommends. Jeannette, you will have to continue all your medical services on standby. Mark, you will need to do some costing. And William . . ." he turned to the Defence Secretary. "I am continuing to leave this in your hands. Should it become necessary to implement your plan, we will have to go on television and explain to the nation exactly what we are going to do and why we are going to do it. Keep me informed."

"And may God have mercy on us all," muttered the Health Secretary.

Not for the first time, David awoke with a considerable sense of disorientation. But this time there were no barriers. Although there was, as before, the cat. They had decided to take Miranda into the bedroom with them, complete with a temporary litter tray of ground from a flowerbed, as she was feeling even more disoriented, and even with them had spent an hour yowling before finally settling down. Not that they had noticed.

Now she was curled up in the small of David's back. He left her there, as he wasn't intending to roll that way. Instead he gave Debbie's inert body a hug, peering round her to look at his watch; his left arm was under her neck. "Good grief! Seven-thirty! I have to rush."

She opened her eyes, then put her arms round him to hold him against her. "Rush where?"

"The office. I never did get back there yesterday. Listen, can I borrow your car? Just until I can get hold of mine."

"And what do I use?"

"Well, you only have to get into Epsom—"

"Epsom!" she shouted, sitting up so abruptly that Miranda sprang from the bed, yowling. "They're evacuating Epsom. The paper! Martin! My job! I must get down there." She sprang from the bed and rushed from the room, apparently making for the shower.

David followed more slowly. "You won't be able to get in."

"Watch me." She re-emerged, towelling. "But I'll really have to use my car. Listen, Daddy might lend you his. We'll ask him."

"Are you sure? What if they decide they want to evacuate?"

She shook her hair free of the shower cap. "As long as you promise not to smash it up and return it by tomorrow, it should be all right. After all, the Trench hasn't moved for a while so it wouldn't get here for a couple of days, anyway."

He took her in his arms. "I know this is total catastrophe, for everyone. But would you believe that I'm a very happy man?"

She kissed him. "You need to shave. You'd better borrow Daddy's razor, too. Then you have to sort out Alison. Today."

Amongst other things, he thought.

John Owen was perfectly happy to lend David both his car and his razor. "And we'll see you back here this evening."

They all clustered round the television set while they ate various breakfasts; the children were in the garden, playing. "The Trench appears to be stationary at this time," said the presenter. "But the Government is going ahead with the orderly evacuation of Epsom, nevertheless.

151

Other areas which might be affected, such as Sutton and Cheam, and Mitcham, are requested to keep calm and attend to their business or jobs but remain close to a radio or television set in case a further evacuation becomes necessary."

"Cheer us up," Elizabeth said.

The phone was buzzing. Debbie took it, as she guessed who it might be. Her end of the conversation consisted mainly of "Shoots," and occasionally something stronger.

"I must get down there," she said, squinting through an old pair of spectacles she had discarded while still at school and found in her bedside table drawer. "We're relocating in temporary accomodation, in Wimbledon. Seems we can share a press with some other local rag. Listen, be careful," she told David.

"You mean, you be careful," he said. "I'm going the other way. At least to begin with. Sure you don't want me to come with you?"

"I'd love you to come with me, but you have things to do." She looked at the Clarkes.

"I think we should make plans," Tom said. "Like for where we're going," he told Penelope.

"I'll call my parents, and see if we can get up there."

"Don't you have a job to go to?" David asked Tom.

Tom nodded. "Eventually. My boss gave me a couple of days off when he realised what was happening. I'll give him a buzz and bring him up to date."

"Well," David said, "I have to rush. Listen, I'll come back down this evening and see how things are."

"I'll be here," Debbie said. "I hope. Where's your mobile?"

"I actually haven't got around to buying a new one yet."

"Oh, you noodle."

"Not to worry, I'll be at the bank all day. Don't you realise that if I'd had my phone Alison would have been on it? All day and probably all night?"

"I think I'd better wish you luck," Debbie said, grinning.

David drove very carefully in John Owen's Escort; the tyres were worn and he certainly didn't want to prang it, and the roads were as busy as ever, while there was a constant parade of helicopters moving to and fro overhead, and in the distance behind him he could make out a couple of blimps obviously filled with eager cameramen photographing and filming the Trench. He supposed he was not being unreasonable praying it had done all it was going to, and would now stop. Even filling in what was already there, and replacing the houses and railways and conduits and general infrastructure, was going to cost a fortune, in both time and money.

It was nine before he reached the bank. "Well, hi," Angela said. "I was just thinking of calling the police."

"The police know where I am," David said.

"I thought that might be the case." She placed a lengthy list of names and telephone numbers on his desk. "One of those is your solicitor, sounding aggrieved."

"Oh, hell," David said. "I had an appointment with him, yesterday afternoon."

"He did mention it. There is also your hotel. I called there, yesterday afternoon, trying to get hold of you, and they said they hadn't seen you since Saturday night. They were quite shirty, wanted to know if you still want the room. Seems there's a queue."

"I can imagine. Call them and tell them yes, I still need the room, and will be there this afternoon. And then get Joe Darling on the phone."

"What about her?" Angela stabbed the sheet of paper; Alison's name occurred six times.

"Darling first."

"And him?" Wayne Bryson.

"Him second."

"And Walden?"

"Did he get his loan?"

"No. Peter turned him down."

"Oh, good grief. Him third; I'll have to sort something out."

"And the boss?"

"He's not after me?"

"I wouldn't say after you. He merely called down to say that if you turned up he'd like a word. He did use the word if, rather than when."

"Shit! Is he in yet?"

"I'll give Caroline a buzz. But I don't think so."

"Then let's start on those calls."

"There's also quite a list of people seeking appointments. They all have financial problems related to this Trench."

"I doubt if I'll have time to see them all. Give them phone appointments. Joe!" he said into the receiver on his desk.

"Where the devil have you been?"

"Escaping the Trench, mainly."

"What has the Trench to do with you, now?"

"It's a long story. I had some things to do close to home, and I got caught up in it. Then I had to go to Ashtead to rescue a friend . . . and one thing led to another."

Joseph Darling sighed, loudly. "Okay, let's start again. If we are going to get you some compensation we simply have to be in on the ground floor, because the list is going to be a mile long within a couple of days. When can you come down?"

"Ah . . . where? Aren't you evacuating?"

"The Epsom office, yes. I'm calling from the City."

"Oh, right. Well, I really feel I have to do a little work. Listen, I'll call you back this afternoon. Put me down for four, tentatively."

"I do not make tentative appointments," Joe said. "If I did that I wouldn't be able to afford my Rolls. I will expect you at four."

That reminded David about his car. "Get me Hawkins Garage in Epsom," he told Angela.

"*Where* did you say your car is, Mr Barnes?" asked the foreman.

"I was trying to get to Ashtead, but the roads were blocked. It's in that little village with a stone cross by the market. A mile outside the town."

"You do realise that Ashtead is a disaster area?"

"Yes. That's why I'd like to get my car out of there."

"Well . . . I'll send a pick-up truck over. But I'm not sure the police will let us through. We'll do what we can."

"I'd be most awfully grateful."

"Supposing we do manage to reclaim the car, where should we deliver it?"

"Ah . . . I'll give you an address in Sutton." He did so.

"The boss is in," Angela said. "And I have Mr Walden on the line."

"Right. Tom! Good to hear you."

"Is it? I'm in deep trouble, David."

"Of course you're not. Listen, come in to see me. Make it . . . eleven. We'll sort things out." He replaced the phone, looked up as Peter pushed his head round the door.

"Ah, you're back in charge."

"In a manner of speaking. Why did you refuse old Walden?"

"Well . . . he didn't have adequate security."

"I see. Sometimes you have to trust people. Walden is as honest as anyone I know."

Peter blew a raspberry.

"David!" Oakley leaned back in his chair. "Had a busy day, yesterday, eh?"

"I'm afraid I got caught up in Ashtead."

"Oh, quite. How did the court case go?"

"I'm for trial."

"Oh."

"My solicitor is quite sure we'll sort it out."

"I'm glad to hear that. Are you going to be around for a day or two?" He was not, actually, being sarcastic.

"Of course, sir. Yesterday really was a blip. Circumstances beyond my control."

"I'm sure they were. Now, tell me, how are we going to handle this situation?"

"Ah—" David was not quite sure which situation he was referring to.

"I am informed," Oakley went on, "that the Government is preparing to consider a package of compensation for houses and property, and now, of course, businesses in places like Ashtead, that have been destroyed by this Trench. I imagine you're in line for compensation yourself."

"Hopefully, yes," David agreed.

"But of course, like you, there are quite a few people who need some financial asssistance right now. There are also people with mortgages, whose properties, their security, have disappeared."

"Have we any idea how the building societies are going to react, sir?"

"Not as yet. But going on the evidence presented by the last recession, we cannot expect them to be very co-operative."

"Ah . . . I seem to remember that we, I mean the banks, weren't very co-operative either," David said. "Of course, I was only a junior then—"

"Yes," Oakley remarked, indicating that he did not really wish to discuss past attitudes. "I have been in touch with Head Office, and they feel that our approach should be sympathetic. But cautious. Anyone who is a customer of the bank, has a good credit rating, is in regular employment, and needs some cash flow to tide him over the next few weeks, is to be considered. But of course we have our profit margins and our shareholders to think of. We certainly don't want to have to create a massive bad debts reserve."

"I understand, sir," David said.

"Good. I'm sure you can handle it. Now, have you put in for a loan yourself?"

"Not as yet, sir."

Oakley raised his eyebrows.

"I'm actually managing to survive at the moment," David explained. "I'm running up a fairly stiff hotel bill, and I shall need help with that, but I cannot possibly give any thought to rebuilding, or buying elsewhere, until this whole Trench thing has been sorted out."

"Hm. Yes, I suppose you're right." Oakley lived in Hammersmith, well away from the Trench – at the moment. "Well, keep me up to date. And I would like a list of all loans you have agreed on my desk every morning first thing."

"Yes, sir."

As if he didn't have enough to do, David thought. "I have Mr Bryson on the line," Angela said. "And Miss Bates has been calling. Several times."

"Bryson first."

157

"It is as I thought, old man," Wayne said. "The insurance companies are definitely treating the Trench as an Act of God. So—"

"We've anticipated that," David said. "I'll get your cheque in the mail today, and of course you must let me have the credit card figure when it comes in. And thanks a million, old friend, for all you've done."

"I just wish it could have been more," Wayne said.

"There is something," David said.

"Yes?" Wayne's tone was suddenly watchful.

David explained about his car. "I am assuming that it is all right and that it will be reclaimed by Hawkins and be waiting for me this evening. But just in case it is not—"

"What are you expecting to have happened to it?"

"Well . . . I left the keys in the ignition."

"Oh, dear God," Wayne said. "Your insurance certainly won't wear that."

"Equally, it could have fallen into the Trench . . . I'm not quite sure how wide it was as it went through Ashtead."

"In which case—"

"I know. Act of God. But it could also have been vandalised, or towed away and dumped, or any number of things."

"Yes." Wayne sounded sceptical. "We don't actually have any idea how far this Act of God thing is going to be spread. I'm sure they will try to have it cover anything remotely connected with the Trench. Listen, let me know the moment you get something definite from Hawkins."

So, David thought. No house. No clothes, save what I bought with Alison. And now no car. And two women! And a cat!!

"She's on the line again," Angela said.

"Alison! Good of you to call."

For a moment she was speechless. Then she said, "I have been calling since this time yesterday morning." Her voice was low and apparently controlled, but he sensed she was on the verge of an explosion.

"I'm sorry. I have been most frightfully busy."

"Your secretary said you were out of the office."

"Well, yes, I was, for a while. I had to go to court, and then there was the horsebox—"

"Court?"

"I'm on a charge of GBH. That fellow I hit, you know. Then there was the horsebox—"

"Have you been seeing that reporter woman again?"

David began to feel just a little bit nettled. "Who I see is really no concern of yours, Alison."

"I see. Well, then . . . goodbye."

The phone at the other end was put down with ear-shattering force. But he still didn't suppose he had heard the last of her.

The day passed in a succession of anxious customers, some of whom he rejected on the phone, knowing they were hopeless cases with overstretched overdrafts even before the Trench had appeared. Others he saw in person, some with their wives, all claiming to have lost everything. As instructed by Oakley, he assisted where he could despite, in some instances, the total lack of security. But, again as instructed by Oakley, he had to act on past performance, and inevitably there were one or two who had poor credit records. These had to be refused, although he tried to sweeten the pill by promising that when the Government had sorted out its compensation package and with how much would be available and on what basis, he might then be able to help them in the short term, while awaiting payment of any guaranteed monies.

But it was unpleasant work, compounded by a sandwich lunch, as he had no time for anything else. He was totally relieved when three o'clock came round. "Print out that list for the boss," he told Angela. "I'll check it tomorrow morning."

"Are you off again?" she asked.

"I have an appointment with my solicitor at four o'clock," he said. "It's to do with claiming compensation, so I'd better get along there now. By the way, where do you live?"

"I thought you'd never ask. I live in Finchley."

"Well away from trouble."

"I should hope so."

"Well, go off home as soon as that list is ready. And Angie . . . you've been tremendous."

"Well, thank you. Holding the fort is what secretaries are for. Have fun with your lawyer."

David cleared up his desk. He desperately wanted to be with Debbie, but he had no idea where she was, right that minute; probably still busy relocating. The phone buzzed. David picked it up. "Yes?"

"There's a Mr Hawkins on the line," Angela said.

"Great! Put him through." He waited, then asked, "Any luck?"

"You won't believe this, Mr Barnes, but we have your car."

"How badly damaged is it?"

"Not a scratch. That Trench is about half a mile away from where you left it. Did you know the keys were in the ignition?"

"Ah . . . yes. I was in a hurry. Can you hold on to it at your garage? I'm going to try to get down as soon as I can, but I can't promise it'll be tonight."

"We'll hold it, Mr Barnes. For as long as we can."

"Just what do you mean by that?"

"Well, sir, my garage is on the main road out of Epsom, and it's just been on the telly that the Trench is coming this way."

"What? You mean it's on the move again?"

"Yes, sir, and changed direction more to the north-east. They're saying it's going to hit Sutton next."

Towards The River

"Oh, my God!" David gasped.

"Tell you what we'll do, Mr Barnes," Hawkins said, with massive calm. "When we leave, one of my chaps will drive your car to a safe place, let you know where it is and make arrangements to meet you when you're able to pick it up."

"Yes," David said, absently. "When do you leave?"

"We've been told to evacuate, sir. Well, they've already evacuated most of Epsom. Now they're starting on Sutton."

"Right. Thanks a million." He hung up, used the outside line himself to call the Owen household. "Mrs Owen? Have you heard the news?"

"Yes, we have. David Barnes, is it?"

"Yes. What are you doing?"

"Well, packing up. The police have been down the street with instructions; they don't want anything like those massive traffic jams outside of Epsom to happen here. We're to evacuate by streets, as they call us."

"But the Trench—"

"They say it can't reach here for several hours, at the very earliest, if it gets here at all, and that there will be ample time to get everyone out." Her calmness was impressive; in the background he could hear one of the Clarke children wailing.

"Is Debbie there?"

"Debbie is in the temporary offices in Wimbledon. But she is going to try to get down here to drive us out."

"I'll try too, to get your car back to you. If she doesn't make it you will need it for your own transport. I know the Clarkes won't have room in their car. It's jam-packed already."

"I don't think you should attempt to come, David. Getting through the traffic will take you hours. And if she can't get through we'll cadge a lift out with our neighbours. I'll ask Debbie to call you as soon as she gets here, shall I?"

"Yes." Then he remembered he wasn't sure where he would be. "No. Can you give me her Wimbledon number?"

"I'm afraid not. I don't know it. They're still only just moving in, and I'm not sure she even has a number yet. She was using her mobile."

"Oh, right. I'll call her on that. By the way, do you have any idea where you are going when you leave Sutton?"

"There's talk about hostels and church halls and temporary accommodation, but it doesn't sound too good to me. We'll talk it over with Debbie when she gets here."

"Oh. Right. So what shall I do with your car?"

"I think you should keep it for the time being."

If he was going to collect his own, there was no way he could drive them both. "When I know where you will be staying, I'll try to get it there to you."

"We'll sort something out. Don't *worry*, David." He replaced the phone, gazed at it. Don't worry!

Angela looked in. "What time did you say your appointment was?"

He looked at his watch. A quarter to four. He was never

going to get across London and into the City in fifteen minutes. "Have you heard the news?"

She nodded. "Do you know people in Sutton?"

"Yes." He punched out the numbers of Debbie's mobile, waited. Nothing. "Damnation! She's switched it off."

"Who's switched it off?"

"Someone with whom I am trying to get in touch."

"About this appointment—"

"Call Joe Darling and tell him I can't make it. Tell him I'll give him a ring in a day or two."

Angela pulled a face. "Judging by his reaction to your failing to turn up yesterday, I'd say he's not going to be very happy."

"Can't be helped." He began trying Debbie's number again.

A minute later Angela was back. "It's a good thing you stayed."

"Did you get hold of Darling?"

"Haven't had the time. The boss wants to see all his senior staff in his office, in half an hour."

When Debbie finished speaking with her mother, she returned to the large main room of the temporary *Courier* headquarters, to find the entire staff gathered around a portable television.

"You get down there, Martin," Editor William Leadbetter said. "See what you can get."

"They're all starting to look alike," Martin grumbled, but he collected his camera and camcorder and draped them about his neck as he headed for the door.

"I need to get down there as well, Harry," Debbie said.

"I think you should take a rest."

"My parents are in Sutton."

"Oh! Shit!"

"Together with all the gear I managed to get out of Ashtead."

"What a fucking awful mess. Right. You'd better go. Take care. And bring me back a story!" he bawled after her as she followed Martin out of the building.

The photographer had already left, so Debbie got into her Vauxhall Estate and went for the Merton Road, meaning to cut down through Morden. There was a steady stream of traffic coming the other way, but southbound it was ominously clear, until she was stopped at the corner by a police road-block. "Where are you going, miss?" asked the sergeant.

"I'm trying to get to Sutton."

"Sutton is being evacuated."

"I know. My parents live there. They need me to help."

"Well . . ." he pulled his nose. "You understand, once you're in, you don't come out until you're given permission by the police." Debbie nodded. "Okay. Take care."

The barrier was lifted, and she drove through. Now the stream of northbound traffic was bumper to bumper, in two lines and taking up more than half of the road, well over the white lines so that she had virtually to drive with her nearside wheels in the gutter. They were moving slowly, horns blaring, people leaning out of windows and yelling abuse at each other. She was going to be in the middle of that lot in a few hours!

But before then . . . she supposed the actual fact of the loss of her home hadn't yet sunk in. It had all happened so quickly and completely. And David had been there to cushion the blow, having suffered the same fate. They had conceived of themselves as isolated orphans in the storm, no matter what mayhem and misery might be surrounding them. Besides, her parents' house had been a haven in that storm, though not quite matching up to the comfort of David's arms. Last night had been the sweetest of her life . . . despite all that was going on around them.

Now her parents' home was also being threatened, with all of their treasured possessions at risk . . . and more of her own. And with Dad having had that minor heart problem only two months ago . . . She felt her throat tighten and tears welling up in her eyes. She sniffed, snorted, and with great determination gripped the steering wheel. David! He would be worried stiff, and was probably charging around the countryside looking for her. But he didn't know where she was, and he hadn't replaced his mobile. And she didn't know the number of his bank. She could of course look it up in the book when she got to Sutton. When! Or if.

Suddenly a car shot out of a side road, immediately in front of her. Debbie braked and swerved. Her offside wing struck that of the car next to her going the other way, and she bounced back to be hit by the madman who had caused the accident in the first place. But he didn't stop, just straightened his car and drove away at some speed. "You stupid bitch!" bawled the man she had hit, getting out of his Jaguar.

Debbie's head had gone forward with the impact, and she was feeling her scalp, very carefully. But there did not appear to be any blood. "You!" shouted the Jaguar driver, banging on her window. "You hit me!"

Debbie rolled down her window. "Because that idiot hit me. Look, I'll give you my number and my insurance."

"My car!" the man shouted. "It's wrecked!"

Debbie attempted to look past him. His fender had certainly been pushed in, and his wheel looked out of kilter. "I'm most awfully sorry. Listen. I'll get to a garage and send you help."

"You—" the man appeared about to have an apoplectic fit.

"Hey, you!" shouted the man in the car immediately behind the Jaguar. "You're holding us up. Get that crate moving."

The man turned round, waving his arms. "How can I move it, with the wing stove in?"

"Right," said the man behind. "We'll move it for you." He had a large Land Rover type vehicle, and this he now drove as hard as he could into the back of the Jaguar, shunting it half across the road.

"You fucking bastard!" screamed the Jaguar owner, jumping up and down. The people in the nearby cars cheered.

"Once more for luck," the Land Rover driver said, and again slammed into the side of the Jaguar, this time pushing it right out of the traffic stream and into the southbound lane. "Ta-ra," he shouted, as the line moved forward.

"You . . . you—!"

Debbie was afraid he was about to have a stroke. "Listen," she said. "I'll get help."

"You—" he turned back to her with surprising suddenness, thrust both hands through her open window, grasped her by the front of her suit, and with an immense heave pulled her right out through the window. She bumped her thighs and her knees, and her shoes came off, and for the moment she was too surprised to react. Nothing like that had ever happened to her before. "I ought to beat the shit out of you," the Jaguar driver snarled, shaking her till her teeth rattled.

"You bastard!" Debbie had got her breath back, and kneed him in the groin.

He gave a gasp and fell forward, and she wriggled away from him and reached for her car door. "No, you don't," he bellowed, and grasped her hair.

She struck back with her elbows. He grunted, swung her round and hit her on the chin. For the second time in a few seconds she was taken entirely by surprise. She sagged against her car, head spinning, only vaguely seeing the people in the cars streaming by . . . but none was showing the least inclination to stop and come to her rescue.

Her assailant dug both hands into her shirt front and dragged her up. She supposed he meant to hit her again, but was too dazed to do anything about it. Then she heard the wail of the siren. "Shit!" the man muttered, and let her go.

Debbie sank slowly down the side of her car, her entire face and head aching, then pushed herself back up to look at the policemen who were getting out of their car. "They wrecked my car!" shouted the Jaguar owner.

"You all right, miss?" one of the policemen asked. He could see that Debbie had taken a beating.

"That b . . . beggar," she glared at her assailant.

"She started it," the Jaguar driver shouted. "She drove into me."

"I was pushed into him," Debbie protested. "Some idiot came out of that road and drove into me. You can see the damage on the other side."

The second policeman had been inspecting her car. "Your passenger door's buckled all right," he said.

"So I was pushed into his beastly Jaguar," Debbie said. "And he got out and assaulted me."

"She hit me."

"Let's keep calm," the first policeman recommended. "So what happened then, miss?"

"The people behind got upset because he wouldn't move his car, and pushed him out of the way."

"I couldn't move my car," the Jaguar driver shouted. "The wheel's buckled."

The policemen peered at the wheel. "Right," said the first one. By now there were several cars waiting on the southbound carriageway hooting and shouting. "We have to get it off the road. Give us a hand."

"To do what?" the driver demanded.

"Push it on to the verge so the traffic can get through. Then we can call for a pick-up truck and get this sorted out."

"Can I go?" Debbie asked.

"She should be arrested," the driver declared.

"Look, I've told you what happened," Debbie said. "You've seen the evidence to prove it. I'll give you my name and address, and the name of my insurance company. But I have to get into Sutton. My elderly parents are there, and they need my help." They weren't that elderly but it didn't hurt to lay it on thick.

"Well . . . I reckon that'll be all right miss." the policeman said. "I'm not guaranteeing you won't be contacted later. We may need a full statement."

"Okay. But not right now."

He grinned at her. "You sure you're fit to drive?"

"Yes, I'm fit to drive. Incidentally, when it comes to statements, I'm bringing a charge against him. Road rage. He hit me."

"She provoked me."

"Oh, rubbish. Can I go?"

"You can go," the policeman agreed. "Take care, eh?"

"Grrr," Debbie said as she got back behind the wheel and slipped her shoes back on.

Sutton was a strange sight. The police were obviously evacuating the streets nearest the approaching Trench first, and they had not yet reached the Owens' area. Every building had cars waiting outside, laden with goods, while anxious people gathered on the pavements muttering at each other. Few vehicles were moving, and Debbie reached her parents without difficulty. Here she saw the Clarkes' car waiting, fully loaded, and as soon as she pulled up her father came out to greet her. "Debbie?" He peered at her. "Your face is swollen."

"Is it? Shoot! Some behemoth hit me."

"Hit you? Someone hit you?"

"It's a long story." She went inside, peered at herself in the hall mirror. The left side of her face was definitely bigger than the right. And it was turning a weird shade of purple.

"Darling." Elizabeth bustled up. "What on earth happened?"

"Road rage. Some fellow I was shoved into got all het up."

"My God! Are you all right?"

"Well, I think so. The police happened along and sorted it out."

Elizabeth peered at her daughter. "Does your head hurt?"

"Like hell."

"I'll get a couple of aspirins."

"No," Debbie said. "I simply can't afford to go all limp. There's too much to be done."

By this time the Clarkes had joined them and had to be told all over again. "The maniac," Tom Clarke said. "I hope they throw the book at him."

"So do I," Debbie said. "Now, what are we doing?"

"We have a bit of a problem, as regards car space," her father said. "Being one short, as it were."

"That nice David rang up and asked if he could come down," Elizabeth said.

"With my car," her husband put in.

"But I thought it best for him not to," Elizabeth said. "He said he'd ring you."

"Damn," Debbie said, "I've had my mobile switched off. Have you any idea where he is?"

"Well . . . the bank?"

"Right. Now, where are you going when you leave here?"

"Well—" the Owens exchanged glances.

"We really don't want to go into a hostel or something like that," Elizabeth said.

"I quite agree. Listen, why don't you go up north, to Granny."

"Ah . . . what in?" John Owen asked.

"Listen," Tom said. "If Debbie can drive you in her car, you can follow us, at least as far as Pimlico. My cousin lives there, and I know he'll put you up for the night. Then you can go north tomorrow. That's what we're planning to do. You really don't want to start the journey up there tonight."

"Hm," John Owen said.

"I think that's a brilliant idea," Debbie said. "I'll take you as far as Pimlico and David can bring the car there. Give me the address in case I lose you."

"Don't you think you had better call your cousin first?" Elizabeth asked Tom.

"Will do. May I use your phone?"

Debbie used her mobile to call the bank. "Debbie!" David shouted. "My God, where have you been?"

"Doing this and that," Debbie said. She didn't want to go into the accident and the road rage incident over the phone.

"Where are you now?"

"I'm in Sutton, with my folks and the Clarkes."

"Shouldn't you be out of there by now?"

"We can't move until the police tell us to."

"Well, I hope they tell you to in time. Where are you going?"

"Into London for starters. Pimlico. I want my folks to get

up north tomorrow to my grandmother's. We'll organise that tomorrow morning. But they'll need their car."

"Heck, yes. Of course they will. Where can we meet?"

"Like I said, we're going up to Tom's cousin in Pimlico. Here . . ." she gave him the address and telephone number.

"That's just down the road. When will you be there?"

"God knows." She looked at her watch; quarter past five. "Not for a couple of hours, at the very least. The roads are solid, northbound."

"Damn! And if the Trench catches up with you—"

"I'm sure they'll get us out ahead of that, even if we have to abandon the cars and escape down diagonal streets," she said, with determined optimism.

"I should be there, with you."

"Well, there is no way you can. And to try would be counter-productive. Listen, I'll keep in touch. Are you staying at the bank?"

"For a while, I'm afraid. The boss has called a high-level conference to discuss the situation. I'm just on my way up now."

"Right. Have fun."

"Debbie . . . can you come to the hotel tonight?"

"You mean you want it at a time like this?"

"I want *you*, safe and sound where I can keep an eye on you. Now and always."

She blew a raspberry down the phone. "I'm a big girl, remember? I can look after myself. But if I can, I'll see about tonight. After I've got this end sorted out." Then she frowned into the phone. "But you won't have any transport after you've delivered Daddy's car! I'll have to drive you back, anyway."

David gave a happy sigh. "So you will! And tell me, is the cat all right?"

"Shoot! I wonder if she's still in my room! She'll be going spare. I have to rush."

"I love you."

"Grrr," she said. "Me, or the cat?"

Miranda had been been playing with the children: or rather they had been playing with her. Being a much travelled cat over the past few days, she had taken to her new surroundings quite happily, at least after being fed. Now she was content to snooze on Debbie's duvet, where the latter left her and returned downstairs. John and Elizabeth hurried from room to room, picking up and discarding various precious possessions. When each separate decision was made, Debbie increased the load in her car out on the forecourt, where Tom was standing watch, waiting for the police to arrive with their instructions.

Penelope was the one looking most stressed. She opened the rear of their car a dozen times, checked the bags and miscellaneous paraphernalia, then closed it again before checking on the children, or fetching some further item from the kitchen which might prove vital on their coming journey. Most of the time Jason and Polly played or fought together with customary disregard for all that was going on round them: only occasionally were they aware of the tense atmosphere and taut expressions of the adults, pausing briefly in their activities to sidle up to a parent for reassurance and comfort before rejecting fear for the fun of exploring this different, temporary environment.

"Okay, folks, this is it," Tom called through the open front door. "They want us in our cars and ready to leave within five minutes." He seems to have aged ten years in the past two days, Penelope thought. Elizabeth smiled gently at her; she and John remained very calm and collected, no matter how they were feeling inside at the prospect of abandoning their home of thirty-five years. Having checked all the doors and window fastenings, John waited beside the front door, keys in hand, until everyone was out before slamming and locking it behind them.

Debbie was last to leave, carrying Miranda in her box and wondering how long the animal could hold out without recourse to a litter tray. Heaven only knew when there might be another opportunity for her to go. She had a small bowl and bottle of water and some tins of cat food in a plastic bag which she stowed alongside the catbox on the rear seat beside her mother, whilst her father occupied the front passenger seat. Though five o'clock in the afternoon, the paved forecourt was still hot; likewise the interiors of the cars, despite the windows being reeled down and doors left open. "Can't we get out until it's time to go, Dad?" Jason moaned.

"You just sit tight and keep your eyes skinned on that end of the road. The first one to spot a policeman gets four Smarties," Tom bribed.

"What does the second one get?" Polly demanded.

"Three. And the third one gets two."

"And the last one only gets one Smartie!" the kids chorussed. "And there he is!" they shrieked together. He was on a motorcycle, red light flashing, with a powerful loud-hailer attached to his wrist. Debbie and Tom switched on their ignitions, watching as neighbouring cars were signalled out on to the street.

At last they were away. And at a considerably better and more orderly pace than they had travelled the previous day. Apart from a few overheated engines and tempers being dealt with at the roadside, progress was a fairly smooth fifteen to twenty miles per hour except at junctions where they ground to temporary halts. "I wonder which bridge they will put us on to cross the river," Debbie said, changing up into third gear again.

"Perhaps they'll give us a choice," her father suggested hopefully.

"Which would you prefer?" Elizabeth asked.

"Putney, Battersea or Chelsea. They all lead to Pimlico."

"Do you know anything about these cousins of the Clarkes' who live there?"

"Yes. I've met them a couple of times when they were visiting Tom and Penelope. Rather arty types. Cara has her hair cut short as a man's at the back but with a long, angled fringe across her face."

"Oh!" her mother sighed. "And what about her husband?"

"Rolf wears a ponytail and Russian-style designer shirts. And Mum, don't go and put your foot in it. They are not married; he has various boyfriends and she has girlfriends but they live together because they understand each other so well."

"And what does he do for a living?" John asked, trying not to laugh.

"Not a lot except write poetry and buy quaint pieces of art," Debbie replied, keeping her eyes on the road. "I believe he has private means. Cara is paid vast sums for doing something spectacular in advertising. Oops!" She swung the wheel to avoid a determined young man on a bicycle. Miranda yowled.

"Thank goodness the sun is going down behind those roofs. It's so hot!" Debbie groaned.

Elizabeth opened the coolbox on the floor. "Here, darling. Have a swig of lemonade."

The bottle was still quite cool. "Lovely. Thanks." Then Debbie spotted Jason and Polly in the car in front, waving. They had bottles of lemonade, too. The twin lines of traffic came to a halt.

"Now what?" Debbie wondered.

John stuck his head out of his window. "I can see a police car parked on the pavement, up ahead."

The two cars edged slowly forward till Tom's drew level with the uniformed men. One of them opened the front passenger door and said, "There are special trains being laid on to take people northbound. Do you wish to get on to one?"

"No thanks," Tom said.

"Are you headed for a specific destination? If so we will direct you into the correct lane of traffic."

"Pimlico," Penelope told him. "Which bridge will be quickest?"

The man laughed. "Lady, your guess is as good as mine. Just hold on and I'll check up ahead." He turned his face away to speak into the radio strapped to his shoulder. "They recommend the Putney bridge. With the number of cars we've had overheating and breaking down, the wider the roadway the better the chance of getting past them." He closed her door and through the window said, "Stay in this lane and follow the road through Putney to cross Upper Richmond Road and the railway. Then once you've crossed the river you must take the right-hand fork and go through Chelsea. Can you follow that?"

"Yes thanks," Tom nodded. "I know the area quite well." He waved an arm at Debbie, who waved back, then moved his car forward.

John Oakley looked around the faces of his senior staff. "I have called you in this evening," he said, "to discuss the situation created by this Trench catastrophe." The men and women gathered round the meeting table exchanged glances; coping with sudden openings of the earth was not included in the training of banking executives.

As Oakley recognised. "Of course we are helpless to do anything practical about it," he said. "That is the Government's business. However, certain factors have been created which is causing Head Office, and I may say the Head Offices of all the clearing banks, some concern. Firstly, it has become necessary to close and evacuate three of our branches south of the river. Preparations are going ahead now to close and evacuate two others, in Mitcham and Wimbledon, areas which could conceivably be affected by this, ah, Trench. David, you've been involved in this thing. Do you suppose the Trench will travel that far?"

"I'm afraid it's impossible to predict, sir," David said. "It shouldn't have reached as far as it has."

"Oh, quite. However, the point is that we here, being the main branch of City and South closest to the, ah, Trench, but in a position of safety, have been requested to deal with all our customers who would normally use those branches south of the river. With this in mind, staff from various of those branches will be coming in here tomorrow morning, and are to be given every assistance and facility. I'm afraid it will mean a certain amount of overcrowding, but that we have to accept. Where possible, records will also be brought for use in handling customers, and especially those needing credit, but of course we can always refer to the mainframe in the City where we have to."

"What about cash, sir?" asked the accountant. "There has already been quite a run. Some people have even been asking for payment in gold."

"Have they, by jove? I was coming to the cash situation. Extra deliveries will be made before we open tomorrow morning, and more will be on call as we need it."

"What will the situation be if the Trench comes north of the river, sir?" asked one of the woman managers. Everyone in the room looked at her as if she had suddenly developed a clear case of bubonic plague. "Well, it could happen," she said, defensively.

"Do you think there is any possibility, David?" Oakley asked.

"I should have thought it extremely unlikely," David said. "But—"

"I am sure Head Office have such a possibility well in mind," Oakley said. "If it will make you any happier, Margaret, I will raise that point when I see the Chairman tomorrow morning, at the meeting of all the Area Managers to discuss the situation. Thank you, ladies and gentlemen. I just wanted to put you in the picture. Stay a moment, David, will you?" The staff filed out, while David waited. "Have you got that list of loans for me?"

"It will be ready first thing tomorrow morning, sir. As you requested."

"Ah, yes. I would like to take it up to the City with me. I'll be stopping by first thing."

"It'll be ready, sir."

"Thank you. Well, have a restful night."

Chance would be a fine thing, David thought, as he hurried for the car-park.

Debbie was almost crying with weariness when they finally arrived in Pimlico. The battered Vauxhall had hiccupped to an overheated halt near Victoria Station and they had had to stop at the roadside for twenty minutes till it cooled down enough to restart. Fortunately, Polly had spotted her problem through the rear window of her father's car and Tom had pulled out of the traffic a few yards further on and waited for her. At least the roads north of the river were not quite so choked. Nor was there a problem finding car spaces when Tom finally signalled he was pulling in beside a row of tall, terraced houses down a side street.

It was Tom who pressed the buzzer and duly announced their arrival to the door phone. An electric beep signalled the door release, Tom pushed, and the party was greeted by a flood of weird, electronic music – and an aristocratic, thoroughbred Abyssinian cat. "Uh uh!" Debbie eyed it as yet another problem.

Jason and Polly rushed into the house calling "Auntie Cara!"

But it was the ponytailed Rolf who appeared. "She's in the shower. Got home late. Busy day. Do come in and have a drink."

Inside, the Victorian brick house was entirely white. White-painted walls, floors and ceilings: twin, white leather three-seater settees, heavy, white folk-weave curtains. A pair of stunted, white Corinthian columns supported the glass dining table-top at the far end of the room, and the electronic music emanated from a stylish, white plastic cabinet in a corner. Light relief was granted the room in the form of a lifeless, leafless tree in another corner, the branches and twigs of which were painted black, and a shallow bowl of red roses which sat on the white coffee table amidst colourful, glossy art magazines. Under the table, a pale blue and white kilim had been laid very symmetrically between the settees. A near fatal situation was caused when Elizabeth and Debbie accidently caught each other's eye; both turned away to smother the threatening explosion of laughter: it all seemed so dramatically overstated. Elizabeth felt a need to stand on her head in an attempt to fathom a charcoal sketch of something, hanging unframed on one wall. Opposite was a vast, unframed mirror. Debbie found herself staring at an array of totally indecipherable metal lumps: presumably Rolf's and

Cara's chosen *objets d'art*. She averted her eyes, straightened her features and practised kind thoughts about these temporary hosts who were offering her parents a safe haven for the night, excusing her levity on near hysteria – of which laughter and tears were twin symptoms.

Cara appeared in a purple turban and kaftan. "So sorry I wasn't down in time to welcome you," she said, kissing Tom and Penelope and Debbie. Tom introduced the Owens and they shook hands.

Rolf disappeared for a moment and returned with a bottle and tray of glasses. "Drinks," he announced.

"What are you offering?" Tom was suspicious.

"Some of my sister's parsnip wine. This is from last year's batch in Cornwall."

"You wouldn't have a beer, or perhaps a cider, would you?" Tom asked hopefully.

"'Fraid not."

So Elizabeth and the men screwed up their courage and faced the parsnips while Debbie and the children sipped Robinson's lemon and barley water. They were discussing the advance of the Trench, with stiff British upper lips, when the doorbuzzer went. It was David, who was ushered in and also plied with parsnip wine. "Wonderful," he said, carefully avoiding Debbie's glance.

"Very good indeed," John agreed, so convincingly that Elizabeth stared at him, anxious to check if he was serious. Actually, she thought it was probably quite good, if one liked that sort of thing, though she would have preferred a stiff gin and tonic in the circumstances. She wondered what the beds were going to be like.

"I have to say I'm jolly glad to see you, David," John went on. "Did you manage to get the car through unscathed?"

"The offside wing-mirror was nudged on one occasion,

180

but it's undamaged. Otherwise, amazingly, not a scratch."
He turned to Debbie. "Now what's the plan? Can you get
me back to the hotel?"

"I think so. But," she smiled sweetly at Cara, "Do you think
it might be possible to leave the cat here? She has been shut
up in a box in the car for hours."

Cara's eyes rolled dramatically. "My dear! Mushtaq would
eat her alive! After he had raped her, of course."

The answer appeared to be no. Debbie looked at David
whose mouth was twitching ominously. Amazing, she
thought appreciatively, how the English invariably found
something humorous in even the most dreadful and tragic
situations, or was he, too, approaching hysteria? "Not
a problem," he said. "She'll have to come with us."
Considering all that had happened and been coped with
in the past couple of days, installing the cat in the hotel
bedroom would be a doddle. He glanced at his watch. "It's
already gone eight-thirty. I think we should make a move,
Debbie."

"Right. But first we will have to transfer Dad and Mum's
luggage into their car. Are you two sure you will be okay
to drive up north tomorrow?" she asked her parents.

"Of course," John frowned. "We may be retired but we
are not senile!"

"We'll be fine, darling," Elizabeth assured her.

"We'll set off in tandem, if you like," Tom suggested,
"Though we may well get separated. I'll try to sort out a
route, later, with the police. They'll advise us which roads
will be best." Debbie gave Penelope a grateful wink behind
her father's back.

After lots of hugs, false gaiety and optimism, David and
Debbie set off to the tune of Miranda's wailing. Compared

181

with the turmoil of earlier in the day, the return to David's hotel was reasonably easy, fortunately. Both were mentally, physically and emotionally exhausted. Drained. And silent. There seemed little to say. All they needed was a simple supper, and sleep. As David parked her car, Debbie asked, "Do you think the hotel will mind us taking the cat into the room for the night?"

"Frankly, I couldn't care less. They can bloody well bend their rules for once. Have you got her litter tray?"

"Yes. And food."

"Good. Let's go. Do you need anything else from the car?"

They walked up to reception, laden, to ask for the key. The receptionist was indifferent to their luggage, so the question of Miranda's welcome wasn't raised. Crammed into the small lift with all the gear, they waited till they lurched to a halt on the second floor and the doors finally slid open onto a pleasantly carpeted and decorated rectangular area. A large Chinese planter containing a plastic palm stood in a recess beside a reproduction *chaise-longue* . . . and sitting on the *chaise-longue*, one arm draped elegantly along the back, was Alison.

Neither of the weary travellers noticed her for a few moments, preoccupied as they were with collecting up all their luggage from the floor of the lift. Then Debbie heard David mutter "Oh shit!" She looked up, recognised the problem and hissed with irritation.

"Hallo! What the hell are you doing here?" David demanded through gritted teeth.

"What's more to the point is what the hell *she*'s doing here!" Alison retorted, uncrossing her legs. "Here, you'd better let me have that," she said, getting up and snatching the card key from between his teeth. "I'll open the door for you."

182

They had no option but to follow her along the corridor to David's room. Alison stood with her back to the door, holding it open as David passed her into the room, ahead of Debbie. "Right," she said. "That's all right, Miss Owen. I'll take the rest of his bags. You can go now." She snatched at the catbox, and Miranda yowled. "What the devil was that?" she squealed, releasing the handle.

"Miranda. My cat" – which David knew was not actually true. He had no idea whose cat she was, nor how the hell he was ever going to locate the real owners; but for the time being she was his responsibility.

"That thing?"

While they were arguing, Debbie sidled into the room and took Miranda straight through to the bathroom, returning to fetch the litter tray and food from David's clasp. Ignoring her, Alison marched up to David, allowing the door to slam shut. "And just how long are you going to wait before throwing her out?"

David was tired, furious that she had turned up here unannounced and more particularly at her tone. As though she owned him. "Probably about forty years. And then only if she wants a divorce."

Alison's mouth opened and shut. Twice. "Divorce? What in God's name are you talking about?"

"I'm going to marry her," David explained, then turned away to sort out the rest of the bags.

"*Her?*" He ignored her. "Don't turn your back on me!" she yelled. "Look at me when I'm talking to you!"

He straightened, sighing. "You are not talking, you are screeching and making a damned exhibition of yourself. Now will you shut up a minute and listen to me. I would far rather have explained the situation to you, quietly, and in a civilised manner and suitable scenario . . . which this is not. However, like thousands of other people across the south of England, my life is in crisis. So is Debbie's. So the ideal time and place in which to tell you is not an option. Alison," he shook his head slowly, voice dropping, "You and I have known each other several months; we have enjoyed meals together, playing tennis and, on occasion, sleeping together. But never has one word of commitment passed between us. We have continued our separate lives and interests. Haven't we?"

She was breathing heavily. "In a manner of speaking, I suppose, but—"

"And," he continued, "I have never once told you I loved you, have I?"

"No, but—"

"I have enjoyed your company and we have been good friends. So please don't let's spoil that friendship by pretending or imagining it was anything more than that."

"Mummy warned me that you were just using me—"

"Like you were using me? Same thing." He shrugged, spread his hands in a gesture of apology, adding, "And now I've moved on to another type of relationship which I have never experienced before. I've fallen in love with Debbie."

Alison frowned, angrily. "You can't have! You've only just met her!"

"True. But already we know we are an item. No ifs, buts or maybes. Furthermore, we are about to ring down for room service, have supper and go to bed. In that bed, together, where we can comfort each other for the loss of our homes and all our worldly possessions."

Alison's mouth was pursed up tight. "I was the one who came shopping with you and helped you choose new clothes—" she hissed.

"You were a very kind friend. And one day, when this Trench no longer wreaks havoc in our lives, I hope we

184

can all be friends again. But at the moment it seems you are unwilling. Now," he moved towards the door, "Are you planning to return home, or would you like me to check if the hotel has a spare room for you?"

"Damn you, David Barnes! I was so looking forward to a lovely summer of tennis with you, and perhaps going off on a nice holiday together somewhere exotic—" Alison's bottom lip was quivering. "And now you've gone and spoiled it all. And Mummy's going to say 'I told you so'!" With an angry flick she hitched the strap of her bag over her shoulder, and David snatched the door open just in time for her to sweep out of the room.

He closed the door and leaned against it.

"Phew!" Debbie crept cautiously out of the bathroom. "I heard all that! Do you think she might come back?"

David's expression was grim as he bolted the door. "No. I don't think so."

Debbie crossed the strip of carpet between them to slide her arms round him and lean her head against his chest. She was so tired she was near to tears, and the emotions he had roused in her with the words he had spoken about loving her and wanting to marry her, were not helping. They stood there in silence for a few moments, holding each other. Then Debbie said, "Tired as I am, I am so hungry that I nearly stole Miranda's supper from under her nose. Come on," she picked up the room service menu. "Let's eat."

They ordered, were able to eat only half the food delivered by a disgruntled waiter, and afterwards were too exhausted, mentally and physically, to do anything more than sleep.

David had booked a call for seven, and was immediately awake. "I have to get to the bank early," he said. "The area manager is asking for all manner of things for his head office meeting this morning."

"I suppose I had better get down to Wimbledon and see if anything's happening," Debbie said, but she switched on the television anyway, and gaped at the screen.

"Just look at this," she shouted.

Mitcham

David ran in from the bathroom. "This is a repeat of the Prime Minister's broadcast of last night," the presenter said.

The Prime Minister appeared. "I wish to speak with you tonight," he said, "to inform you as to the measures this government proposes to take in order to deal with this very strange phenomenon that has appeared in the south London suburbs. It is an unprecedented situation, and one that was quite impossible to foretell or forecast. However, it is there, threatening lives and causing immense damage and disruption to those people who live in its vicinity. This Government has never shirked from its responsibilities, from dealing with hard issues firmly and decisively, no matter how difficult these issues may have been. We have ended the crisis in our hospitals . . ." ("That's a bit of an optimistic assessment," Debbie muttered.) ". . . as we have ended the crisis in our schools. We have dealt with the law and order issue. We have reformed our taxation system."

"What is this?" David asked. "A party political broadcast?"

"Now we propose to deal with this Trench," the Prime Minister said. "I will tell you frankly, we do not as yet

187

know the cause of this phenomenon. Our experts, and experts from all over the world, are working on it, but we have determined to grasp the nettle by the forelock, as it were . . ."

"I do feel," Debbie said severely, "that if one is going to use clichés, one should not mix them up."

". . . and settle the matter once and for all. Some thing, some agency, has caused this Trench to appear. We do not yet know what this agency is, but we know how to deal with it."

"Talk about woolly thinking," David remarked.

"To this end," the Prime Minister said, "we intend to halt and destroy this monstrosity. The matter is in the hands of the army, and they intend to use high explosives to achieve the end we all desire."

"How the devil do you blow up a hole in the ground?" David asked.

"The designated area is Mitcham Common," the Prime Minister said. "It has been calculated that should the Trench continue its advance, at the rate it has maintained over the past few days, and in the direction it has followed for the past twenty-four hours, it will reach Mitcham Common in the middle of tomorrow morning."

"That's today," Debbie said.

"Should it do so, the army will be waiting for it with sufficient high explosives to end its advance once and for all. An orderly evacuation of the area is being carried out now. We will minimise damage to property as much as is humanly possible, which is why a large open area has been selected. Now, there is absolutely no need for alarm. This is a carefully calculated action, designed to end this crisis at a stroke. Should, by any chance, the Trench cease its activity, or divert to a new direction, then we will call off

188

the proposed action, and all those evacuated will be returned to their homes. We must hope and pray that this may be the case. But should the extension of the Trench continue, I ask you to have confidence in your Government and your Army, who will cope with this horrendous situation and enable you all to resume your lives. I may add that for all of you who have lost homes and possessions as a result of this Trench phenomenon, a package of compensation is being prepared by the Chancellor—"

"First sensible thing he's said," David commented.

The presenter returned. "We are informed that the Trench is indeed advancing, and has cut through the centre of Sutton. It seems certain, therefore, that the Government plans will necessarily be implemented, and the area around Mitcham Common is at this moment being evacuated."

Debbie switched off the set. "Mitcham Common," she muttered. "Mitcham Common."

"No, Debbie!"

"Yes! I must!"

In bare feet and boxer shorts he pulled himself up to his full height. "You can't!"

Her brows drew fiercely together. "And why not?"

"Because . . . because you have to drive me to the bank. You promised."

"And then? Are you proposing that the little woman sits twiddling her thumbs while the busy banker gets on with his business, and the biggest story this country has ever known unfolds a few miles away?" Her naked breasts were quivering with rage. "You joke!"

It was the first time he had seen her really angry. With him! He dragged his eyes off her enchanting chest. "My darling! I can't bear the thought of you driving down there into danger, and with no one to look after you."

"What danger? The police and army will keep the press away at a safe distance."

"I dare say they will. But what about the road ragers waiting to beat you up?" He had been appalled when she told him the story over supper last night.

"I keep telling you. I'm a big girl! I can look after myself!"

"And a bloody rotten job you make of it, judging by that bruise," he argued. "Just look at yourself in the mirror, will you?"

"You haven't seen what my knee did in his groin! He is probably a eunuch this morning!" They fell into each other's arms, laughing.

"Then I shall phone the bank, say I haven't any transport and can't get there till later, and I'll come with you."

"You mean you insist on nursemaiding me?"

"Try stopping me!"

"Well then, let's hurry."

"We don't leave till we've had breakfast."

"Oh, Da–vid!" she complained.

"We have no idea when or where the next meal will be. So let's fuel up while we have the chance."

"Okay. Anything to keep you quiet," she huffed. But he was making sense. They ate in the dining room, theorising that it would be quicker than ordering room service. Afterwards they unloaded the remaining gear from Debbie's car into the bedroom, fed Miranda and left her loose in the bathroom, putting a 'Please-do-not-disturb' notice on the door before leaving, in the hope that the chambermaid wouldn't let her out.

Debbie drove. Traffic north of the river was no worse than any morning rush-hour, moving slowly, but after crossing the river and heading south they ran into problems. First was an ancient, broken-down lorry with a vast family aboard, most of whom were sitting in the back on a pile of mattresses and clutching all their worldly goods. The rear axle had collapsed and no amount of pushing and shoving with the help of other heavy vehicles would budge it to the side of the road. So all the cars behind it were pulling out to pass, denying passage to southbound traffic. In the end, after a long wait, David got out, walked forward fifty yards and stood in the road halting the northbound vehicles until a dozen or so in the southbound lane, including Debbie, had slowly edged through. "You see I do have my uses," he commented, getting back in beside her.

"Mmm. Lots of uses," she agreed. And patted his knee.

Ten minutes later, having advanced only as far as The Oval, they realised that a number of people were turning left towards Camberwell. "Do you reckon they're making for Folkestone and Dover?" Debbie suggested. "Or maybe the Dartford Tunnel and East Anglia."

"Not a bad idea, either way. Get out of the country while it's still in one piece."

"Rats leaving a sinking ship, more like."

"One might wish this lot in front of us would follow," David growled. There was a line of scruffy-looking New Age Travellers, or whatever they cared to style themselves, in a variety of vans and old buses.

"Where do you suppose they are going?"

"Probably to Mitcham Common to protest at the decision to blow up the Trench. Defacing the environment or blowing another hole in the ozone, they'll claim."

Debbie looked around at the buildings. "I wonder if I can get any reception here on my mobile. I'm going to try to raise the office."

The traffic was barely moving. David listened while Debbie

spoke to her editor, explaining where they were and asking for a link-up with Martin. When she switched off she smiled at him. "Martin is already down there," she said. "There is a proper Press Area, apparently, from where we can watch the bang, but we will need to wear our official badges to get in." She leaned across him and opened the glove compartment. "Here, you'd better pin yours on now, before we get stopped. And mine."

It was a quarter to nine. David used Debbie's mobile to call the office. "Listen," he told Angela. "Something has come up and I won't be able to get in for a couple of hours."

"Oh, yes?" she asked, suspiciously.

"Have you got that list of new loans ready?"

"It's printing out now."

"Then as soon as it's checked, take it up to Caroline, will you. The boss wants it first thing."

"And when he asks after you?"

"I'll be in before lunch," he assured her. Her eyes were raised to the ceiling as she replaced the phone.

The traffic ground to a halt, and there was much shouting and swearing. "Where are we?" David asked.

"Brixton," Debbie told him. "Looks like an air show over there."

David squinted through the glass. To the south the sky was filled with aircraft. Helicopters were hovering, blimps seemed almost stationary, and even some light aircraft were buzzing around. "Air Traffic Control must be going spare," David said. "I don't suppose we have a frequency for them?"

Debbie gestured at the car radio. "You can try." She pushed her head out of the window as the driver of the car in front of them got out. "What's the hold up?"

"Police barrier," he said.

"Shit! Listen, I'm going down to talk our way through," Debbie told David. "You stand by to bring the car up."

Fiddling with the frequencies, he didn't have time to protest before she had disappeared into the gathering throng of disconsolate would-be spectators. He couldn't find the right band, was left with the disconcerting feeling that he might have lost her for good, or at least the rest of the morning, when she came hurrying back. "Any luck?" he asked.

"You bet." She opened the boot, took out a large sign which said PRESS, and stuck it on her windshield, held in place by the wiper on David's side.

"Hey," bawled the driver behind them. "Where the hell do you think you're going?"

Debbie ignored him as she carefully swung her car out of the stream and into the empty right-hand lane. "Hey!" shouted the man in front of her as she drew level.

Debbie gave him a bright smile, and kept driving. Now they were attracting even more shouts and protests, but fortunately a few minutes later they encountered some policemen on foot who, having checked Debbie's identity, waved her through and walked beside the estate car to prevent any risk of trouble. They reached the barrier, which was guarded by a large number of policemen, and even a platoon of soldiers, wearing full battle gear.

An inspector looked into Debbie's window and checked her Press pass. "You understand anyone entering this area does so at his, or her, own risk," he said.

"We understand," Debbie said.

"Right. Now, keep on this road to Lower Streatham. You'll be stopped again and directed to the Press Area. But in no circumstances must you leave this road. Understood?"

"Aye-aye," Debbie said.

The inspector was not amused. "You must also bear in

mind that beyond this checkpoint all of Mitcham is under martial law. You must obey, instantly, any command issued by any policeman or soldier. The army are empowered to shoot looters or anyone acting suspiciously."

"We will obey instantly," Debbie promised.

The inspector glared at her for several seconds, then stepped back and waved them through. "And drive slowly," he bellowed.

"I don't think he approves of us," Debbie remarked.

"I don't think he approves of anything, right this minute," David said. "My father used to have one of those phrase books issued to British servicemen when they anticipated the invasion of Germany during the last war."

"Was that the one with the first phrase, 'Please help me, my postilion has been struck by lightning'?" Debbie asked, concentrating.

"Well, they weren't quite up-to-date. But only just lower down there was one, 'I am a British officer. Lie down and do exactly what I tell you.' You won't forget you promised to obey, instantly."

"That depends on how good-looking the British officer happens to be," she riposted. "Jesus! Look at it."

They seemed to have driven into a dead world. The streets were empty, the houses obviously evacuated; doors were firmly shut, windows firmly closed. There was absolutely no sign of life, save for a couple of stray cats, scampering along the pavement.

"There's going to be an awful amount of glass lying about by lunchtime," Debbie commented.

David continued to look up at the milling aircraft. He could guess that the RAF and police were trying to keep order up there as well; every so often RAF helicopters would close on one of the private or Press ones, and the offenders would go whizzing off, but only for a few miles, before turning and trying to come back; every photograph was worth a fortune. Debbie and David crossed the railway line, which was as silent and deserted as everywhere else; all trains had been cancelled, even where the lines were not actually at risk from the Trench.

Then they heard a shot.

Debbie braked so suddenly that David, still leaning forward to peer through the windshield, bumped his head. "Sorry," she said. "Someone shot at us."

"Of course they didn't," he protested, and then gaped at two men who came running round the corner, directly in front of them. One carried a plastic bag slung over his shoulder, the other what looked like a baseball bat.

They checked at the sight of the car, then gave a whoop and ran forward. "Drive!" David snapped at Debbie.

She thumped down, it seemed both her feet together, and the engine stalled. "For God's sake!" David shouted. "How can you stall an automatic car?"

"I can stall anything," Debbie said, twisting the ignition key.

But the two men were up to them. "Out!" the one with the bag shouted. "Get out!"

Debbie got the engine started. "Bitch!" The second man swung his bat, aiming at the windshield, but missed and struck the roof instead, with such force that the bat shattered and the car shook.

"Don't stop," David said.

Debbie gunned the engine, then braked again, hard, as out of the street in front there emerged three soldiers, armed with automatic rifles. "Stop there!" one of these shouted, unnecessarily.

He advanced on the car, weapon thrust forward. His

companions moved to either side. "Halt!" one of them bellowed at the two looters.

"Halt or we fire!" called the second.

A moment later there was another shot, and a shriek from behind the car. Debbie and David both twisted in their seats, which meant that Debbie took her foot off the brake. The car moved forward, and the soldier in front of them had to leap to one side. David hastily grabbed the handbrake and brought them to a halt. The soldier moved up to Debbie's window, and thrust his rifle barrel at her. "What the fuck were you playing at?"

"I'm sorry," Debbie gasped. "My foot slipped. Look, your pals have just shot someone."

"Looters," the soldier said. "And who the hell are you?"

"Press." She pointed at her badge.

"That doesn't prove anything."

Debbie reached for her handbag. "Just check it," the soldier shouted.

Debbie checked the hand in mid-air. "You wanted me to prove who we are," she said. "I was going to show you my pass."

"Well, do it," he said. "Moving nice and slow."

Debbie moved very slowly, opened her bag, and took out the plastic card. The soldier studied it, rifle barrel still thrust into the car. "What about you?" he asked David.

"He has one too," Debbie said, and, holding her breath, produced another piece of plastic.

"Right," the soldier waved it away. "I suppose you've come to see the explosion. Take the next on the left and you'll come to a police checkpoint. They'll direct you to the Press Area."

"Thank you," Debbie said. "Would you mind moving that thing? It's getting up my nose."

The soldier withdrew the rifle barrel, and Debbie switched off the ignition and opened her door. "Just what do you think you are doing?" the soldier inquired.

"I am going to see what happened to the man who was shot," Debbie pointed out.

"That's no business of yours."

"Of course it's my business. It's news, right? And I'm a reporter. You coming, David?"

The soldier hesitated, uncertain, and David joined Debbie to hurry back to where one of the looters was writhing on the ground. His companion was also on the ground, unhurt but spreadeagled beneath the rifle of the second soldier; his plastic bag had burst and he was surrounded by miscellaneous pieces of silver and ornaments. The third was talking into his radio. "Is he badly hurt?" Debbie asked.

"He's not good," the soldier said. "I've called for an ambulance."

"He's not armed," Debbie said.

"He was looting a house round the corner," the soldier said. "And when called upon to stop, ran off."

"And he had that baseball bat," David pointed out, entirely on the side of the army.

"Ha," Debbie commented. "I shall be reporting this."

"That's your right, miss," the soldier said. "We had our orders to carry out."

"Aren't you going to give him first aid?"

"The ambulance is close by. Here it is, now." Siren wailing, the ambulance came round the corner.

Reluctantly, Debbie allowed David to draw her back to the estate car. "Like the man said, he was given his orders, and he was only carrying them out," David said. "It's past nine. We'd better hurry."

They got into the car, David nodded to the waiting soldier,

and Debbie drove off. "That really upset me," she said. "I've seen dead bodies, from time to time – goes with the job. But I've never seen anyone actually being shot before."

"It had to be done," David insisted. "All of these people left their houses on trust; it's up to the army to maintain that trust. And by the way, I didn't know you had an official Press pass made out in my name."

"I didn't. I handed him my sports club membership card. He just didn't bother to read it."

"Who'd be a soldier?" David wondered.

They turned at the indicated corner, and saw the road block. Debbie's card was checked again, this time against a list the inspector in charge was holding. "Deborah Owen, *Epsom Courier*," he said. "And assistant. Right ho. Just follow the road."

"Have you any idea where the Trench is now?" Debbie asked.

"I know it's just wrecked St Helier Hospital," the inspector said. "Don't worry, it was evacuated last night. So its present position is about a mile away from the Common. Now, if you swing to the right down there, you will find the Press Area."

"Are we going to be able to see anything?"

"Certainly. You have been allotted a large building, the upper floors of which overlook the Common. The distance is about a mile. You'll be briefed when you get there."

Debbie nodded, and eased the car forward. "Bloody hell!" David said.

Debbie braked again, and looked up following his gaze, to stare into the sky – as all the service personnel in the street were doing. The chaotic situation above the south London suburbs had only increased with the arrival of more private helicopters and even a few small aircraft, undoubtedly breaking every rule in the book in their anxiety to see and photograph. Amidst them, the RAF and police helicopters buzzed like bees. Now one of the aircraft suddenly seeking altitude to get away from the attentions of one of the helicopters and rising rapidly, had clipped the edge of a television blimp with a wing tip.

The watchers on the ground could only stare in horror as the gas-filled balloon erupted into a huge fireball, which entirely consumed the light aircraft – and then the flaming mess plunged earthwards, seemingly only a short distance from where they were sitting. The inspector had grabbed his radio mike. "Everything you have!" he shouted. "Principally fire engines. You," he told his sergeant, "hold this checkpoint and let only service personnel through. I'm getting over there."

He ran for his car, and Debbie gunned her engine to turn down the nearest street to her left, and get there first. They swung round two corners, and gazed at a scene of the most utter destruction. The blimp had come down on several houses and these were already ablaze, flames shooting everywhere. Debbie braked and leapt out to run forward, but was checked by the heat. David grabbed her arm and pulled her back. "People!" she shouted. "There may be people!"

"Those houses were evacuated," he shouted back. "Thank God. As for the people in the blimp or the aircraft . . . there's no way they could have survived that."

Sirens wailed and fire engines surrounded them, hoses immediately being connected to hydrants. But there was no water. "I need supply!" the chief fire officer shouted into his radio. "I don't give a fuck if the council has said all mains must be sealed off. Give me water, goddamit!" A few seconds later the hoses were in action.

By now several ambulances had arrived, but the crews could only stand and stare as the houses blazed. Debbie snatched her bag through the car window and withdrew a tiny digital camera. David watched as she aimed it at the varied scenes around her, clicking until the film ran out. "I don't know if any of that will come out. I couldn't stop shaking," she said.

"Shall we try and find our way back to the main street and follow directions to the Press building?" David was feeling pretty fazed himself: this continuous chaos was way out and beyond his accustomed banking scenario. Though with all that he had survived in the past few days he should have been immune by now, he thought.

"We can have a go," Debbie said, wearily, sliding back into the car.

Martin was there, waiting, along with a platoon of other *paparrazzi*. "Don't know what the police imagine we can get from here," he grumbled, screwing on an additional telephoto lens. "This is all pretty useless from this range. What we'll need is something out of Jodrell Bank!"

"Did you get anything of the crash?" Debbie asked.

"What crash?"

She stood on tiptoe to peer over someone's shoulder at the two walls of plateglass windows. "You couldn't have seen it from in here. Aren't you able to get up on the roof?"

"Not until the police give us permission. They say they are boarding up all the windows in this building. What crash?" he repeated.

"A private plane and a blimp. A terrifying sight."

"Oh shit! And to think we didn't get it!"

"Don't worry. I did. With this." She held out the camera in the palm of her hand.

"With that! You are not serious!"

"Shot a whole film," she added. "May not produce the most perfect definition, but it will be a damn sight more than any of these boys got." She stared at the backs of the necks of all the photographers double-banked facing the windows. Martin looked indignant.

David sighed, and smothered a wry grin.

"Ladies and gentlemen, your attention, please." The crowd of journalists and film crews turned to face the army major who had just come into the room; the boarding-up of the windows had been completed and it was distinctly gloomy. "Just thought we'd put you in the picture," the major said.

"We going to be allowed upstairs?" someone demanded. "Can't see fuck-all down here."

"You will be allowed upstairs," the major assured them. "Now—" he gestured to one of his aides, who stepped away from the large ordinance map they had been pinning to the wall, and on which they now shone their flashlights. "The Trench is presently at Beddington Corner, and is travelling at a rate of about a hundred yards every fifteen minutes. That is to say, it is half a mile away from us, and we expect it to be here at about a quarter to eleven. Now, you'll see that we expect it to cut the railway line before it enters the common proper. That is, if it continues its present course and speed, which we are assuming it will do. Then it will cross the road. Now, our lines of explosives are situated immediately beyond the road, and are spread right across the common, at hundred yard intervals, so you'll see that we can, as it were, arrest the enemy no matter which exact direction it may take."

"They really do believe it is a living organism," David whispered to Debbie, who was making notes.

"Now, our aim is just that," the major continued. "To terminate the growth of the Trench; blast it out of existence, as it were. We are, to use a naval term, crossing the enemy's T. Now, this building is a mile from the line of explosives. It will undoubtedly be affected, and there may well be debris. We have on hand a supply of hard hats, which must be worn, and also flak jackets, which must also be worn. You will be sheltered by the parapet at the top of the building, and we have reinforced this with sandbags, but I must make it perfectly clear that you are all here of your own free will. Her Majesty's Government cannot and will not take any responsibility for injuries that may arise as a result of the explosion."

"What happens if the building comes down?" someone asked.

"There is no risk of that," the major declared. "We have had this building inspected and it is very well built, a structure of enormous strength. That is why we chose it for your, ah, use. Are there any questions?"

"Who is going to fire the detonators?" someone asked.

"Ah . . ." the major's chest swelled. "I am."

"And the best of British luck," Debbie muttered, as she and David and Martin trooped upstairs in the middle of the now huge gaggle of media people, many lugging enormous cameras; above them TV crews were already shouting at each other as their gear was installed and prepared. Much of the shouting was in foreign languages, as the Trench had now become a worldwide sensation.

They arrived on the large, flat roof, which in normal times was apparently a garden: part patio with wooden furniture and potted plants, fenced off from neighbouring clothes-lines. The garden was not going to survive, as journalists and cameramen stomped across the gravelled paths and uprooted from the various pots any shrubs obstructing their line of vision. "I wonder if the owner is being paid compensation," David muttered, his banking instincts coming to the fore.

He didn't suppose anyone heard him as, although following the collision most private aircraft had had the sense to withdraw to a safe distance, the sky immediately overhead still buzzed with a few of the more intrepid private helicopters as well as official ones. But not even the roar of the engines could drown the collective Ooooh! of the journalists as they crowded the parapet and stared across the common at the approaching Trench.

It was something of a surprise to David to realise this was the first time he had actually seen the whole phenomenon in action. Previously he had been too close, both at home and when he had looked back as they were leaving Ashtead and he had seen only collapsing houses. Now he could see the great gash as far back as Beddington Corner and beyond, and watch it advancing steadily. He swallowed. The earth was simply splitting apart. Presumably the noise down there was tremendous – he remembered the dreadful groaning noise on Sunday morning – but now whatever noise there might be was still lost in the snarl of engines overhead. And the sight alone was sufficiently terrifying, as he watched a house collapsing into the depths, and then another, watched the railway line buckle over sideways and disappear taking with it the station and some rolling-stock that had not been moved to safety in time.

"Suppose it doesn't stop when it's blown up?" Martin enquired, video-camera pressed to his shoulder.

"It's not heading straight at us," his assistant replied. "It should by-pass us by a good half-mile."

Now the road had crumbled away, extending to both sides

of the huge pit. "Ladies and gentlemen, stand by!" came a voice over a loudspeaker. "Fifteen seconds."

David found himself counting, and Debbie suddenly held his hand. "Five, four, three, two—" he stared at the steadily advancing opening. "One!"

The entire common disappeared in a vast cloud of smoke and dust, flying earth and rubble. The building shook, and trembled; glass shattered in front of the shutters and in all the unprotected windows around the common. A couple of Press girls screamed as they were thrown flat on to the roof. David found Debbie in his arms, gasping from the shock wave; Martin had dropped his camera; he was scrabbling after it amidst a forest of panic-stricken feet, cursing.

Still clutching Debbie, David looked up, and gained the impression that the blast had even affected the aircraft; they definitely seemed to have gained altitude. "The army must have miscalculated that!" he said, angrily.

"Surely not! They couldn't—"

"They most certainly did. There is no way any responsible official would have allowed all these people so near if they had known the explosion would be that big. We could all have been killed!" The noise was abating now, and the dust and debris was settling. Debbie freed herself and turned to look at the Common. It had been split in two by the multiple explosions, a huge man-made gash across the green; trees had been uprooted together with shrubs, a children's playground now only a mass of splintered wood and twisted plastic. Leading away from the bomb craters to the south, the Trench remained. But it no longer appeared to be moving.

"Well that's somewhat gratifying." Debbie rested her short-hand notebook on the edge of the parapet and scribbled rapidly. She was still very pale but had recovered her composure.

David continued to eye the Trench with suspicion. He couldn't believe the army's ruse had actually worked. "We should think of getting out of here," he growled, "as soon as we can."

Much to his surprise she agreed, slipped the notebook into her bag and headed for the door down through the building, taking off her hard hat and flak jacket. Despite the wooden shuttering their shoes crunched on the glass shards as they passed through the lower rooms. Martin was bringing up the rear. "Two of my lenses are wrecked," he complained. "I only hope I got something worthwhile before they went."

"Don't worry," Debbie called over her shoulder, "We can always give Billy my pictures. It should be far more spectacular than shots of the explosion."

"If Mr William Leadbetter prefers snaps to real pictures for his newspaper, I might as well look for a better job."

First of the three to exit the building, Debbie stopped and gasped. The scene at road level was utter carnage. Clods of earth and chunks of masonry littered the tarmac, together with tree branches and door frames. "Wow! Did we have a lucky escape up there – or did we?"

"I guess the flying debris just didn't fly that high." Martin could be relied upon to state the obvious.

"I suppose the Press were allowed as near as possible so that the government could be seen by the media to have done the maximum possible," Debbie mused.

"Talk about a gamble!" David said angrily. "They would certainly have been left with egg all over their faces if we'd all been killed."

"Nonsense. We would have been blamed for causing our own demise through getting far too close. Having been warned!" She laughed, her voice still slightly shaky. "Now let's see what state the car is in."

The Vauxhall didn't appear to have suffered any further damage than had already been inflicted by offensive drivers and baseball bats. They waved goodbye to Martin and climbed aboard. The engine fired at David's first turn of the key. "Now where?" he asked.

"I want to get to Wimbledon to file my report and hand in my film."

"Won't be easy getting there from this direction. Let's get north of the river first, then we can work our way along the embankment and turn back south." He steered into line behind other Press cars.

There were endless holds-up: army vehicles waiting to be loaded, road-blocks that no one seemed keen to move. A dilapidated old building, for whom the explosion had proved the last straw, had collapsed across the main road. Debbie was getting impatient. "What about your friend in the docklands area? Might he have an up-to-date computer system?"

"Absolutely not. He wouldn't know one end of an old-fashioned PC from the other, let alone really modern stuff. But anyway, why?"

"If I could access the Internet, I could get all my stuff into the office without having to go to Wimbledon."

"What about your film, though?"

"I can load that through, too."

David was not a computer enthusiast himself: most of his spare time was devoted to sport, but he remembered being at Wayne Bryson's place one evening after golf, and being shown the latest toy, a device which screened photographs when the camera was plugged in. He thought for a few minutes while he negotiated a stationary vehicle. "Come to think of it, there are several floors of offices below Simon's apartment. They should be open for business. Shall we give it a try?"

Debbie gave a sigh of relief. "Please!"

Once they turned right they made good progress, crossed the river by the Dartford Bridge and threaded their way towards the block where Simon Harkness was housing David's treasured picture. David was in no mood to worry about the legality of his parking. "Here we are. How does this place take you?"

They stood outside the double, plateglass doors of Mega-Visual Advertising plc. peering across an impressive expanse of marble floor. "Looks as good as any. Let's give them a whirl." Debbie moved up the wide, shallow steps causing the doors to slide aside.

The receptionist looked dubious at Debbie's request, but when a smart young woman with fashionably cropped hair and very high heels heard the story repeated, she immediately led the way to a small, glass box of a room where the very latest in computer technology awaited Debbie's bidding. "Simon's number is one five seven one," David told her. "I'll go on up and you follow when you've finished down here. How long do you reckon you'll be?"

"About twenty minutes or so, I imagine." She was already engrossed with her task. "See you later."

Sailing up in the lift, David was smiling to himself thinking what a splendidly laid-back girl she was. To have coped with all that had happened to her in the past few days and still be so keen and on top of her job, was really cool. "Hi!" Simon exclaimed as the door opened. "Come to claim your property?"

"No. Just to see your kind face and beg a drink, actually." Then looking at his friend's garb he added, "Hope I'm not interrupting a working session."

Simon was wearing an old, paint-daubed shirt over an

equally elderly pair of jeans. "No problem! I was just about to clean my brushes. Come into the studio and meet my model."

David glanced into a mirror in passing, smoothing back his hair and hoping she hadn't had time to put her clothes back on.

A very elderly man was sitting on a stool beside a high table, with his gnarled hands resting on its plain, blue cloth. "That's it for today, Ernie," Simon said. "You can pack it in now and meet my friend David whose house fell down the famous hole a couple of days ago."

Ernie sat back with a sigh and a nod. " 'Owjado."

David swallowed his disappointment as his visualisation of the perfect model dissolved into a brown, craggy face under long, whiskery eyebrows. He returned the nod. "How do you do."

"Got time for a beer before you go, Ernie?" Simon asked as he stuck the brushes into a pot of turpentine.

Ernie wasn't usually the type to refuse a drink but he wasn't much into the gassy, canned stuff he knew was on offer: if this artist fellow was prepared to pay him silly money for the privilege of painting a picture of his hands, he preferred to spend some of it on real beer, syphoned straight up from a barrel in the pub cellar. "Better get goin'. The wife'll 'ave me dinner ready," he lied.

Simon accepted the polite way his model declined the offer and showed him out. "Great character, that," he said, coming back into the room with two cans of Heineken. "Crewed cargo coasters for years. Now he hangs about the dock and his local pub, willing to recount a string of unlikely sea yarns in return for the price of a pint. Now tell me, what the devil are you doing here when you are supposed to be lording it over your minions at the City and South?"

David was still attempting to explain when the door buzzer interrupted. "That will be Debbie," he said.

She bounced into the room. "Right. That worked out very well. Now I must get back to the scene and find out what is happening, if anything."

David drained his can and stood up. "And I must get back to the bank. To my minions," he added to Simon. "I'm sure they are quite lost without me."

"Did you want to take your painting with you?" Simon thought it was a long shot.

"Er . . . not if you don't mind hanging on to it a bit longer. It wouldn't fit in the car, even if the car wasn't already full of our worldly goods."

"I thought you didn't have any!"

"Well no, I don't. But Debbie managed to get some gear out of her place before that went, too. It's all in the car."

"Awesome!" Simon said as he saw them out. He fetched another beer and stood holding it, gazing out of the window – into space. He hadn't offered any mushy sympathy, knowing David wouldn't have wanted that. Anyway, what could one possibly say that could be of any use in such a crisis. Better to maintain the stiff upper lip.

Amazingly, they had not acquired a parking ticket. "The wardens are all at home watching events on TV, I imagine," Debbie remarked. "Now I'll drive, drop you off at your bank, and get on down to Mitcham again. If I can."

He didn't like the idea. "Have you got to?"

"Stop worrying. The police aren't going to let anyone get near enough to fall in the Trench again."

"I'm more worried about the rotters roaming the streets at the moment, looking for trouble."

"I'll keep my car doors locked and windows shut, if that

209

makes you feel any better. Even if it means slow suffocation in this heat."

He supposed he would have to be content. "When do I see you again? Can you come back to the hotel for the night?"

She braked at a traffic light and took the opportunity to lean across and kiss him. "Could I resist?"

The River

"Nice to see you," Angela remarked, with only a touch of sarcasm.

"I got held up."

"You were at the big bang," she said accusingly.

"Well . . . I told you, I have a kind of personal interest in that."

Don't we all? she thought, but she didn't say it. After all, he was the only person in the building, so far, who had actually lost his home. Her tone softened. "The boss isn't back yet, so there's no problem there. But I have a queue of customers a mile long, all needing money. Peter hasn't really been able to cope."

"Where is he?"

"Gone off for lunch."

"Lunch! My God, that's where the continuous rumbling is coming from. Okay, start telephoning and get the customers in here. Quarter-of-an-hour a time. And can you rustle up a sandwich?"

"And?"

He winked. "A glass of beer. I really do need it."

Angela went to the door and glanced over her shoulder. "Miss Bates has been on the phone."

211

"Oh, good lord. What on earth for?"

"I didn't ask."

"I think I can probably have her for harassment," David said. "Ignore it."

"Right. But she'll certainly ring again."

"What about Joe Darling?"

"Nothing from there. I have an idea you may need a new lawyer."

"I'll have a word with him later on this afternoon."

Still Angela hesitated. "You were at the bang. Is it really all over?"

"That's what they're saying."

"The Prime Minister is making a statement to the House this evening."

"I imagine he's going to take all the credit. Well, why shouldn't he, if he's pulled it off."

David munched his sandwich and then began seeing customers. But his mind was only half on his job. Today was . . . he had to look at his desk diary to discover exactly what day it was. Wednesday. Good God! Only Wednesday? In five days his life had been picked up, turned upside-down, and then dropped down a hole. He seemed to have lost all touch with reality. There were moments when even Debbie seemed like a figment of a tortured imagination.

And there remained so much to think about. His house, and what he was going to do about it, for a start. His car! He had not heard from Hawkins again. Which might mean nothing, or might mean that it had got caught up in the Trench. "Excuse me one moment, Mr Smith," he said to the man sitting across his desk, and pressed his intercom. "Angela, could you get hold of Hawkins Garage?"

212

"That's in Epsom," Angela pointed out. "Epsom has been evacuated."

"I know that," David said. "But there must be some way of getting hold of him. Be a dear." He gave Mr Smith a bright smile. "Now then, ten thousand was it—" he punched the man's file up on his computer, checked his collateral. "Yes, I think we can manage that, with usual terms and conditions, and current rates of interest—" Another satisfied customer, he thought. "Any luck with Hawkins?" he asked into his intercom.

"I'm working on it. I have Mr Tobey waiting."

"Right send him in." Tobey! There was something vaguely familiar about that, although that could go for nearly all the bank's customers.

Miranda! Now why did the name Tobey make him think of Miranda. But Miranda . . . he pressed the switch. "Angela! Get me the Crown Hotel."

"Eh?"

"Just do it. Hold Tobey for a moment."

Buzzes and clicks. "Crown Hotel," said a female voice.

"David Barnes," David said. "I have a room."

"Yes, Mr Barnes." Suddenly the voice was frigid.

"Listen," David said. "In my room, there is a cat."

"We know that, Mr Barnes."

"Ah!"

"The maid found the animal half an hour ago when she went in to make up your room. She thought you must have left the Don't Disturb notice out by mistake."

"No. No mistake. Is she all right?"

"Well, she received quite a shock."

"I am talking about the cat," David said.

"The cat! It's still in there."

"She must be starving. I hope she's been fed."

213

"Mr Barnes," the receptionist said. "It is against the rules of this hotel to have pets in the bedrooms."

"Even four-legged ones?" David could not resist that. "Listen! I'll pay for the cat as if she were human. But if anything has happened to her, I'll sue. Now I want her fed."

"And the mess?"

"What mess? She has a litter tray. But if there is any other problem, put it on the bill."

"Are you coming in this evening, Mr Barnes?"

"I'll be in as soon as I can."

He hung up. Poor old Miranda. She was having an even more traumatic time than he was. One thing was certain, he was determined to adopt her if possible. Of course, when all this débâcle was over he would have to make an effort to find her real owners. Judging by the amount of time she had spent in his house in the past, they didn't give the impression of being terribly caring, but on the other hand, if some kid was distraught at the thought of the beloved Miranda buried in mud at the bottom of the Trench, it was only fair to put him or her out of their misery and return her. If, however, the owners could not be traced or were willing to part with her, then she would share a . . . house, a flat, a home of some sort, with Debbie and himself. He smiled to himself. Or was he being too presumptive?

"Are you ready for Mr Tobey?" Angela asked.

"Oh, yes, send him in." David stood up. "Sorry about the delay, Mr . . . Good God!"

Richard Tobey was equally gaping at him. "I must be in the wrong bank," he mumbled rather than spoke.

"If you're a customer of City and South, then you're in the right bank," David said. "Sit down. How's the jaw?"

"Mending," Tobey muttered.

"Good. I do apologise for hitting you quite so hard," David said. "But you did attack me. Now," he was anxious to get off that topic, "First of all, where was your account?"

"The Epsom Branch," Tobey said.

"Right." David punched his computer, accessed the branch through the central mainframe, and then the account. It revealed a considerable background of unauthorised over-drafts. "Hm. Did you live in Epsom?"

"I had a flat," Tobey said.

"And it's gone in?"

"I don't think so, judging by what they're showing on TV. I'm about a mile away from the Trench."

"Then what's your problem? Or is it merely that you haven't been allowed back yet to see if it's been broken into?"

"My business has gone in."

David studied the screen. "Antiques. Not very large."

"It did quite well."

David continued to look at the screen. Tobey was being optimistic. "So I will need some funding to get it going again," Tobey said. "But I suppose I've come to the wrong person."

"Because you're trying to stick a charge on me?"

"Well—" Tobey touched his chin, and winced.

"It won't happen," David said. "The only witness, Miss Owen, will testify that you assaulted me, and that I was only defending myself."

"You know this, do you?"

"Yes," David said. "So we needn't let personal feelings enter into this. How much do you need?"

"Well, fifteen thousand would help me rent a site and get some stock together. I'm insured, of course, but—"

"They're not coughing up right this minute."

"But there will be compensation from the Government."

"So they say," David agreed, and grinned. "I'm in the same boat myself. What security are you offering for the loan?"

"Well . . . I don't have any, really; save for the certainty of Government compensation."

"Which could be months, or even years, down the pipeline."

"Well . . . I've been a customer of City and South for quite a few years. Ever since I left school."

"I see that," David agreed. "But the fact is, you see, that you seem to have a record of exceeding credit agreements." David studied the computer.

"Well, most of those were unavoidable. And I've always straightened them out."

"After some hassling."

"Look, would it help if I agreed to withdraw my charges against you?"

"You'd be in trouble with the police for wasting their time."

"I'll chance that. If it would help the situation."

"Mr Tobey," David said. "I cannot ask you to drop the charges against me, nor can I allow the possibility that you may do so to affect my judgement as regards your credit status. I am prepared to allow the loan, but only on your signing an agreement that it shall be repaid out of either your insurance or Government compensation, whichever becomes available first. Is that agreeable to you?"

"Oh, yes. Very. Thank you."

"And this limit is not to be exceeded, under any circumstances. Otherwise the loan will have to be called in immediately."

"Oh, no. It won't be."

David nodded. "I'll have the letter of agreement drawn

up. It should be ready by tomorrow morning. Good day, Mr Tobey."

Tobey stood up, half held out his hand, then thought better of it, and left the office. Angela came in; David had left his intercom key open. "Was that really the fellow you decked?"

"It was."

"And you're giving him money?"

"I am lending him money, Angie. Not quite the same thing. You'll print up a standard agreement for fifteen thousand in his name, please." An instruction rather than a request. David was still irritated by Tobey's attempted bribe.

"Right away." Angela got the message. "Ready for another customer?"

"I am bound to say," the Prime Minister said, surveying his colleagues around the table, and smiling at General Briginshaw, who had been asked to attend the meeting and was seated at the far end, "that this has turned out far better than I had dared hope."

"There has been some comment that the explosion was far larger than was really necessary," suggested the Health Minister.

"Media speculation, madam," Briginshaw said, knowing perfectly well that some of the charges were incorrectly placed. But he had no intention of admitting the fault.

"It is the end result that matters," the Prime Minister said. "I really feel this is a matter for congratulations, and I shall say so when I address the House this evening." The Defence Minister beamed.

"There is the matter of cost," the Chancellor remarked.

"Have you done your sums yet?"

"That will not be possible until all claims and estimates

have been made, which will take some time," the Chancellor said. "However, we are looking at several billions."

"That much?" asked the Home Secretary.

The Chancellor checked his notes. "The Trench extends for eleven miles, from just outside Stoke D'Abernon to Mitcham Common, following a slow north-easterly curve. It was quite narrow when it began, but where it enters Mitcham Common it is a hundred yards wide. It is also a hundred and fifty feet deep, in places. That is actually less a trench," he glanced at the Defence Minister, "than a chasm. Its path has cut right through the centres of Ashtead, Epsom, Cheam and Sutton. Now, if you merely add up the houses and other buildings that have actually collapsed you get an alarming number; not all of these have necessarily gone into the Trench remember, but every house, office and shop destroyed has lost virtually its entire contents. And there are an equal number of buildings which have merely been weakened by the action of the Trench, and thus partially collapsed. Immediate opinion is that these will have to be pulled down and rebuilt.

"There is also the matter of foundations, many of which, in buildings which appeared untouched by the Trench itself, may well require serious under-pinning to make them safe. We also have the business situation. A large number of businesses have been destroyed, including several factories which have ceased production. The unemployment figures for Surrey and south London are not going to look very attractive next month. This not only means an increase in benefit payments, but also these businesses are all going to need a considerable injection of capital support, either to relocate or rebuild, not to mention re-establish. And this has to be done pretty quickly.

"There is also the immense amount of damage done to the

public services and infrastructure. Quite apart from railway lines and stations, roads, bridges and flyovers, the entire underground network of conduits, pipes, tunnels, not to mention what goes through them, is going to have to be relaid. This is all before we can consider filling. Now, that is the big one. I suspect we are talking in years, and years of financing, too. I'm afraid I will have to prepare an emergency budget and present it to the House. But in any event, a lot of already agreed expenditures will have to be shelved for this fiscal year at the least."

He looked from the Defence Minister, who had on his budget two squadrons of the new European fighter-bomber, to the Health Minister, who had four new hospitals in the pipeline, to the Home Secretary, who had recently obtained Cabinet approval for a comprehensive system of payments to the victims of crime. Each of them exchanged glances. "Won't do our standing in the polls much good," the Home Secretary grumbled.

"That we will have to accept. And I don't think we'll suffer all that much if the situation is properly explained, and accounted, to the public. This is, after all, a national emergency."

"What sort of a time scale *are* we talking about?" some-one asked.

The Chancellor shrugged. "As I have said, years."

"Our ordinance survey maps may have to be redrawn," the Home Secretary mumbled gloomily.

The Prime Minister cleared his throat. "I entirely agree that we are facing an immense task," he said. "But it is less onerous than it could have been, now that the Trench has been, as it were, sealed off. Now I think we need, in addition to the practicalities and problems Mark has just outlined, to consider also the public relations side of this catastrophe.

No one can reasonably blame this Government for what has happened. However, human nature being what it is, once the shock of the Trench, and the euphoria of its being capped, wears off, people will become angry, rather than distraught, at the ruination of their homes and the disruption of their lives, and they will seek to lay blame at somebody's door. We therefore need to handle this whole thing with the softest of kid gloves. General Briginshaw, can you categorically state that the Trench no longer presents a threat?"

"As the situation stands at the moment, and in light of the fact that there has been no further advance since the explosion, I can, sir." It was said with a pomposity to match his girth and rank.

"Then I propose that we allow all genuine property owners and occupants to return to the homes from which they were evacuated, where they have been undamaged and may be considered safe, and that those who have lost their homes are also allowed to revisit the sites on which their properties stood, under proper supervision, of course. I am certain most people would wish to do this, perhaps to see if any precious possession is left, perhaps to help in arriving at a decision on what to do next. Obviously, there can be no indiscriminate crawling over the Trench, but as long as the police and the army remain firmly in control this should be possible." He looked around the table.

"The Trench remains a dangerous area," the Health Minister pointed out. "It may no longer present a threat in the sense of advancing and destroying, but we have to remember the severed sewers and drains and the subsequent health hazards as well as the infestation of the dislodged rodent population. Also, as you say, it is up to a hundred and fifty feet deep in places with steep sides in some sections, and these sides are liable to crumble."

"As I said, the people will have to be closely supervised," the Prime Minister said. "But I do feel it is essential. John? This is your pigeon."

The Home Secretary drummed on the table with his pencil. "I suppose it can be done. If you wish it. It will entail a great deal of work by the police and the army."

"I do wish it," the Prime Minister said. "And that is what the police and the army are there for, surely. You and William can liaise on this."

The Home Secretary and the Defence Minister gazed at each other, while the rest of the Cabinet smiled surreptitiously – the two men's dislike for each other was well-known.

"I would also like those estimates of costs, and proposals for the immediate payment of compensation, on my desk as soon as possible, Mark," the Prime Minister said.

"Immediate payment, Prime Minister?"

"Well, as immediate as is possible. When I speak to the House this evening, I would like to be able to say that compensation is going to be paid without delay." The Prime Minister looked around the table. "Thank you, ladies and gentlemen."

"That's the last," Angela said. "But there's a full list for tomorrow. You *are* going to be here?"

"Hopefully. Any calls? Apart from Miss Bates."

"Yes. Mr Hawkins."

"Thank God for that. Where is he? And my car?"

"He's relocated with his brother, who also has a garage, in Windsor."

"Good lord!"

"He wishes to know if you are going out there to collect your car, or do you wish it delivered to you at an address in London?"

221

"Would you be a dear and call him back, and tell him to deliver it to the Crown Hotel, Fulham."

"Will do." Angela checked her list. "Then a Miss Owen called—"

"What? When?"

"At half past two."

"But that's two hours ago! Why didn't you put her through?"

"You were having a meeting at the time. And she said it wasn't important. She just said to tell you she won't be able to make it before seven." Angela looked up from her notes. "Does that make sense to you?"

"Yes, it does. Right. I must be off."

"Ah—"

"What?"

"The boss is back, and would like a word before you leave."

"Shit!" David said.

"Well," Oakley said, leaning back in his chair. "All's well that ends well, eh?"

"Yes, sir," David said doubtfully.

"Oh, I know there is a great deal to be done yet," Oakley said. "We are still going to have to carry the can for those lost branches, for the foreseeable future. But I have no doubt we'll cope. And I want you to know, David, that I think you have done a magnificent job, and will say so in my next report."

"Thank you, sir."

"So, I think you should knock it off now."

"Ah—" David decided against telling the Area Manager that he had just done that.

"You need some fresh air," Oakley said.

"Thank you, sir. I shall endeavour to get some."

"I thought that you and I might take a drive together."

"You and—" David realised his jaw had sagged and hastily brought it up again.

"I'd like to have a personal look at this Trench," Oakley explained. "With someone who knows what it's all about. You do, don't you, David."

Thoughts of Miranda and Debbie raced through David's mind. "Yes, sir. Unfortunately, I do not have a car at this moment."

"I do," Oakley said.

"I think the best thing to do is take the Fulham Bridge and then the Portsmouth Road down to Kingston-upon-Thames, thence Long Ditton and Oxshott. That's the way I usually go home. Or I did, up to last Friday."

"You're the boss," Oakley said, jocularly.

"Mind you," David said. "I don't know how close we'll be able to get to the Trench. The police have been keeping people a good way back."

"We'll have to see," Oakley said, confidently.

David was praying they'd be turned back at the earliest possible moment; time was passing. The traffic was surprisingly light, most of the sightseeing now being concentrated on Mitcham. But there was a road-block immediately outside Oxshott. "I suspect this is it," David said, hopefully.

"Nonsense," Oakley said, and drove up to the barrier. "We'd like to get through," he told the police sergeant.

"Are you residents?"

"My friend is. Or was."

The sergeant peered at David, and David's heart sank. "Why, Mr Barnes. Yes, you can come through." The barrier was lifted.

"I thought you were keeping people away?" David asked.

"Just received a directive that former residents of the area can be allowed in to inspect their properties," the sergeant said.

"How can you tell who are genuine property-owners and who are ghouls or would-be looters?" Oakley asked.

"Well, sir, one of my men is supposed to accompany everyone who wants to have a look around. But in the case of Mr Barnes, well, now, we all know him."

"Sometimes it pays to be notorious," Oakley murmured.

"But mind how you go, gentlemen."

"We will." He drove along the road, braked when he came to the hastily improvised fencing. They both got out, climbed through the fence, and gazed at the original sinkhole, and the burnt-out remains of David's house. "Astonishing. And heartbreaking."

"Yes," David said.

Oakley looked at the Fosters' house, on the far side, col-lapsed into the original hole. "Did you know those people?"

"Very well."

"Where are they now?"

"Do you know, I have no idea. Things have been rather fraught, the past couple of days."

"Of course." Oakley looked along the Trench, which stretched out of sight, at this point in an easterly direction, marked by the rubbled houses, the fallen trees and telegraph poles, and by scattered groups of people, accompanied by policemen, who were picking their way through the chaos. "Remarkable," he said again. "A sight we shall never forget. Thanks for bringing me down here, David. Now I think we should get back."

"Yes, sir," David said thankfully. They returned to the car.

"What are your plans for rebuilding?" Oakley enquired as they drove back through Oxshott.

"Well, that rather depends on what sort of compensation the Government are prepared to pay. I will rebuild, of course, but probably nothing quite as large as before."

"Just good enough for a wife and children, eh?"

"I suppose so."

"When were you planning on getting married?" Oakley asked, gazing at the road unfolding in front of them.

David glanced at him, frowning. "Well . . . we haven't really considered it, at the moment. There's been so much going on—"

"I think you should consider it," Oakley said. "If only from your own point of view. As I said earlier, I think you have handled yourself, and your job, magnificently, over the crisis. I would like to recommend you for promotion. But the fact is, the bank likes its senior staff to be married. This is important on the social side as well as, well . . . everything else." His turn to glance at David.

"Well, if you put it that way," David said. "I'll see what I can do. Although I'm not sure her parents are really in the mood to discuss weddings right now."

"I can tell you that they are very eager to have it happen, David."

Now David turned his entire head to look at him.

Oakley grinned. "You didn't know I play bridge with Alec, every week?"

"Alec?" The penny dropped. "Oh, my God!"

"Nothing to worry about. He thinks you're the ideal husband for Alison. He's only concerned that you have never popped the question. I'd charge ahead if I were you."

"Ah . . ." David took a deep breath. "I'm not marrying Alison, sir."

"Eh? She thinks you are."

"Actually, I'm not sure she does, any more. We broke up, last night."

"What on earth for?"

"Because I'm going to marry someone else."

"Good grief! Anyone I know?"

"I doubt it. Her name is Deborah Owen."

"Never heard of her."

"She's a newspaper reporter with the *Epsom Courier*," David explained.

"Good grief!" Oakley repeated. "This has all been very sudden! You'll certainly have a lot of explaining to do to the Bates'."

"Alison and I were never more than good friends," David said defensively. "Er . . . very good friends."

Oakley turned his large, white head to frown at him. "That is not the impression Alec gave me. But then Alec is a bit old-fashioned, I suppose."

Fortunately, David remained the blue-eyed-boy during the drive back to the bank: not even Alison Bates's ruined aspirations could spoil Oakley's mood of *bonhomie*. It was nearly seven when David crossed the hotel foyer, sidling past the receptionist while she was attending another customer and unable to buttonhole him about the cat. Three times he passed the plastic card through the key slot in the door: why was it these damned things acted up when one was most tired? As he pursed his lips to try again, the door was opened from the inside by Debbie.

"There you are! At last!"

"What a loving greeting," he commented with a touch of sarcasm, throwing his jacket onto a bed and loosening his tie.

"I'm not in a very loving mood!"

226

He took a deep breath. "Now what have I done?"

"Failed to convince your dear friend Alison that the affair with her is terminated. She has been on the phone every ten minutes for the past hour demanding to speak to you."

"And you said I wasn't here."

"Yes. And she remains convinced that I am lying through my teeth and you, you heartless cad, are stretched on the bed beside me, laughing your head off."

"Oh shit!" He grabbed the hotel phone chart. "What's the room service number? I need a beer." He reached out to grab the phone . . . which buzzed under his hand. He recoiled, sighed, and picked it up. "Hello?"

"David! At last! Why wouldn't you speak to me before?"

"Alison! For God's sake woman! The reason was because I was several miles away with my boss, a friend of your father's, who can verify that statement. What do you want?"

"Oh David! Please don't speak to me like that," she whined. "I know you have had a most traumatic time, darling, but I can't believe you really want us to split up. I'm sure this Debbie person is a very nice girl and all that, but you know, in your state of mind one does reach out to a sympathetic soul as a stop gap. You cannot be really in love with her. The feeling is going to wear off."

With the receiver still held to his ear, David 's head sank onto his free hand. "Do you want me to leave the room while you talk?" Debbie asked.

He tucked the mouthpiece under his chin. "No. No way. I want you right here."

"David? David! Are you there?"

"Yes, Alison I am here, trying to think of a new verbal format which might convince you that I am in a sane and sound state of mind, though extremely tired right at this minute, and also a way to make you understand that

Debbie and I are an item. Nothing you can do or say will alter that."

"Oh David!" she wailed.

He didn't believe the tear treatment. She was not the sort of girl to cry, genuinely. He waited till she stopped and spoke again. "David! Are you still there?"

"Yes."

"Then I think I ought to tell you that I think I may be pregnant."

Although he knew that was impossible, nevertheless a nasty shiver ran down his spine. And he began to feel really angry. "Who by?" he demanded. "It certainly wasn't me, as well you know!"

"You damned sleaze bag! You confounded swine! I hate you!" the girl screamed, and slammed down her receiver.

Debbie clapped her hand over her mouth to stifle a laugh. "I heard that! Loud and clear!"

David shook his head, depressed the call button and dialled room service. Debbie came and sat on the bed beside him. "Are you sure, dearest? Are you one hundred per cent certain that the chaos of the past week hasn't upset your emotions, prompting you into making a terrible mistake?"

"No. More like a thousand per cent sure." He ran his fingers through the gold strands of hair cascading onto her shoulders and gazed long and seriously into her eyes. "What's more, Deborah Owen, I am getting a bit brassed off being surrounded by doubting women! Have you caught Alison's disease or is this just a temporary aberration?"

She slid her arms round him and together they fell backwards across the bed, kissing frantically, until they heard a knock on the door and a voice called "Room service, sir!"

Over dinner, downstairs in the dining room, David said,

"You still haven't explained how you got into the room? I had the key card in my pocket."

"They weren't keen at first, but when I told them at reception it was essential for me to attend to the cat they couldn't open up the door fast enough!"

"Amazing cat, Miranda. I always understood that cats couldn't bear to be relocated, and would run off at the first opportunity. But this one . . . well, you've seen her. She eats well, then curls up and goes to sleep. Anywhere. Perfectly happy."

"I think some cats latch onto people rather than places. As long as your smell is around the place she is happy. Wherever she is."

David ate in silence for a few minutes, thinking. Then he said, "You know, I believe I may have some of that feline instinct you just mentioned. When I saw my home burnt up in that hole I was devastated. I simply couldn't imagine living anywhere else. But now I realise that I could live anywhere in the world, as long as your scent is around the place."

She smiled at him adoringly. "David Barnes, I not only love you but I feel you doing terrible things to my old-fashioned sense of morality."

He could scarcely wait to finish the meal before hastening upstairs and putting her statement to the test. He felt almost hysterical, so difficult was it to accept that it was all over. In less than a week his entire life had been torn apart – and then put back together in the most miraculous fashion. He could envisage the two of them, planning and building their new home . . . he wondered where it would be.

"And so I say to this House," the Prime Minister declared, "that by taking prompt and decisive action, a catastrophe of unimaginable consequences has been prevented."

The Chamber was packed, late as it was. "We've had a catastrophe anyway," someone called from one of the back benches.

"We have had a great misfortune," the Prime Minister retorted, having to shout.

"Order, order!" called the Speaker.

"I know," the Prime Minister said, "that there are those saying that before undertaking so drastic a step as blowing up Mitcham Common we should have reconvened Parliament and debated the matter. But time was not on our side. Time was against us. With every minute that passed, the Trench was growing, extending, threatening to destroy more property, cost more lives. A decision had to be taken, and this Government took it. On that basis, we are prepared to stand before the judgement book of history." He sat down to cheers from the Government supporters, although not even all of them were happy with the way the crisis had been handled.

The Leader of the Opposition stood up. "As the Prime Minister has just said, a great catastrophe has been averted. Exactly how, we are not sure, and we cannot be sure until the cause of this calamity has been ascertained. What we can be sure of, however, is that the cost of repairing the damage caused by this Trench is going to be astronomical. Will the Prime Minister tell this House just when we may expect a statement on the cause of this phenomenon, and whether or not it is likely to recur, and secondly, when will he be able to give this House a figure as to the cost, both of repairing the damage and of compensation to those who have lost homes and property because of the Trench, and whether such compensation will involve additional taxation."

The Prime Minister stood up. "To take the second question

first, the Exchequer with its related departments is at this time correlating returns and invoices. I am sure my Right Honourable friend will understand that this is an immense task and will take time, but I am hopeful that a full statement will be made within a fortnight. As to the first question, I must tell you that all the experts we have working on the Trench, and they are now worldwide, have been unable to account for its appearance. However, an answer will be found, and it will be found shortly. I can assure this House—"

There was a rustle as a folded piece of paper was passed along the Government front benches, having just been handed in at the door of the Chamber. "You'll excuse me," the Prime Minister said, as he took the paper from the Chancellor, and opened it.

Then he sat down.

The House waited, in total silence.

Slowly the Prime Minister stood up again. His face was ashen. "I am afraid I have very grave news to give this House. The explosion we activated this morning was not, after all, successful. I have to tell you that the Trench has resumed its movement. It has also changed direction, and is now travelling almost due north. It is expected to reach Battersea, and the Thames, by noon tomorrow."

Evacuation

They slept curled close together, a tangle of warm arms and legs, waking to an early dawn and urgent demands for more. "I must get up and go to the bank," David said reluctantly, looking at his watch, which showed six-fifteen, and kicking aside the sheet.

"At this hour?"

"There's still a hell of a lot to be done. We're fielding all the customers from south of the river. Did I tell you that your friend Tobey was in?"

"Good Lord! What did he want?"

"A loan."

"And you threw him out."

"I did not. He's a customer."

"Grrr." Debbie sat up and stretched. "And I too must go and earn my humble crust. It looks rather overcast this morning. Let's see if we can find a weather forecast." She reached for the remote control on the bedside table while David went off to evict Miranda from the shower stall.

The cat greeted him with a *Brrr!* stretching her paws and foreclaws before stepping daintily onto the bathmat to sit and scratch an ear.

David's despair and disorientation of the past few days

had truly disappeared: as water sluiced over his face he was smiling happily to himself. The wonderful relationship he had found with Debbie filled him with confidence and hope that they could now start to build a future together. Today was the first day of the rest of their lives!

Then he heard her shout. "David! David! Oh God!"

He turned off the water and thrust the shower curtain aside. "What is it?"

She was standing there naked, eyes agape with horror. "It's the Trench. It's started opening up again. It's heading for the river!"

"Oh no! Surely not!" He grabbed a towel, the balloon of euphoria bursting under a new leaden weight of anxiety.

Suddenly they both became aware of a hammering on the bedroom door. "Stay here," he told Debbie. "I'll get it." Towel hitched round his waist, David opened the door.

A dishevelled waiter was standing there. "Please to leave the 'otel, pronto! Is the big 'ole, coming!"

"Here? This way? It's south of the river and way over to the right."

"Si, si, Signor. But the manager, he say, too close. So we shut down, eh? You go, now. Pronto!"

David nodded, "Okay," and made to close the door.

"No, no, Signor. Is not permitted to close door. All doors to be open." And the panicky waiter crossed the passageway to hammer on the opposite door.

David pushed his door sufficiently to allow dignity to their dressing, called Debbie and hurriedly grabbed his pants. "The Trench is coming this way and we're told to evacuate," he said.

"I told you! Now don't forget your things. Your new suit. And Miranda! Thank heavens we still have her box!"

Miranda was not keen to get into the dreaded box again,

David having to resort to force when persuasion failed. Then he put on his suit and shoved the rest of his clothes, hangers and all, into the shop carrier-bags. His shaving gear was squashed into his briefcase. "Ready?"

Debbie had also put on her suit and was dragging a comb through her yellow tangles. "I'll finish this in the car." She picked up her overnight case, slung her shoulder bag. "By the way, have you got your car back yet?"

"It should be in the car-park with the keys under the front seat. According to the garage people. Where are we going?"

"I want to get as near to the Trench as possible, to report on what is happening."

"Don't be an idiot! You've covered all that. One stretch of Trench is going to be much the same as the next."

"What? With the Thing approaching the Thames? You joke!"

"Look, darling. Be reasonable. I must get to the bank, but I cannot go off and leave you wandering around alone in danger."

"I won't get too near, I promise. I've been down the Trench once, and that was one time too many!"

"It's not just the Trench. Remember there is going to be a mad stampede of terrified people out there. With and without cars. You could be jumped, your car hijacked. Anything could happen."

Debbie glowered at him. "I still want to get a bit nearer, anyway. And you certainly don't have to come!"

David read the stubborn determination in her body language and sighed. "We'll cross the river together, cars in tandem, and see what is happening. Then decide what to do next."

"Well all right. But just remember you are my lover, not my mother!" she warned.

The lift was jam-packed, plus a queue outside on the landing, so they walked down the stairs with their gear, Miranda complaining all the way. But no one heard her above the wailing children and voices raised in complaint and alarm. The foyer was full and David headed straight for the doors. "What about the bill?" Debbie panted beside him.

"What about it? They have my card number. If their computer survives they will doubtless bill me."

"I wonder if they will also charge for Miranda and me?" she giggled. "Talking of which, does she go in your car or mine?"

"Mine. I'd better take her to the office. At least she won't have to stay in the box all day while you wander around reporting!" He did a three hundred and sixty degree turn. "Where the hell *is* my car?"

"There's another parking area round the back. It could be there." Debbie unlocked her car and threw her bag onto the passenger seat.

David edged through the crowd of departing hotel guests and their luggage, finding his car in the farthest corner. Miranda was placed beside him on the passenger seat and he drove out gingerly to avoid all the anxious pedestrians. Drawing level with Debbie's car he called, "Chelsea Bridge?"

"Yes," she yelled back. Well, it was the nearest.

But it was easier said than done. Traffic, two and three lanes wide, was surging towards them, leaving them barely room to pass southwards. David kept one eye on the rear mirror, checking that Debbie was able to keep up, but she was an aggressive driver and seemed to be having no problem – until they approached the bridge. There, the northbound traffic was solid, leaving no room for southbound vehicles at all. David pulled up beside a pair of parked police motor bikes whose riders were attempting to keep the cars moving. "Hey!

What's happening here? How do we cross southwards?" he asked one of them.

"You don't. All southbound lanes are closed to allow extra movement for northbound traffic."

"Which bridges are taking southbound traffic?"

"None, as far as I know. But what the devil do you want to go south for?"

"I'm Press," Debbie called from the car behind. "I'm wanting to get down there for reporting."

The young policeman gave her a look which suggested a psychiatric couch might be more appropriate. "Well, you won't get there this way." He wandered off to disentangle a pair of bumpers.

The northbound cars were moving very slowly: people were shouting through their open windows, their dogs barking and children crying in the tense heat and humidity. Though it wasn't raining, the sky was overcast, dark and felt thundery. "The question is, how do we turn round and get out of here?" Debbie said.

"With great difficulty, I imagine!" As it was, their two cars were becoming increasingly unpopular, blocking the way of the cars in the most easterly lane. "I think if you back up there and turn onto the pavement," David suggested, "I might be able to follow suit."

"When you've backed in I'll back up to allow you out in front of me, otherwise we'll get separated." David nodded. "And darling," she called, "Thank you for not saying I told you so!"

He blew her a kiss. "And where are you heading now?"

"I'm very worried about Daddy and Mummy. I thought we might check that they have got away safely."

"Can't you get them on your mobile?"

"No. The battery is flat."

"Shall we stop at a phone box?"

"Haven't seen one without a queue, yet. Have you?"

David sighed. "Okay! So we are heading for Pimlico."

It took them nearly an hour to cover the half-mile. "Debbie!" her mother exclaimed in Cara's and Rolf's surrealist hallway. "What on earth are you doing here?"

"What's more to the point, what are you doing here? I've come to check up that you got away safely on your journey north."

"We've been on the telephone, making sure we have somewhere to stay when we get up there."

"And have you?"

"Well, yes," John Owen joined them. "We will be fine for a week or so until this thing settles down."

"If it does. You know it's on the move again."

"Yes. We've been watching it on the early news."

"So when are you leaving?" Debbie pressed.

"Right now," her father replied. "Come on, Elizabeth. Time to say goodbye to everyone and get into the car."

David looked at his watch. It was nearly eight. "Look, darling, I really must get to the bank! Why don't you come with me so we can stick together?"

"Ye-es. I might just do that. But can we just see what Tom and Penelope are doing? I can hear the children's voices upstairs somewhere."

"Good grief. Are they still here, too?"

"They've been dithering a bit," Elizabeth said, "But now they've made the decision to press on. They are just rounding up the youngsters."

Rolf appeared, barefoot in baggy cotton pants and a voluminous smock. "We are staying. I don't imagine there will be any problem here, other than burglars."

David had thought of asking the Clarkes if they would

like to adopt a cat, but seeing their tightly packed car he realised they were in no position to take Miranda on board. He stood with an arm round Debbie, waving them goodbye as they drove off to join the stream of fleeing evacuees. "Poor dears. What a ghastly experience for them, with the responsibility of the children, and no home," Debbie muttered.

"Terrible for everyone," David said, watching the Owens bringing their gear down, while Cara and Rolf fluttered around them like moths, eager to help but constantly getting in the way.

John and Elizabeth were making progress, very slowly, in loading their car, as though they were reluctant to leave London. "Look, I think I had better hang about here and make sure they get away," Debbie whispered. "I'm sure they won't want me at the bank."

David frowned. "How do we keep in touch, if your mobile is out?"

"There are phones here. I'll call you as soon as they're away. Or you can call me whenever you're free."

Reluctantly he agreed.

"Now tell me, as we seem to have lost your hotel, where do you plan to sleep tonight? I don't think you're going to find it easy to get another hotel room, if all of south London is moving across the river."

"Ah . . . I don't suppose your friends would take us in for a night or two? I mean, with the Clarkes and your parents gone—"

"I'm sure they probably would, if we could stand it. But what about that cannibal cat of theirs?"

"Well . . . Miranda could stay in our room. She's quite used to staying in strange rooms."

"Grrr," Debbie said. "Look, go to work, and I'll call you."

Although the bank was only a few blocks away, the traffic was so jammed, bumper to bumper, that David pulled into the first available parking space – the end of a bus lane, but all the buses were heading out of town as well – and abandoned the car, this time remembering to lock it. Then he hurried up the street, cat box in one hand, briefcase and plastic bag of litter and tray in the other. He had covered half a mile and the bank was in sight, when someone said. "Room for four more where you're going?"

He glanced at the car on the inside of the several lanes of traffic. "Good God! Is this as far as you've got?"

"Don't even talk about it," Tom Clarke said. "At this rate we won't get out of London until tomorrow."

"Well listen," David said. "I think it might be a good idea for you to call your friends Rolf and Cara on your mobile, and warn the Owens about the situation. Debbie may be able to work out an alternative route for her folks."

"Will do," Tom said.

David dashed into the bank at twenty-five to nine, having to pass an already forming queue of anxious customers, to find the entire building in a state of chaos. "What the hell—?" he asked Angela.

She was busily packing up his desk. "Orders from on high," she said. "We are to evacuate."

"They surely don't expect the Trench to come to Victoria, do they? What about the Thames?"

"I only work here," she said. "What is that dreadful noise?"

"This is a cat box, and inside it is a cat."

"Say again?"

"This cat and I have been through hell together," David explained. "We are firmly attached. Now, I would be pleased if you would take her into your cubby-hole and look after her until I get things straightened out."

"A cat," Angela said, perhaps to herself. "Does she always yowl like that?"

"She's agitated. Aren't we all? Look, just feed her from time to time, and do whatever else is necessary. Here's her cat litter. Let her loose in a closed room, but just don't let her out."

"Judging by the pong, I would say whatever is necessary is necessary now," Angela said. But she took the box. "Okay, Fred."

Several overalled and amused men moved in to remove the various cabinets. David stared at them, open-mouthed. "We're only transferring what might be called current essentials," Angela explained. "Computers and other hardware are being left for the time being. We'll have to share up in Marylebone."

David scratched his head. "Oh, by the way," Angela said. "The boss wants all senior staff upstairs at half past eight. That is, five minutes ago."

David ran for the lift. "And there are phone calls," she shouted after him.

He waved at her as the lift door closed.

"Ladies and gentlemen," Oakley said, surveying his managers and under-managers. "I know you have all seen the news and received your directives. Now, we cannot have any panic. I personally am not even sure this evacuation is necessary. I mean, this Trench is hardly going to cross the Thames, is it?" He looked around their faces with a confident smile.

"However, Head Office wishes the branch evacuated until, as they put it, the situation becomes clear. This is especially annoying in view of the large amounts of cash we have recently received, anticipating a run. This money will now have to be transported up to our Marylebone Branch. I have requested police protection for this as our usual security people are unable to help, but they have not yet arrived. However, we must be ready to move the moment they do. The office equipment will start at once."

"With respect, sir," someone said. "What do we do about our customers."

"We will deal with customers as usual, up to ten o'clock, or the arrival of our security escort. Then we will have to tell them to go to our other branches, where they will receive attention."

"That's not going to make any of them very happy," someone else remarked.

"I know, but it cannot be helped. I don't think we will actually lose any business, as Head Office tells me that all the other clearing banks in the area are doing the same thing. However, there is one more matter. The branch is going to be locked up and left as it is, just as if it were a weekend. But we can't be sure what the, shall we say, mood of the people might become if the Trench *were* to cross the river. Now, Alfred and his people have volunteered to keep an eye on things, but I feel that they should be supported, and if necessary, directed, by members of the senior staff. I, of course, will remain here until the police arrive to escort the cash transfer, but I feel I should go with it. Volunteers to remain on duty should be unmarried men, as I am sure all of us with families would prefer to make them our top priority."

Good grief, David thought; he's looking at me. "Of course I will volunteer, sir," he said.

"And I will," Peter said. "I assume we will operate on some sort of a rota system?"

"You can sort that out for yourselves."

Two more of the male managers volunteered. "Thank you," Oakley said. "That is very gratifying. Well, then, if there is nothing more—"

"Excuse me, sir," David said. "But has anyone been outside recently?" Oakley raised his eyebrows. "I know I was late this morning," David said, "but that is because all the roads leading north are jammed solid. I had to abandon my car half a mile back. Traffic is moving at a rate of a hundred yards an hour. That means it may take us several days to move up to Marylebone."

"Oh, I'm sure it's not as bad as all that, David," Oakley said. "What we have is a normal rush hour traffic jam with some added elements from south of the river. The police will soon have it cleared away. Now, ladies and gentlemen, you all know what you have to do. It's time to do it."

The lift was crowded, so David took the stairs, along with Peter. "Banking is never going to be the same again," Peter remarked.

"You'd better believe it."

"Well, at least you can move out. I can't believe there'll be any applications for loans in this mess."

"You joke. Who's going to draw up this roster?"

"I will, if you like," Peter said. "There are four of us. Shall we say, six hours on, eighteen off?"

"Right. Don't put me down for the first half; I have some sorting out to do." He returned to his office.

"All set?" Angela asked, carefully closing her door behind her as she emerged from her office.

"How is Miranda?" David asked.

"Eating," Angela explained. "Are we taking her with us to Marylebone?"

"I am not going anywhere," David said.

"Ah. Does that mean I'm not going anywhere either?"

"I'd be grateful if you could hang around a bit. Actually, neither of us would find it very easy. This idea of moving everything up to Marylebone is absolute codswallop. All that will happen is that the entire bank is going to be stuck in a monumental traffic jam for the rest of the day."

She nodded. "I've been looking out of the window. My God, what's that?" A huge noise came rumbling up the stairwell.

"Someone has opened the doors," David said, looking at his watch.

"Thank God for that," Angela said. "For a moment . . ." she stared at him. "There's no real chance that thing could come this far, is there?"

"None at all," David said, with more confidence than he actually felt. If the man-made chasm at Mitcham Common hadn't stopped it, would the Thames? But there was no comparison between the two, at least for size.

"Phone calls," Angela said, consulting her notebook, and anxious to return to normal. "Your friend Miss Owen."

"What? Why wasn't she put through?"

"You weren't here, remember? You were upstairs with the boss."

"Damn and blast and—"

Angela raised a finger. "She said she'd call back. Mr Bryson?"

"Okay."

"Mr Darling?"

"Is that a fact. Him in front of Bryson."

"Several people seeking appointments."

243

"Make them, but also make sure they understand that these are subject to circumstances."

"Do I make them for here, or for Marylebone?"

"Oh. Jesus . . ." he rubbed the back of his neck. "Here for an hour. Marylebone after that, but their man will have to handle them. I don't know when I'll be able to get up there."

"You have a list for this morning, as well. Starting in five minutes."

He nodded, wearily. "As I said, I'll see the first in here."

"Then there's Miss Bates."

"You have got to be kidding. Miss Bates is yesterday's news."

"I don't think she knows that. She sounded quite agitated."

"Aren't we all? Definitely, no Miss Bates. However, I would like you to get hold of Miss Owen for me. There's the number."

"Miss Owen. Right. Where does she rank in the list?"

"Top," David said. "The word is now."

"What about . . ." she looked at her list. "Mr Evans. Your first appointment?"

"He can wait until I've spoken with Debbie . . . Miss Owen."

"Debbie," Angela said, obviously doing a lot of deducing "Half a tick."

She went off, and returned in a couple of minutes. "Miss Owen isn't at that number."

"Say again?"

"She was there," Angela explained. "But she went out. I spoke with a right weirdo. He said she'd gone off with her parents, and he didn't know when she was coming back, or if." She gazed at David, eyebrows arched.

"Shit," David said. "Look, get the weirdo . . . his name is Rolf, and let me speak with him."

"There," John Owen said, with some satisfaction. "All set." The little car was loaded.

"So . . . we'll see you when we see you," Elizabeth said, giving Debbie a hug. "Do take care."

"I always do," Debbie said; her mother didn't yet know about her falling into the Trench and nearly drowning. But she was preoccupied, and worried. This whole business had been a ghastly experience for her parents. Having to abandon their house, not know when they were getting back or if it would still be there, and now setting off into utter chaos – Dad was already looking utterly exhausted, his face grey, and they hadn't even started yet. "Are you sure you'll be all right?"

"Of course we'll be all right," Elizabeth said. "It's you I'm worried about."

"Well, just drive carefully. Don't be impatient. Don't let other people's antics upset you." She kissed them both and closed the doors on them, and Rolf appeared in the doorway.

"There's a phone call for you, Debbie."

"That'll be David. Half a tick." She ran inside. "When are you free?"

"Free? My dear girl, we are totally walled in, by traffic."

"Tom? Tom! I thought you were David."

"David! Just saw him."

"You saw David?" Debbie was totally confused. "Where?"

"He walked by five minutes ago, on his way to work."

"He walked . . . look, where *are* you."

"Trying to reach the Brompton Road. We thought this would be a better bet for getting round the Park than Buck House. But the road is absolutely solid. David asked me to

245

call you and tell your parents not to use it. There must be another way."

"Shoot," Debbie commented. "Right. Thanks a million. Keep in touch." She put down the phone and ran outside. Her father had just started the car. "Hold it a moment," she said. "The roads immediately north are jammed. Come inside and let's look at a map."

The Owens dutifully obeyed their daughter, and returned inside.

Cara produced coffee. while they peered at the atlas. "I'd say cut across to the Embankment," she suggested.

"That's jammed solid with traffic coming over the bridges from the south," Rolf argued.

"How about going west, into Chelsea, and trying to get up to Kensington," John said. "Then we could swing back and pick up the Edgware Road."

"You don't suppose that's solid too?" Debbie said.

"I think we'd do just as well to stay here," Elizabeth said.

"No," Debbie said definitely. "You are getting out." She couldn't tell the poor old dears that she wanted them out of her hair, out of her sphere of responsibility. But for the moment, they were still *in* that sphere. "Okay," she said. "It seems whichever route we take is going to be a bore. So we'll follow the Clarkes."

"We?" asked her father.

"I'm coming with you. I'll do the driving."

"That's not necessary," he protested.

"I feel like it."

"But how will you get back for your own car?" Cara asked.

"I'll get back. I'm just going to see the folks through the worst of the traffic. Just let me make a phone call first."

She dialled the bank. "Mr Barnes, please."

"I'll put you through."

This took a little time, as there were apparently other people trying to get hold of Mr Barnes. But at last a prim voice said, "David Barnes' office."

"I'd like to speak with Mr Barnes, please."

"I'm sorry, he's not available at the moment."

"Oh, blow it. Well, would you . . . no, don't bother. Tell him I'll call back." David would undoubtedly go spare if he learned she was setting off into the traffic jam, and there would be no way he could contact her – her parents were not into mobile phones.

"Of course," Angela said. "Who shall I say called?"

"Deborah Owen."

"Ah," Angela said, meaningfully.

Debbie put down the phone. "Okay folks, let's go."

Debbie felt like a driver about to leave the pits in the Grand Prix. The road outside the house was busy enough, but once they joined the mainstream, with much blowing of the horn and shouting and swearing, she felt they had descended into hell. There were cars everywhere, as well as trucks, lorries, motor bikes and bicycles; they hadn't gone twenty yards when someone scraped their rear bumper, but neither driver was prepared to stop and get out. "You know something," John Owen said. "I'm damned glad you're doing the driving, Debbie."

"Grrr," Debbie said.

They advanced a few feet. "Look!" Elizabeth exclaimed from the back seat. "Isn't that David's car?"

It was off the road in a bus lane, neatly ticketed. "I knew he'd abandoned it," Debbie said. "Not for the first time. Amazing to think he's just over there in the bank."

She glanced to her left as they reached a corner; the lights were against them. But the street to the left looked reasonably clear. She made an instant decision and swung round the corner, drove for about fifty yards, and was back in another stream. Nor could she change her mind; the cars behind her had followed her and were now bumper to bumper back to the lights. "Sod it," she muttered.

Now they really were stopped; they weren't being allowed to rejoin the major road up ahead. "Remember what you said, dear," Elizabeth said. "Patience."

"Grrr," Debbie growled. The line of traffic moved a few feet, and suddenly there was a bumping, grinding sound. "Oh, no!"

"I had an idea that tyre was going," her father said.

"And you never told me? Oh, Dad—"

Horns were blaring behind them as a gap opened up in front of them. Debbie got out to survey the tyre. It was certainly flat. "Hey," the man behind her shouted. "Get a move on!"

"I can't," she shouted back. "I have a flat. I don't suppose you'd care to help me change it?"

"I'll help you get it off the road," the man said, and got out, followed by several more drivers in the queue.

Debbie suddenly felt as that Jag owner must have, was it only yesterday? "What are you doing?" John Owen protested, getting out.

"Moving your crate," said one of the men, as a dozen pairs of hands seized the car and bodily lifted it from the road to dump it on the pavement with a breaking of glass.

"You bastards!" John Owen shouted.

"Easy." Debbie caught his arm. The men were all bigger, and younger, than he was. And his face was too red for comfort.

248

"John!" Elizabeth was scrambling out of the back. The men had rejoined their cars and were filling the gap. "Take their numbers," she said.

"Oh, really, Mother, what good would that do?" Debbie surveyed the car. It had been dumped with one wheel hanging over the quite steep edge of the pavement; an ordinary jack wasn't going to get that up. She raised her head to gaze at the stream of traffic. The men who had dumped the car had moved on, their places filled by other faces, some grinning at her, some looking sympathetic, most merely looking angry and bored.

"Can we fix it?" John Owen asked.

"Not where it is," Debbie said, and turned to look at the steady stream of pedestrians, making their way along the pavement, also heading north, each carrying a suitcase or a bundle, some pushing baby carts laden with gear; they made her think of photos she had seen of French and Belgian refugees fleeing from the advancing Nazis in 1940.

"I don't suppose anyone would care to help me get this car up?" she asked loudly.

One or two people looked at her and continued on their way; most ignored her. "Oh, the rotters," Elizabeth said.

"You can't blame them," Debbie said. "They're scared stiff."

"So what are we going to do?" Elizabeth asked. "Walk with them?"

They had three options, Debbie supposed. One was to walk, as Elizabeth had suggested. But that really wasn't on; Dad would never make it more than a mile or so, then they'd have a heart attack on their hands. Number two was to walk to the bank. She didn't reckon that was more than half a mile. But would that get them anywhere? She didn't even know if David was still there; the television had said, just before they left the house, that the banks just north of the river were evacuating. And if he was there, how was he going to help, with his car parked down the road, probably vandalised by now?

The third alternative was to walk back to Pimlico. That wasn't much more than half a mile away either. Once there they could transfer to her car, and try again – at least all her tyres were in good shape. She glanced at the high roof of Victoria Station, only a block away – but it was closed because it served the south. "We'll go back and get my car," she said, opening the boot and taking out the overnight bags, "Think you can make it?"

"Out?" David demanded into the telephone. "Gone with her parents? Why, in God's name?"

"I think she felt they might not be able to cope," Cara explained. "You know her father isn't all that well."

"Shit!" David commented. "I beg your pardon."

"I don't blame you," Cara said.

"What time do you expect her back?"

"I really have no idea. Her idea was to see them through the heaviest traffic and then let them get on with it."

"And how was she going to get back?"

"I have no idea. I think maybe she was going to walk it."

"Oh, my God! Look . . ." he glanced at his watch. Half past nine. The bank was officially closing at ten. But he didn't have to go up to Marylebone; he was one of the guard dogs. "Call me as soon as you hear anything, okay?"

"You'll be at that number?"

"I think so."

He hung up, but was too agitated himself to attempt to do any work, or to contemplate speaking with either Bryson or Darling – Mr Evans had abandoned his appointment and gone off – so he went outside and stood on the landing and watched the packed floor below, as customers tried to get to the tellers and porters were putting up large signs saying THIS BANK WILL CLOSE IN HALF AN HOUR – TRANSACTIONS WILL BE CONTINUED AT OUR MARYLEBONE BRANCH.

From the shouts and yells he didn't feel that was making anyone very happy.

John Owen was just about out on his feet by the time they regained Rolf's house. Quite apart from the walk carrying the suitcases, they had been bumped and jostled by all the people going the other way. He collapsed into a chair in the lounge, while Cara peered at him. "Should we call a doctor?"

"How is one to get here?" Debbie asked.

"I think a large whisky would probably do just as well," Elizabeth recommended.

"Ah—"

"I don't think he'd go for parsnip wine," Elizabeth said. "But you can try him."

"Now, Debbie," Rolf said, "there have been several phone calls—"

"David?"

"Oh, indeed."

"I'd better call him and bring him up to date."

The phone rang. "That'll be him now," Rolf said. "You'd better take it."

Debbie picked it up. "Listen," she said. "Things didn't quite work out."

"Deborah! Where *are* you?"

"Bill? Good lord! How's it with you?"

"With me?" William Leadbetter shouted in his best editorial voice. "Listen, where are you?"

251

"Bill, you are speaking with me, having telephoned me. You know where I am."

"Listen. One of the girls tracked you down. They got hold of a fellow named Clarke on his mobile. Martin said he was a neighbour of yours."

"Once," Debbie said. "Where is he at this moment?"

"Somewhere in London. On the road, apparently."

"So was I," Debbie said. "Now I'm about to have another go."

"No, you're not. For God's sake, woman, where *are* you?"

"Pimlico."

"Pimlico! That's ideal. You're north of the river."

"However did you guess?"

But sarcasm was always lost on William Leadbetter. "And close to it," he said. "Now listen, the Trench is only half a mile away from the river. It's by-passed us here in Wimbledon, but all roads north have now been closed. Martin's gone off on foot to see what he can shoot. But you're the only person I have north of the river."

"Suppose I wasn't?"

"You are, dear girl. Action stations. Get down there and do me a piece on what happens, what you see. Chelsea Bridge is the place to be."

"But . . . what about my folks?"

"What about your folks?"

"I am trying to get them out of London."

"Listen, this thing will be over in another hour. They can wait another hour. Maybe they won't have to go anywhere, after it hits the river."

"Why? What's going to happen when it hits the river?"

"Nobody knows. That's why I have to have someone there to report on it. This is the big one, Debbie. Don't

252

let me down. Phone in your report; we're putting out a special evening edition." The phone went dead, and Debbie was left staring at it.

"David?" Elizabeth asked. John was actually drinking parsnip wine, and looking better for it.

"Work," Debbie said. "Look, I have to go out for a while. As soon as I can, I'll be back to drive you out of town. Is that all right?"

"Of course, darling," Elizabeth said. "In an hour or two the traffic may have eased."

Still Debbie hesitated, unwilling to leave them, but equally unwilling to turn her back on her job . . . or to admit that she was excited at the prospect of seeing what happened when the Trench met the Thames. "You still going to call David?" Cara asked.

"Oh, shoot," Debbie muttered. But to call David and tell him what she was doing would drive him round the bend. She'd only be gone an hour, anyway. "No," she said. "I'll call him when I get back."

David stamped into his office, shut the door to keep out the racket from downstairs, and listened to Angela talking to Miranda, who, as was her wont, seemed to have settled into her new habitat now she had been fed. "Nothing?"

"Dozens," Angela said. "But I didn't think you'd be interested. The Bates female heads the list."

"Stuff her," David said. "What about Debbie?"

"Not a word."

"Okay, get me that house."

He sat at his desk. "Hello? Cara? David Barnes. Anything yet?"

"Well," Cara said, "she did come in, but she went right out again."

"Where now, in the name of God?"

"Something to do with work. Her boss called her, and she dashed right off."

"Work?" David shouted. Shit, he thought. That could only mean . . . "Right. Thanks," he said, and put down the phone.

Angela hovered in the doorway. "Do you have any idea where the Trench is now?" he asked.

"I think it's coming up to Battersea."

"Right. I'm going out for a while."

"To Battersea? That's across the river."

"To the Embankment. Well, Chelsea Bridge, anyway."

"Looking for Debbie?" She'd listened in to the conversation.

He glared at her. "Yes, if you must know."

"Just checking. I do feel we should keep in touch. If only for the sake of the cat."

He never could tell when she was pulling his leg. "Right. Let me have your mobile. And you stay here."

"Until when?"

"Until I get back, I shouldn't be very long."

"I'd say you'll be gone forever. Looking for Debbie? How on earth do you suppose you are going to find her in all that throng?"

"She'll be at Chelsea Bridge. I'll find her."

"And the best of luck. What happens if the Trench comes up here?"

"It won't."

"Suppose it does," Angela persisted.

"If it does, grab the cat and run like hell. Call me as soon as you can get to a phone."

She looked him up and down. "God save us from men in love," she said. "But . . . do come back, you silly old goofball."

Beyond The River

D avid ran down the stairs, into a continuing hubbub. The tellers' stations had all been closed down, and the last of the cash was being carried out of the vault, although there was as yet no sign of the requested police protection for the transfer north. People continued to mill in front of the glass partitions, shouting and swearing, while the porters and Oakley himself tried to calm them, repeating time and again that there was no risk to their money, and no difficulty in obtaining it, if they would just go to one of the branches in the north of the city.

David himself was set upon by angry customers as he reached the bottom of the stairs, and he had to fight his way through them, trying at the same time to avoid being spotted by Oakley, until he could gain the street. Not that he was that much further ahead, for the street was packed, with people trying to get into the bank, and others trying to make their way north, laden with suitcases and various parcels. Once again he had to fight his way through them in his attempt to make his way south.

Just down the street from the bank he came upon his car; it had apparently been struck several times by vehicles trying to overtake others on the inside; there were dents and scratches wherever he looked. Something else for Bryson to work on; no one, not even an insurance company, could claim he had abandoned the car this time.

He made his way down the street, and now found himself in the midst of people going the same way. They were nearly all younger than himself, although small children were conspicuously absent, unlike amongst those going north. These looked like a crowd of soccer fans intent on seeing what was happening, and with them, some forty-five minutes after leaving the bank, he debouched on to the Chelsea Embankment, to find himself in the midst of an even vaster crowd, looking across the smooth-flowing Thames at the towers of Battersea Power Station. Directly in front of him was Chelsea Bridge, but this was firmly blocked off and a large force of policemen and soldiers were holding it; it had apparently even been closed to traffic coming up from the south, for there were more troops and policemen at the other end. To David's left, the railway line also crossed the river, but this too was clearly out of action.

The noise was enormous, as people jabbered and shouted and asked questions, while overhead the unceasing accumulation of helicopters, airships and light aircraft droned and zoomed and roared. Various yachts and other craft moored in the river were also packed with people.

Finding Debbie was going to be just as difficult as Angela had predicted, but he was certain she would be in the vicinity of the bridge. He began to push his way forward, and his bleeper went. "Yes?" he shouted into the phone.

"The boss wants a word," Angela said.

"Tell him I didn't reply," David said. "I'll call you back in a few minutes."

"What's it like down there?"

"Noisy," he told her, and switched off.

He continued to force his way forward, and had reached the end of the bridge, when the human noise around him slowly died. Like everyone else he stared, opened-mouthed, as the buildings in the park at the far end of the bridge started to tilt and collapse, accompanied by the trees.

Then there was a huge "Ooooh!" as the first of the power station chimneys went down, with a huge rumbling roar. And now they could hear that dreadful tearing sound, coming closer.

The police and army personnel at the far end of the bridge now came across it, running or driving their vehicles. The barriers on the north side were opened to let them through, while the crowd continued to stare, as another and then another of the chimneys came down in a huge roar of rubble and dust. Then they saw the Trench itself, a sudden split in the embankment immediately to the right of the bridge as they looked at it, an opening now some hundred yards wide and at least a hundred feet deep, like a huge, unfinished drain.

Any human noise was still subdued by the continuing rumble of the collapsing power station, as well as by the tearing sound of the Trench itself, but now there was another immense "Ooooh!" For the Trench had reached the river, and slowly, almost it seemed hesitantly, the water turned away from its normal flow and into the fissure.

It was obviously hot down there; clouds of steam rose out of the depths, but few noticed that. It was the sight of the water draining off, forming a new river bed, and a new river, that fascinated and horrified the watchers. In a matter of minutes the whole downward flow had been diverted, to go rushing and foaming into the crevasse, and now the water downstream of the bridge also began flowing, backwards, into the opening. People on the boats began to scream for help as the water level under their craft went down with terrifying rapidity. There was really no human danger at that moment; the bottom of the river was mud, and the various craft settled easily enough, although several went over onto their sides, leaving their erstwhile occupants floundering in the shallows as they tried to get to the north bank, where willing hands pulled them out.

Upstream, looking at the corner of the river at Battersea itself, water continued to flow towards them, but it was now nearly all pouring into the Trench as soon as it passed Chelsea Bridge. Downstream, water kept coming, the river flowing backwards, as water was pushed up by the tide. But the sea was a long way away, and this level too was dropping, although several of the boats were swamped. David calculated that the whole river bed would be exposed at next low water, and wondered, irrelevantly, if the new river would flow as far as his home. At least, the Trench seemed to have been stopped by its encounter with the water . . . but then there was another "Ooooh!", as the bridge itself started to break and fall into the water, and the downwards flow could now seen to be extending into the river itself. "It's coming across!" someone shrieked. "It's coming across!"

One of the police inspectors at the bridge shouted into a loudspeaker. "Evacuate!" he bawled. "Evacuate this area at once. Evacuate!"

The Trench was half-way across the river and still advancing. David was thrown to the ground and had to fight off people who would have trampled on him as the entire mob surged away from the water and made north. Breathless and dishevelled, he regained his feet, and pulled out the phone, switching it on and punching numbers almost in the same movement. "What's happening?" Angela shouted. "We're hearing all kinds of wild rumours."

"They're not rumours," David said. "The Trench is crossing the river and could be coming straight up to Victoria. Listen, get out. Leave now."

"Ah . . . to go where?"

"Go home. You said it was in Finchley."

"That is in a straight line going north from Chelsea Bridge," she pointed out.

"It's also several miles away. We'll have time to think. Go up there and wait till you hear from me. And don't forget to take the cat."

"How could I do that?" she wondered. Then said, "Oh, Lord. Mr Barnes, Mr Oakley wants a word." Her sudden formality indicated that Oakley had obviously come in while she was speaking.

David sighed. He was now being crowded by policemen, and urged away from the embankment – and he had still not seen hide nor hair of Debbie! "Yes, sir."

"David! Where are you?"

"Just leaving the Chelsea Embankment. It's going. And the Trench is coming straight at us."

"Good heavens. Well, listen, I've had Alec Bates on the phone. He needs help."

David was tempted to suggest he send his friend up to Marylebone. "What sort of help?"

"His wife has fallen down the stairs and broken her leg. Poor Alison is going spare. I want you to get along there and help them out of their house. Get them up north of the Park."

"But—" David wanted to tell the old sod that he no longer considered Alison, or her family, any responsibility of his.

"Good lad," Oakley said. "I won't forget this, David. Keep in touch." The phone went dead, and David was left staring at it in impotent outrage.

"Come along now," said the police inspector. All his colleagues were already hurrying up the streets leading away from the bridge, collecting stragglers as sheepdogs might have herded strays. "That thing is going to arrive any minute now."

David swallowed. "Listen, there was a girl here, a woman, with long yellow hair. A reporter. You must have seen her."

"Sorry, chum," the inspector said. "Can't place her. And anyway . . ." he turned to look back at the now deserted embankment. "She surely isn't here now."

David ran up the street with him. He felt like the centre of a triangle, Pimlico to his right, Brompton to his left, and Victoria and the bank straight ahead. At least he felt he could rely on Angela. And presumably Debbie would have gone home to collect her parents and the Clarke cousins. While he . . . But he had been virtually given an order.

Like everyone else, Debbie had stared at the approaching horror; attempting to use her recorder in the din would have been quite ridiculous, so she scribbled notes on her pad, constantly jostled to and fro by the people around her. When the Trench broke through the south bank, she couldn't help but wonder where Martin was, but as far as she could see the entire neighbourhood on the far side of the river had been evacuated along with the power station. Her job was to telephone this copy through – it was quite sensational.

But would there be any telephones between here and Wimbledon? She had to get hold of a mobile and hope that Leadbetter had his switched on. Vaguely she wondered where David was; he'd be sorry to be missing this.

Then the Trench resumed its advance, coming straight across the river. "Evacuate," bellowed the police loudspeaker.

Debbie turned and ran with everyone else, stuffing the
notepad into her shoulder bag and clutching it to her chest.
It was coming straight across. Which meant that if it kept
its course it would cut straight through the heart of Pimlico.
"Buck House!" someone was shouting. "It's making straight
for the Palace!"

To hell with the palace, Debbie thought, running for
Rolf's house.

She arrived there, panting. Rolf had seen her coming and
opened the door for her. "What's going on?" he inquired.
"All this shouting—"

"Haven't you been watching TV?"

"The electrics have gone. Just like that."

"That figures." Debbie ran inside. "Listen, I'm afraid we
are going to have to move out. I don't see any chance of
getting anywhere by car, so we'll have to walk." She peered
at her father. "Can you make it?"

"Of course." He stood up, then sat down again with
a bump.

"Oh, my God! Johnnie!" Elizabeth knelt beside his chair.

"He's a funny colour," Rolf remarked.

"I'll get some more wine," Cara suggested. She had just
come downstairs, having changed her clothes, and was as
usual amazingly dressed, this morning in tight-fitting gold
lamé pants and a loose, flowered silk blouse; clearly she
meant to meet the Trench in style. "What were you saying
about leaving on foot, Debbie?"

"That Trench is coming straight at us," Debbie told her.

"Oh, come now—" she poured the wine, and gave the
glass to John Owen, who took it somewhat reluctantly.

"It is, I tell you," Debbie shouted. "God—" her brain
seemed to have gone blank. To attempt to make her father

walk out of here would be to risk his life. To stay here would be to risk all of their lives. Unless, by some miracle, the Trench missed them. But it was a hundred yards wide . . .

"We need an ambulance," Rolf said, pontifically.

"And how is one going to get here?" Debbie asked.

"Well—"

"David! He'll think of something."

Cara and Rolf exchanged glances.

Debbie ran to the phone, and waited. "No reply."

"They must have followed fashion and evacuated," Cara said.

"I think the phone is dead." Debbie tried again. "Absolutely dead." So much for my story, she thought. "Don't you have a mobile?"

"Never needed one, dear girl."

"Listen," Elizabeth said. "You all get out. John and I will stay here. We don't know that thing is going to come through here anyway."

"Mother, it's coming straight at us," Debbie said.

"It's changed direction before."

"We can't risk it." She made a decision. "We're going to leave. We'll take it nice and slow. We'll walk up to the bank and David will get us out. I know he will." She looked at Rolf and Cara. "You coming?"

"Well," Rolf said. "If it really is coming straight at us—" he had apparently changed his mind about offering it a drink.

"What about Mushtaq?" Cara asked. "He so hates crowds, or being moved about. I couldn't possibly abandon him."

Debbie raised her eyes to heaven – but David had had the same attitude about Miranda. Miranda! She wondered where she was now?

"Well, we are going," she said.

"But . . . all our things," Elizabeth protested.

"I'm sorry, Mother, we'll just have to get new things."

Elizabeth and John gazed at each other. They didn't know if their home had been totally destroyed. Now they were being told to abandon their very last possessions. The not very large balance in their savings account was never going to be able to cope with that.

"Come *on*, please," Debbie begged. "We're talking about our lives!"

From the street outside there was a sudden increase in the shouts and screams, and the morning was once again distorted by the obscene tearing sound.

David panted and pounded up the Brompton Road, jostled by fleeing people. Others leaned out of windows and called for news. Thankfully, he turned into the side street and reached the Bates' forecourt, where two cars waited, loaded with gear.

"David!" Alison threw herself into his arms before he could fend her off. "I knew you'd come for me."

"I've come for your mother," David snapped.

"Oh, she's in terrible pain. We called for an ambulance, but they said they couldn't get to us. David! What are we going to do?"

David managed to push her away and went into the lounge. At least there were no cats to be seen.

"I put them in the cattery, two days ago," Alison said, reading his expression. "Just in case. But Mums—"

Mrs Bates, who David had never seen without a twinset and pearls, was lying on the settee, weeping – wearing a twinset and pearls. Her leg was bound up rather inexpertly on to a stout wooden spatula, and she was clearly under some kind of sedation, although she continued to groan and weep. Her husband stood above her, looking desperate. He wore a moustache which seemed much whiter than David remembered. "Barnes!" he shouted. "Thank God you've come. I spoke to Oakley—"

"I know," David said grimly.

"What are we going to do? I'd thought of driving out, but we've been warned about the traffic. We'll never get out."

"I don't believe you need to," David said.

"But the Trench—"

"Is going up through Pimlico," David said.

"How do you know?" Alison demanded.

"I've just seen it. Look, I have a lot to do. I believe if you just sit tight here you'll be perfectly safe."

"But you can't be sure," Alison wailed. "David, you have to help us."

"Oh, for God's sake," David said. "Look, there is only one way out of here, and that is to go north. If you're determined to get out, as your mother can't walk, I suggest you get in your car and chance the traffic. Like I said, you may not get very far, but I don't believe the Trench is coming this way. Just stay off the Brompton Road."

"You'll come with us!" Alison clutched his arm, while Alec Bates looked embarrassed.

"I can't. Where's Jimmy?"

"He went out. Oh, my God! Jimmy!"

"He'll be all right," her father said, reassuringly.

"Then why hasn't he come back? He went to look at the Trench. Oh, Jimmy—"

"Good luck," David said, and went to the door.

"David! Mr Oakley said you'd help us. He said he'd make sure of that—"

"Stay off the Brompton Road," David said again, and ran out into the street.

Now he could go back to Pimlico. He was again fighting his way through crowds when his phone went. He backed against a wall. "Don't tell me," he said. "Debbie?"

"I'm sorry. It's Angela."

"Right. Where are you?"

"At the bank."

"The bank?" he shouted. "Don't you realise the Trench is only a quarter of a mile away?"

"Is it coming this way?"

"Of course it's coming this way!"

"Oh. Well, Mr Oakley says he can't leave while all of this cash is still here. The police never did come. He says the cash is our prime responsibility."

"Your lives are your prime responsibility," David shouted. "Where is Miranda?"

"Here with me. Where are you?"

"About half a mile away."

"Well, can you get here? We may need your help."

Shit, David thought. But Pimlico was closer, and he could hear the ripping sound as well as the rumble of collapsing buildings, just as he could see smoke and dust rising above the rooftops only a few blocks away. Despite the cutting of electricity and gas mains there were still little fires popping up, about which no one could do anything. "I'll be with you in five minutes," he shouted, optimistically, and plunged once again into the crowds.

These were mostly fleeing now, and he felt like a salmon fighting its way upstream. The noise was louder than at the bridge, screams and shouts and wails as people ran, were pushed, fell, and were trampled on. David was knocked down twice, but he was a big man and managed to reach the corner of the street on which Rolf's house stood . . . and gaze at the Trench, which was at that moment entering the street from the other end. "You can't stay here!" a policeman shouted. "Go on, get out."

"My fiancée is down there," David shouted, and pushed past him.

"It's your life," the policeman shouted, and himself retreated up the street.

David ran forward, gazing at the Trench. He could understand how the Army had presumed it must have a life of its own, or some agency driving it onwards. It approached like a rising tide, only it was tearing the surface open. There was no one on the street. He ran forward again, and again checked; the Trench had reached Rolf's house. The street was actually splitting in two, one edge just inside Rolf's front gate. David stood still and watched the forecourt just open up, the two cars, Debbie's estate car and Rolf's Honda, plunge down into the depths, then the front wall collapsed downwards, followed by the rest of the front of the house.

He thought he could hear screams coming from the wreckage, and ran across the road to get on the house side of the split. Now chimney pots were coming down and he had to hurl himself into the shelter of the neighbours' house and crouch against the wall to avoid the hail of stone and timber falling all around him. The edge of the Trench was now only a few feet away from him as it moved relentlessly onwards. David forced himself up again and ran into Rolf's back yard, through an open gate. He gazed up at the house, which had been sliced in two as if struck by a tornado. The entire front portion had collapsed into the Trench, but the back wall still stood, although for how long he couldn't tell.

He ran at the back door, but it was jammed. He took off his jacket and threw it on the ground, then hurled his shoulder against the door, and brought down a fresh cascade, this mostly small stuff, which bounced off his head and shoulders. But the door gave, and he found himself in the kitchen. There was a terrified miaow, and Mushtaq shot past him into the garden. "Debbie!" he shouted. "Are you there? Debbie?"

The door from the kitchen into the hallway stood open, but beyond it there was nothing but space; the hall had fallen into the Trench. So it seemed had the lounge, but now he heard a scream. "Help me! Oh, help me!"

He was sure it wasn't Debbie's voice. He ran forward, checking himself just before where the floor had given way, while from behind and above him there was a dreadful creaking noise as the exposed joists beneath the bedrooms began to sag. "Where are you?" he bellowed.

"Here. Please—"

The voice came from immediately below him. He knelt and peered downwards, and saw Cara. She had apparently gone down with the floor, and was caught up in a mess of broken floorboards and dislodged foundations – these had prevented her falling right down to the bottom of the trench, a huge distance below her, from whence steam was rising as water seeped into the hot earth. But her position was precarious in the extreme. Her hair was scattered and her clothes were torn, and from the way her face was twisting David estimated she was in considerable pain. He lay on his stomach. "Hold my hand."

She reached up, and their fingers touched. He stretched a bit further, and locked his fingers on her wrist. Then he exerted all his strength to pull her up. Cara screamed again, in the purest agony, but he wasn't going to stop. Another immense effort and she was sprawled on the floor beside him; her pants had come off and her legs were dripping blood where the flesh had been torn.

David looked up, and saw the timbers splitting. "Get

out at the back," he shouted. "Into the garden. You'll be safe there."

"Rolf," she panted. "Rolf. He's down there!"

"Jesus! What about Debbie and her parents?"

"They left. A few minutes ago."

Relief swelled through his system, but only momentarily. They could still have been caught up in the advancing Trench, which was now almost at the end of the street. Meanwhile . . . "Get out of the back," he told Cara again.

"But Rolf—"

"I'll get him. You get out."

She crawled away from him, sobbing, leaving a trail of blood. David lay down again and peered over the edge, and saw a head, grotesquely sticking out of the earth and rubble, some feet lower than Cara had been. "Rolf," he shouted. "Rolf."

There was no movement. The rest of Rolf's body was buried in the rubble. Even his hands were down there. David swallowed, cast another look up at the sagging timbers above his head, then down at the immense, seething pit waiting for him, and then swung his legs over the edge of the remaining floor and dropped down the side of the trench. The floor had not broken off evenly, and jagged bits of wood bit into his stomach and tore his shirt. But he found a purchase, close by Rolf's head, beyond which the slope continued down into the Trench itself, over a hundred feet deep, still smoking and sizzling as water poured into it.

Taking deep breaths, David knelt beside Rolf, but he needed only a look to ascertain that he was dead. "Shit," he muttered.

He looked up. The floor seemed to be sagging even more, but he hoped that was an optical illusion. Certainly he had to get out, and he couldn't reach the lower floor to pull himself up. He made his way along the side wall of Trench, slithering and sliding in the mixture of mud and earth, digging his fingers and feet into the soft ground, almost prepared to believe that it *was* alive, and that at any moment he would feel a demonic hand closing on his ankle to jerk him down into the depths. He was just in time, for he hadn't travelled more than a few yards when the remainder of Rolf's house came down, the upper floor and the roof crashing into the Trench, and completing the burial of Rolf's body as it tumbled down the slope in a mess of wood and stone and mortar.

David reached the next door neighbours'; they had a much larger forecourt and the house seemed undamaged. He was able to clamber over the collapsed concrete and reach the surface, where he lay for several seconds, panting, bruised and battered.

And desperately anxious.

He pushed himself up, again made his way round the rear of the property, and into Rolf's back yard. The early overcast had disappeared and the sun blazed down out of a noonday sky, with not a cloud in sight, although above him it remained filled with buzzing aircraft and drifting – and no doubt filming – blimps. He found that incredible. He knelt beside Cara, who was curled up into a ball; blood still seeped from her torn legs.

She lay close to his jacket, from which there was a steady bleep. He grabbed the phone. "David!" Angela was breathless. "Where are you?"

"Pimlico. I ran into a bit of trouble."

"Well, listen, the boss wants you back here immediately. That thing is coming up the street, and we have to get the cash out, escort or no escort."

"Where?"

"Anywhere," Angela said. "That's why he needs all the senior staff."

"Shit," David said. "He doesn't need you. Or the cat. For God's sake get out."

"I'll wait for you," she said, and switched off.

Damn and blast and hell, he thought, and knelt beside Cara. "Listen," he said. "I have to go. I'll send help . . ." supposing I can find any, he thought. "But my people need me."

Cara opened her eyes. "Rolf," she muttered.

David licked his lips. "I didn't see him," he lied. "I'm sure he's all right." The last thing he felt he could cope with was a traumatised woman.

"Mushtaq," she said. "Where's Mushtaq?"

"He went past me like a bolt of lightning," David said. "I'm sure he'll be back."

Cara and Rolf having flatly refused to leave their home, or their cat, Debbie managed to get John and Elizabeth out on to the pavement. The street was still crowded with people, being shepherded towards presumed safety by various policemen. Of the Trench there was as yet no sign, although they could hear it, the dreadful sound being accompanied by the roaring rumble of collapsing buildings. "Come along, dears," Debbie said, holding an arm each. "Look, take it easy," she shouted at two youths, who ran past, cannoning into Elizabeth's shoulder and all but knocking her down.

"Don't panic," said a policeman, walking beside them. "Don't panic." It occurred to Debbie that *he* was panicking.

They reached the corner. Back to square one, she thought; they had been here only half an hour ago. To their left was the Brompton Road, still packed and hysterical. To their right was Victoria Station, presumably empty. Ahead of them was David's bank. And behind them was the Trench. They needed to get to one side, in the hopes it would pass them by. But she had no idea where exactly it was going, which direction it would take. And her father was already flagging.

She determined she would stick with her original plan, more than ever felt an enormous urge to be with David. If they were going to get out, they would do that together. "Up there," she said. "The bank."

"That's not our bank," John Owen protested.

"It's a great big solid building," Debbie said. "And it's got David in it."

They stumbled onwards, still being jostled by fleeing people, still pursued by the dreadful noise, the crashing of catastrophe, shrouded in smoke and dust. The bank door was firmly shut. Debbie banged on it.

"Hello!" she shouted. "Is there anybody there?"

"The bank is closed, miss," said a voice through the letter box.

"Listen," Debbie said. "Do you know David Barnes?"

"I know Mr Barnes," Alfred said.

"Well, I'm his fiancée. He told me to come here. Go ask him."

"He's not here, miss."

"Not there? Oh, dear God. Well, won't he be back?"

"We are expecting him, miss."

"Then let me in to wait for him. He'll want that."

"My orders are to let nobody in, miss."

"Surely you can let me in," Debbie shouted. "I told you, Mr Barnes told me to come."

There was a muttered consultation behind the door, then she heard the bolts being drawn. The door swung inwards. "They're opening the bank!" came a shout from behind her.

"There's cash in there!" somebody else shouted.

Debbie was struck on the back, so hard she fell to her

hands and knees, while John Owen went sprawling. "Dad!" she screamed, grasping for his shoulders as there was a rush of bodies from behind her. Elizabeth shrieked as she was thrown to one side.

Alfred had two other porters with him, and they attempted to stop the inrush and push the intruders back out. Fists flew and there were snarls and shouts of pain and anger. Debbie managed to get her father away from the stamping feet and got up herself, swinging her shoulder-bag against the head of the would-be robber nearest to her and sending him staggering. But there were at least six of them, and she felt the numbers were too great, when there was another intrusion from the doorway.

The battling men and women turned to stare in consternation at the apparition who stood there, a tall, gaunt man with bloodstained face and jacket, the jacket itself torn as were his pants. "David!" Debbie screamed, in a mixture of consternation and relief.

David stepped forward, seized the first intruder by the collar, and hurled him against the wall. He subsided to the floor without a sound. David stepped up to the second intruder, picked him up bodily by the shoulder and the crotch, and hurled him after his friend.

David then faced up to the third intruder, who ran for the door. By now, Alfred and his assistants had recovered their wind, and the other three robbers were evicted into the street, watched in amazement by the hurrying passers-by, and the door was slammed and locked. "David!" Debbie was in his arms, being hugged.

"John!" Elizabeth knelt beside her husband.

"Mr Oakley was asking after you, Mr Barnes," Alfred said.

"I'm on my way," David said. "But Debbie . . . God, I've been worried about you."

"Snap. What *happened*?"

"I've been down in the Trench. Trying to help Rolf. I'm afraid he didn't make it."

"Oh, no! Cara?"

"She's all right. In a manner of speaking." He joined Elizabeth beside John. "How is he?"

"He seems to be all right," Elizabeth said. "Just exhaustion."

"We'll have to get him out of here. Alfred, how many people are in the building?"

"Just us, Mr Oakley, and Mr Stanton. They're guarding the money. And Miss Brooks, and some animal."

"Miranda!" Debbie and David said together.

David ran through to the vaults, where Peter Stanton was standing guard, looking apprehensive but resolute. "David! Thank God you've come back. What was that rumpus?"

"A rumpus. Where are all the others?"

"Couldn't raise them. It's just you and me. And the boss, of course."

"We have to move."

The elevators were out, so he ran up the stairs. "David!" Oakley stood in the doorway of his office. "What in the name of God have you been doing?"

"This and that." David looked past him at a white-faced Angela. "Where's the cat?"

"In her box. Can't you hear her?"

"We simply have to get out of here, sir," David told Oakley. "The Trench is very close, and coming straight at us."

"'We can't leave all that money," Oakley insisted.

"There is no way we can get it out," David shouted. "Not the four of us. Even with Alfred's help. And our lives are at risk if we don't go. Now!"

Oakley was the picture of indecision, years of banking

priorities conflicting with alarmed common sense. "Angela," David said, "get on downstairs. I'll bring Miranda."

Angela gave Oakley an apologetic attempt at a smile and ran down the stairs, high heels clattering. David picked up the catbox. "Now, sir," he said. "Do I have to carry you as well?"

Angela stumbled down the stairs, out of breath. Her somewhat sedentary lifestyle had not prepared her for a series of shocks like this. At the foot she gazed at the Owens. Elizabeth had propped John sitting against the wall, had loosened his collar, and was fanning him. Debbie was totally dishevelled, her hair scattered. "Hi," Angela said. "I do believe you're Miss Owen."

"We've spoken on the phone," Debbie said.

"I feel we're old friends," Angela said. "Here's David now."

David was following Oakley, Miranda's box cradled in his arms. "Check the front," he told Alfred.

Alfred hesitated. "I don't think there'll be anyone there now," David assured him.

Alfred opened the door, and stared down the street. "Oh, my Gawd," he said.

The Trench was coming straight for them, the entire street opening up, as it had done in Pimlico. Hastily, Alfred closed and locked the door, as if they could keep it out.

"The back room window," David shouted. "Here, take the cat." He thrust the box into Angela's arms, and knelt beside John Owen. "We have to move you," he said.

"Come on, Dad." Debbie knelt on his other side. Elizabeth fluttered, as they lifted John Owen to his feet.

Now the noise of the approaching Trench was very loud, together as usual with the crashing of collapsing buildings.

Alfred and his porters hurried to the back, followed by Oakley, who stood staring at the huge mound of bagged notes and coin which waited there.

Angela ran behind him, carrying the yowling Miranda, followed by Peter. The Owens were last, as John Owen was put on his feet. "Easy now," David said. "Easy—"

There was an almighty crack, and the great front door of the bank split open, as did the floor beneath it. Elizabeth could not resist a scream; the head of the Trench was only feet away. And above their heads the ceiling was disintegrating.

"Run for it!" David shouted at the two women, seizing John Owen and driving his shoulder into the older man's stomach to give him a fireman's lift.

Elizabeth ran for the back, where the others were waiting, open-mouthed, Oakley's face a picture of dismay as he watched the collapse of the bank. David glanced up at the first floor ceiling, which was sagging, then down at the steadily opening floor. "Listen, get out while you can," John begged.

David ignored him as he carried him across the floor, feeling the Trench snapping at his heels. The entire front of the bank had gone in, just like Rolf's house, or his own, for that matter. And still the opening, constantly expanding, advanced. Now with a rumbling crash the first floor came down – and there were three other floors above that. Debbie screamed as her father and lover both disappeared in a cloud of dust. Peter ran forward to find them. David had fallen to his knees, but had retained hold of John Owen. Now he was helped to his feet by Debbie and Peter, and half carried through to the back. "Only seconds!" David shouted.

Oakley was gallantly holding the window open. Angela was already through. "Run!" David screamed at her as he thrust John through the window into Albert's arms. "All of you. Keep on going!"

Angela kicked off her shoes and ran up the alleyway behind the bank. Elizabeth followed, then the porters and Oakley. Debbie and Peter stayed by David and John Owen. They reached the open air, deafened by the huge noise behind them as the upper floors of the bank caved in over the Trench. Masonry and wood and plaster and machinery sailed through the air. David was struck several times and went down again, but was dragged up by Peter and Debbie. "It's gone," Peter gasped.

"Run!" David shouted again.

They stumbled up the alleyway and reached the road beyond. This was still filled with fleeing people and harassed policemen. "It's heading straight for the Palace," one of these said.

Oakley and Elizabeth were also waiting for them. "What can we do?" Oakley said.

"Look out for ourselves," David told him. "Just keep going, and move to one side or the other as soon as we can."

Oakley stared back at the huge smoking wreck that had been his bank. "All that money—"

"They can always print more," David said.

A police inspector peered at them. "Is that man hurt?"

"He needs hospitalisation," Debbie said.

"There are some ambulances up the road," the inspector said. "They can't hang about, so you'll have to hurry."

They found the ambulances and gained a place in one of them for John Owen. Elizabeth went with him; David wasn't sure she wasn't on the verge of a heart attack as well. Oakley and David, Alfred and his men, Debbie and Peter and Angela, and Miranda, continued with the crowd, fleeing north, first of all into Green Park, and then when it was obvious that that too was at risk, continuing to Hyde Park, where at last they were able to escape from the path of the Trench and collapse on the grass, physically and mentally exhausted. By then they had watched part of Buckingham Palace collapse into the Trench.

It was now mid-afternoon, and the park was a mass of people, all similarly exhausted, all confused by the catastrophe, all uncertain what to do next. And all both hungry and thirsty; many were drinking from the Serpentine. Mobiles buzzed, but there was seldom anyone on the other end.

"I must get to Marylebone," Oakley said.

"I'll come with you," Peter volunteered.

"And we will, sir," Alfred said.

"You stay with the women, David," Oakley said. "I'll give you a buzz when we have something sorted out." The five men wandered off through the throng.

"Cara," Debbie said. "What can we do about Cara?"

"We should try to get back to her," David said.

They looked at each other. Their clothes were in ribbons, as well as covered in dust and dirt. Debbie's hair was a snarled mess. Beside them, Angela looked almost spic and span, although her dark hair, which she invariably wore in a bun at the office, had come down onto her shoulders. Miranda yowled.

"The poor thing is absolutely starving," Angela said.

"Aren't we all," David said.

A loudspeaker rumbled across the afternoon. "Food is available at the east gate," the voice said. "And drink. Please be orderly. Food is available—"

"Let's do that first," David said.

They joined the remarkably patient queues, and finally obtained some orange juice and sandwiches; they were even able to provide some milk for Miranda.

"I wonder where the Trench has got to now?" Debbie asked.

They stared to the south-east, unable to see what was left of Buckingham Palace, but Park Lane and the Hilton and the Inn on the Park appeared undamaged. Nor was there any evidence of damage further east.

"It's stopped again."

The word was taken up by others, and there began a movement towards Green Park and the Palace.

"Are we going?" Debbie asked.

"No," David said. "Once you've seen one Trench you've seen them all. Angela, I think you should go home. Can you do that?"

Angela made a face. "I think so." She looked down at her bare feet; her tights were in rags. But she was not the only one around lacking shoes. "I assume you wish me to take the cat?"

"Could you. Just until we can get ourselves straight."

"And when the Trench comes up to Finchley?"

"Just get out."

"With the cat." She gave Debbie a hug. "It's been great knowing you. Maybe I'll come to your wedding."

"You bet," Debbie said. "And us?" Turning to David.

"We'll go find Cara."

They made their way south, once again through throngs of people, many of them home-owners whose property had been in the path of the Trench. They gazed at the most utter destruction in a swathe perhaps a quarter of a mile wide, as some houses had come down, others had just lost roofs and chimneys; cars littered the street, abandoned by their fleeing owners, some fallen into the Trench itself. "The Clarkes!" Debbie said.

They tried the mobile, and eventually got a reply. "Where are you?" Debbie asked.

"Regent's Park," Tom replied. "Where are you?"

"We're trying to get back to Rolf's house, to see what we can do. You know Rolf is dead?"

"Oh, no! Look, do you want me to come down?"

"No," Debbie said. "You stay with your family. We'll cope."

They made their way on, and reached Rolf's house. But Cara had gone. "Oh, the lady?" asked a watching policeman. "She was all cut up. We managed to get her to hospital."

"Keep your eye open for her cat," David told him.

"What do we do now?" Debbie asked.

The rest of the house had subsided into the Trench, and by standing on the end of the slope they could just make out the Vauxhall Estate, crushed and shattered. "All my wordly goods are in there."

David put his arm round her. "So we'll start from scratch. Together."

"When?" she asked.

"When the Trench stops moving. Meanwhile, let's see if we can find some place to sleep."

But the Trench had already stopped moving. People waited throughout the night and the next day, and then the next. Very slowly, away from the vicinity of the Trench, life returned to normal. Debbie and David found their way up to the Marylebone Branch, where temporary accomodation had been fixed up for the bank staff. Debbie managed to get in touch with Leadbetter and Martin, and confess to them that she had lost her notepad and observations.

"Doesn't really matter now," he said. "We can't print without electricity."

She also managed to get hold of the hospital, and learn that her father was recovering well; Elizabeth was at his bedside.

When on the fourth day the Trench still had not extended, the tension began to ease. David's car was a write-off, but they managed to get John Owen's Escort jacked up and the tyre changed; it was dented and scratched but still usable. On the Sunday they drove down, first of all to Sutton, to discover to their delight that the Owens' house was untouched and undamaged, and then to Ashtead, to look at the wreckage of Debbie's apartment building. "There's a lot to be done," Debbie said. "But at least there's a roof over our heads."

"You mean I'm to start my married life by living with my in-laws?" David asked.

"They'll be happy about that. What do you want to do first?"

"Go up to Finchley and get Miranda. We may as well start as we mean to go on."

"And then," Debbie said, "we can collect my new glasses. It'd be nice to see what's going on."

"Plates," said Professor Murray. "The whole world is composed of plates, some near the surface, others well down. Think of California."

"But do we have plates under England?" asked the interviewer.

"Of course we do. We have even had earthquakes, in the past. Small earthquakes."

"But this wasn't an earthquake," the interviewer persisted.

"No it wasn't. It was a phenomenon. But it was clearly caused by plates. Just a tiny shift, enough to open up a crack in the surface. Now the plates have stopped moving, the crack stops growing. It's very simple, really."

"Then may we expect the Trench to close?" asked the interviewer.

"I doubt that. It will have to remain as a newly-formed valley, after all the water is drained off, which will be after the dam has been built to restore the Thames to its normal flow, which will be after the ground has been surveyed, which will be after the infrastructure is put back into place—"

"Do you believe him?" Debbie asked.

She and David and Miranda were curled on the bed in her room, watching the television.

"Not really," David said. "About the Trench. But I suppose they have to have a theory. But he's right about what needs to be done. I think it'll be our grandchildren who'll complete the job."

"And meanwhile," Debbie said, "there's another question—"

Which the interviewer was at that moment asking. "Finally, Dr Murray, is there the remotest possibility of a phenomenon like this ever happening again?"

"Who's to say?" Murray said. "I would say there is every possibility. But when, and where . . . who's to say?"